I pricked my fin

He dropped the

waited for the cells to start bursting. Nothing happened.

Several beats passed. I glanced up to meet Jax's confused look. Unsure what to say, I turned back to the microscope. Tiny lights began to appear inside each blood cell. In a matter of seconds, they glowed like miniscule stars flying through the solution. The light intensified, glaring out of the tiny cells.

"What the hell?" Jax asked.

I couldn't take my eyes off the blood. Finally, I straightened, tears running down my face from the blinding light. I met his wide-eyed gaze over the top of the gleaming scope. The slide cast pink light up to the ceiling, leaving the room in a rosy glow.

"How?" he stammered.

I opened my mouth without a clue as to what to tell Jax. A loud *pop* saved me the trouble. Smoke curled up from the cracked slide as the light faded. A nasty burned-meat smell wafted up to my nostrils. Only one thought made it through the frozen neurons in my brain. Get out of here.

Praise for Emily Bybee

Two Time Winner RMFW Colorado Gold Contest

Fractured Magic

by

Emily Bybee

Unstable Magic, Book 1

Fractured Magic

Cover Art by *Kristian Norris*

The Wild Rose Press, Inc.
PO Box 708
Adams Basin, NY 14410-0708
Visit us at www.thewildrosepress.com

Publishing History
First Fantasy Rose Edition, 2018
Print ISBN 978-1-5092-2280-3
Digital ISBN 978-1-5092-2281-0

Unstable Magic, Book 1
Published in the United States of America

Dedication

For my mother, who gave me strength to pursue my dreams and so much more.

Chapter One

The grape in my palm glowed an eerie green, its molecules buzzing with my energy. I urged more power into the fruit until it shown bright as a miniature sun.

"Good." My mom coached from her observation point a few feet away—out of the danger zone. "Now, picture where you want it to go."

My control over the spell faltered, and the grape's light flickered like a candle. This was the point where I always lost it. My breath refused to leave my lungs.

"Careful, Maddie. Don't let any other thoughts in your mind. Doing great," my mom urged, but took a small step back.

A picture of the dented wooden chair formed in my mind. I latched onto the image and held it like it was my only lifeline to keep me from falling to my untimely death. Which, given my mother's mood lately, wasn't too far off.

The grape jumped in my hand. Pressure built from the air trapped in my chest. Light poured from my palm and, with an audible *pop*, the grape disappeared.

I gasped, releasing the stale breath. My eyes darted from my empty hand to the still empty chair. "I did it."

"Where did you send it?" Mom asked. Her eyebrows pulled together while her gaze searched the basement. Barren of furniture, except for the old chair, the room had white walls and a plain cement floor. It

1

made for easier clean-up from my magical studies. There was always quite a mess when I was involved. My younger brother could have, and often did, practice in the living room with no problems.

Another *pop* sounded. The grape reappeared in my hand and promptly exploded. Warm grape jelly splattered across my face and chest, which only added to the half-dried globs left by its predecessors. I sucked in a lungful of the sickeningly sweet air.

The butterflies of hope, fluttering in my chest, transformed to ninja razor blades of death. I couldn't stand to look my mom's way, but I knew the disappointed expression on her face by heart. My hand closed into a fist around the sticky mess.

Untouched by the fragrant shrapnel, Mom sighed. "Go get another one."

I bit back the snarky remark begging to jump off my tongue and instead refocused my frustration on the noise that came from the basement window. The neighbor's dog, which looked like someone crossed a long-haired hamster with a mountain goat—minus the horns of course—wouldn't quit barking outside. How the neighbors slept through it was beyond me.

Animals could see through our magical tricks. That dog was absolutely certain something fishy was going on in our house, and he was determined to let the world know. Concentrating with all that yipping and yapping was like having a phone conversation at a rock concert.

I glanced at my watch—6:45am—we'd been at this for over two hours. "I'm going to miss school again. Can't we work on transference later?"

Mom's jaw clenched, and she pushed her hair behind her ears. Never a good sign. "If you worried about your magic half as much as you worry about your school work we wouldn't be having this problem."

"Yeah, because getting a grape facial every day for the last six months has so helped my progress. I'm not good at much but I'm good at school. I want to go to a decent college," I said.

"You can be good at magic too," she insisted. "This afternoon maybe we can try transferring oranges again. You did a little better with those."

I shook my head. "I have to go do that lab at the campus. Dad already set it up with Professor Cho."

She bit her lip, obviously weighing the importance of me getting my AP Biology grade up with an extra assignment against more hours of practice. I wouldn't need an extra assignment if I could actually make it to class more than twice a week.

"You can get it done today if you use the college lab instead of the one in your high school?" she asked.

I nodded, not trusting my tongue to hold onto a particularly snide comment.

"Try to be home early and maybe we can get in at least an hour of practice."

The dog abruptly stopped its yap alarm. The silence did little to soothe my frayed nerves. Grape juice oozed from my tightening fist, but I kept my voice level. "Have you ever considered that I may just be no good at witchcraft?"

Her voice softened from the *professor voice* to *mom voice*. "Maddie, you can't talk that way."

My mouth opened before my brain could catch up with my tongue. "Why?" I threw my hands out to the side and raised my voice. "Are you afraid someone might hear that your daughter sucks at being a witch?

They already know I'm a Defect."

"Don't use that filthy word," she said, her cheeks shifting from white to red.

"Oh no, another scandal for the family. Maybe, if I'm really lucky, they'll cancel my betrothal to Mr. California Surfer Boy..." I ranted.

A tingling sensation in my mouth stopped my tirade. "Mom don't—" was all I could get out before I lost the ability to control my tongue.

She stared for a moment, the warning evident in her eyes. "Stop calling him Surfer Boy. You should be grateful we were able to arrange such a good match for you."

I poured my helpless rage into the bowl of fruit on the stairs. Grapes exploded like popcorn in the microwave. Chunks splattered across the wall in an arc.

"Are you finished having a tantrum?" Mom asked. "Now, if you can't control what you say then I will have to do it for you. One of these days the spell may be permanent."

My eyes widened, and my mouth opened in a reflex to protest. With no way to tell her what I thought, I crossed my arms and felt the outline of the locket that hung around my neck, safe from the mess, under my shirt. The gold locket had been my grandmother's, the one person in the world who thought I was perfect just the way I was.

Her gaze rested on me for a moment, then, after a deep cleansing breath, she pointed to the stairs. "Now, get another grape."

My teeth snapped together with a sickening crack. I waited a beat then stalked to the stairs and plucked a slime covered grape from the nearly empty bowl. The muscles in my legs trembled, signaling that I had used up most of my energy already. Around the year 1700 witches lost the ability to pull power from the earth. Without that source we were limited to the finite amount of power in our own bodies—unless we killed someone. Not an option I was completely opposed to at the moment.

"Try again. And don't use so much power. You only need a tiny bit to transfer something so small. You should be able to do this a hundred times and not be tired," she said.

An hour later we ran out of grapes. Their remains smeared my face and hung from my hair in gloppy dreadlocks. My knees threatened to buckle, but I forced myself to remain upright. No matter how I tried to throttle back I always seemed to use too much of my power.

I stood covered in the evidence of my own failure and glared at Mom in an attempt to retain the last tattered shred of my self-worth.

I waited for her to speak, still unable to do so myself, and afraid that she would tell me to go grab the fruit bowl from the kitchen. It wouldn't be the first time I ended up smelling like a smoothie. Although, I had to admit, fruit was way better than last week when she decided I might do better transferring meat. Raw hamburger is hell to get out of your hair.

We could use any organic body for this spell, it just had to be carbon based and for some odd reason she wouldn't allow me to practice on anything live yet.

Mom paused at the bottom of the stairs. She didn't turn to look at me, but I heard the tears straining her voice. "I know I'm hard on you. I hate it but…they'll be coming for you soon. We won't be able to protect you much longer."

My sullen anger vaporized at her words. Though I'd known the truth for a long time, it was different to hear her say the words out loud. Fear swept over me like cold water. I stood motionless, speechless, even if my tongue had been working, and watched her disappear around the corner.

****

Twenty minutes of furious scrubbing later, I pulled a baggy long-sleeved shirt over my wet hair and rushed downstairs, still shaky, but caffeine and sugar coming to the rescue. There was no time for the blow drier if I wanted to catch the last half of my Biology class. Good thing the bed head look was in.

"Wow, what happened to you?" my ten-year-old brother, Parker, asked, pausing in his attempt to stuff his lunch into an overfull backpack. With Mom working on my magic most mornings it was Parker's responsibility to get himself ready and out to the bus. He was about as good at that as I was at transference.

I glared my response, unable to deliver the scathing remark in my mind.

His smile grew wider. "Mom freeze your tongue again?"

If only I could talk. I grabbed my own backpack and stalked out the door, as the school bus chugged down the snow-covered street. A devious grin spread over my face. He was going to miss the bus again. Served him right. Mom would be furious, especially in the mood I had put her in.

I paused. The corners of my lips fell at the image of Parker facing wrath that was meant for me. With a silent groan I spun on my heel and rushed into the house.

Still struggling with his backpack, he shot me a wide-eyed stare. "What?"

I threw him his coat, smashed his snack into the backpack, and yanked the zipper shut. Goldfish crumbs taste the same anyway. He ran in my wake out the front door and down to the street where we watched the bus pull around the corner and out of sight.

The usual snarkiness left his voice. "I guess I better go tell Mom."

With a glance at my watch, I debated. I'd miss all of second period Biology, not something my C minus grade could really afford. Really, why did high schools have to put all the AP classes first thing in the morning? One look at his face made up my mind. I opened the passenger door on my car and threw in his backpack.

The corners of his mouth shot up, and his eyes crinkled. "Really? Awesome! Hey can I come watch you practice tomorrow? It's way cool."

I glared sideways at him, but the look didn't pack much heat. Parker had always thought my *talent* of blowing stuff up was great.

He stopped next to the open door. "Mom doesn't appreciate you."

I was momentarily glad Mom had frozen my tongue, and he didn't expect me to answer. It saved me from lying.

Mom's warning about them *coming* for me sped up my pulse. I pushed the fear aside. I'd known it would happen someday. I'd just hoped it would be much later.

I forced a smile to my unwilling lips and waved to our neighbor, my best friend Emma's mom, who stood

7

on her porch looking up and down the street.

"Have you guys seen Sparky?" she called.

I shook my head and noticed Parker ducking into my car a little too quickly at the mention of the annoying mutt. I filed away that thought for later. He had a habit of *practicing* on the neighbor's dog.

Emma's mom put her hands on her hips and glanced up the street. "Well, he got out again—somehow. Let me know if you see him."

With no voice to question Parker about the disappearing dog, I waved goodbye. I settled behind the wheel and encouraged the engine of my hunk-of-junk car while it struggled to life.

Parker slammed the door. "Hey, can we go through the drive-thru and get me a bacon and egg biscuit? I didn't actually have time to eat breakfast."

I momentarily considered banging my face against the wheel. Okay, so maybe I'd be able to catch the last half of third period. If I was lucky.

****

I trudged across the campus at Northwestern. Probably the only perk of having parents who were professors was that they could arrange for time in the well-equipped lab.

Both my parents worked as History professors at the university but their real jobs involved the history of our kind and most importantly, finding the answer every witch except me was so desperate to discover. How to access the unlimited power beneath our feet. I wouldn't know what to do with it if I found it. Probably unintentionally blow up a city.

College students hustled by me in groups of twos and threes, laughing and chatting. Oh, to be a simple college student, where if you failed your finals, evil witches didn't fry your brain.

I cleared my throat and pasted a smile on my face. Thankfully, the spell my mom put on me that morning had worn off by the end of my fourth period class so at least I could speak again. As I rounded the corner to the Biology lab, I stopped in the doorway. At the desk, with his feet propped on the corner was not the slightly overweight, perpetually rumpled, Professor Cho that I'd met at faculty dinners. Instead of polyester, the long legs were covered in faded denim and in the place of Dr. Cho's cowboy boots there was a pair of well used Chucks.

He glanced up from the worn textbook he held. Brown eyes, so deep and vibrant, they looked more like molten copper, met mine. And held. My feet were still rooted in the doorway, while my neurons sputtered to a halt. I forgot how to talk, how to smile, how to even think.

He blinked, breaking my trance, and returned his attention to the book's pages. I filled my straining lungs with air, only then realizing that I'd also forgotten how to breathe, while I took in the rest of him. Let's just say concentrating on my lab might be a problem.

I could only describe him as dark. Hair, eyes, clothes, and attitude. He continued to read from the book in his hand. "So, I hear you like to ditch class then make people stay late to help you get your grade up."

The deep rustle of his voice elicited a surprisingly warm tingle in my stomach that his words quickly eliminated. "I missed class because I was sick, not that it's any of your business."

His gaze lifted from the page and meandered up

my body to rest on my face. One eyebrow and matching corner of his lips pulled up. "Yeah, you look pretty bad. You should have stayed in bed."

Already taut, the muscles in my shoulders and neck tightened like guitar strings. The tension spread to my skull, ready to snap. Coping skills, remember your coping skills. Whenever I was nervous, or in most cases angry, my tongue tended to completely bypass my brain, and no telling what would fly out. I counted to ten and managed a civil tone. "Did you have somewhere you needed to be?"

He dropped his feet to the floor, and laid the textbook, a well-used copy of *Human Genes and Disease*, on the table. A clown-like smile spread across his face and forced joviality filled his voice. "Are you crazy? Why would I want to go to a study group for my midterm when I could be here with you?"

I glanced back at the textbook and the pages of notes spread across the desk underneath. I walked to the microscope on the bench, got out my notebook, and tried to swallow the acid in my throat. While his words smarted, I could understand the frustration behind them. "Feel free to go."

He set two beakers on the bench with more force than necessary. "The professor had better places to be so he asked me to stay, and when he asks you to do something you don't say no if you want to get a good recommendation for grad school. You won't have to worry about recommendations, I'm sure. Your parents will bail you out then too."

All right he needed to be knocked down a peg or three. I cocked my head to the side. "Let me make sure I got this right. Professor Cho is the scientist and you run around doing whatever he says. So that makes you…what? His little minion?"

He paused, as if a bit shocked I'd come up with a stinger.

I let a saccharine grin spread across my face before I turned my attention to my research project on blood cells. If he wanted to think I was some spoiled little rich kid, let him. I didn't have the time or inclination to prove otherwise. I dropped my notebook on the lab bench. With his looks he was probably used to girls falling all over him, unable to come up with a coherent sentence, much less a comeback. Newsflash, not this girl.

After a few minutes of silence, his voice startled me. "I'm Jax, by the way."

I glanced up from focusing the microscope. A truce? "I'm Maddie."

He nodded then waved to the high-tech scope in front of me. "Let me know if you need help. Those can be a pain to get in focus, but they are way better than what you are used to in the high school lab."

"I think I've got it, but I'll let you know."

He crossed his arms then started pacing.

I pricked my finger and squeezed a drop of blood on the slide. Disk-like red blood cells floated through my field of vision under the scope. With my notes out and timer ready, I placed a drop of 10% saline solution on the blood while watching the cells under the microscope. Almost immediately the cells shriveled, or crenated, turning into tiny blood cell raisins. I documented the reaction and time it took and went to the next solution, a 9% saline.

Ten drops of blood and ten slides later, Jax finally

quit his pacing and leaned against the wall with his book. From his vantage point he could watch my progress.

I forced my brain to shut out everything but the blood cells in front of me. Well, almost everything. I couldn't keep myself from glancing up to see if he was watching me. Flippin' distracting. Plus, his biceps flexed in an oh-so-luscious way every time he turned a page. Not that I was watching. He was a total jerk.

His hovering grated on my already frazzled nerves. I wanted out of there even more than he did. Thirty minutes later, my rushed fingers fumbled the beaker of pure water, my last solution, and sent it flying to the floor with a crash. Shards of glass flew in a twelve-foot radius around the puddle of water.

Both of us jumped.

I covered my eyes with a hand and blew out a breath. "Genius Maddie, maybe a monkey would have been better at this experiment."

Jax's attention settled on me, and for a moment his eyes seemed to assess me. Without the expected snide comment, he grabbed the broom from the corner and swept the shards into a pile.

"Sorry about the mess," I apologized. I was used to making messes but it was way worse in front of hot college guys.

I got more distilled water from the dispenser on the counter and rushed to finish the last slide. My hands trembled, from embarrassment or anger I didn't know. I focused the lens and dropped the water. The cells immediately burst, or lysed, leaving a red fog under the scope. I scribbled the result and slammed my notebook shut then gathered up my equipment to put it away.

"Hey, you want to see something cool?" Jax asked, in a voice that had considerably less of a jerk undertone than before.

I blinked a few times and tried to figure out if he was making fun of me or trying to make me feel better for breaking the flask. "That's okay, you have to get to your study group."

He waved it off, and what seemed to be a genuine smile rested on his lips. "It was over twenty minutes ago. This is cool, just watch."

Must be a guy's version of an apology, I thought. Still hesitant, I stepped to the side. He pricked his finger and squeezed a drop of blood on a clean slide and set it under the double-sided microscope. It had two sets of oculars so we could both see the slide at the same time. He took a brown vial from the store room and motioned for me to look through the lens.

Curious, I bent my head to my set of lenses while Jax adjust the scope. His floating red blood cells came into focus out of the red haze. With his head only a few inches from my own, my nose caught a spicy scent. My stomach tightened. So what if he smelled good. He was still a jerk.

He opened the vial and squeezed out a single drop. The instant the solution hit the blood not only did the cells begin to explode one at a time, they produced bubbles until the entire slide was a bubbling foaming mess. I'd never seen blood react that violently.

"Cool, what's in there?" I motioned to the vial.

"My own special cocktail. Professor Cho asked me to mix something up to impress the freshmen on the first day of class." He wiggled his eyebrows at me. "Want to see it again?"

I paused but found it impossible not to return his grin. "Definitely."

I pricked my finger and got the slide ready. He dropped the solution on my blood, and we waited for the cells to start bursting. Nothing happened.

Several beats passed. I glanced up to meet Jax's confused look. Unsure of what to say, I turned back to the microscope. Tiny lights began to appear inside each blood cell. In a matter of seconds, they glowed like miniscule stars flying through the solution. The light intensified, glaring out of the tiny cells.

"What the hell?" Jax asked.

I couldn't take my eyes off the blood. Finally, I straightened, tears running down my face from the blinding light. I met his wide-eyed gaze over the top of the gleaming scope. The slide cast pink light up to the ceiling, leaving the room in a rosy glow.

"How?" he stammered.

I opened my mouth without a clue as to what to tell Jax. A loud *pop* saved me the trouble. Smoke twisted up from the cracked slide as the light faded. A nasty burned-meat smell wafted up to my nostrils. Only one thought made it through the frozen neurons in my brain. Get out of here.

Chapter Two

The questions Jax would ask were none I could answer. My lungs seemed to be filled with cement, I struggled to breathe and took a step back.

That broke him out of his daze. He rushed forward. "What was that?"

If anyone found out this could be the end of my family—attention was no friend to a witch. They pounded that most important rule into our brains from a young age. Never tell a human about your powers.

My family was already under a microscope of our own. I couldn't let the council find out about this. If only my parents were here to do a memory wipe. I couldn't risk scrambling his brain. Or blowing it up.

I snapped my mouth shut and forced myself to sound normal. Well, as normal as I could manage.

"What are you blathering on about? I didn't see anything special." I hoped the snark in my voice would mask the truth in my eyes.

His brows pulled together. "You've got to be kidding. You saw that."

I shoved my notebook into my backpack and yanked the zipper up with trembling hands, while I tried to surreptitiously wipe the moisture from my cheeks. "Nice try, but I'm not falling for your joke. Try it on one of the freshmen next time."

Jax held his hand up in front of me. "Wait, I'm

serious. I know you saw the light."

"Ha, very funny." I pushed past him. "Get a life."

****

I didn't stop shaking until several miles lay between me and the campus. Thoughts raced around my head like little hamsters on a wheel. I'd put my family in danger—again. I hadn't meant to, but I'd also put Jax in danger. Jerk that he was, he didn't deserve what the council would do to him if they found out.

A blaring horn alerted me to the fact that I was sitting at a green light. I waved my apology and pulled off onto the next side street and parked. Obviously not in any condition to drive.

Deep breaths, more deep breaths. A light-headed feeling spread over me. Who the hell came up with these so-called coping skills anyway? One thing was for sure, they obviously didn't have anxiety.

Everyone had been right all along, there was something seriously wrong with me. Now even my blood blew up. The thought of telling my parents I'd made yet another mess for them to clean up seemed about as appealing as jumping in a tank full of starving flesh-eating Piranhas. No, the piranhas sounded less painful, and at least that would be over quick.

I could easily picture the exhausted sigh Mom would try to hide, and the "It's okay, everyone makes mistakes," from my dad. Yeah, but not everyone was a walking explosive.

I drove the rest of the way home half hoping I'd get in a car accident. Then at least I wouldn't have to tell them about the bubbling blood. No such luck.

With my best ever I'm-not-a-freak-that-blows-everything-up impression, I walked into the house and strode into the kitchen. I tossed my backpack on a chair with what I hoped mimicked careless abandon and turned to face…an empty room.

No demands of practicing, no inquisition about my day, and no dinner. Only a note on the table. "We were called in on an emergency call from the council. Parker will stay at a friend's tonight. There is a pizza in the freezer. We will be back tomorrow, please try to get some practice in."

I sank into the chair and looked up to the ceiling. A day of rest before all hell broke loose. There is a God after all.

****

I gripped the freezing metal handrail of the stairs leading to the school. Got to love February in northern Illinois. The last thing I needed today was to slip and break my leg. Actually, that didn't sound so bad. Then I could get some sleep.

I really shouldn't have missed my first three classes, again. And I couldn't even blame it on Mom this time. In my freaked-out state, I'd forgotten to set my alarm. In my defense it is exceedingly difficult go to sleep when you're worried that you might explode at any moment. I found myself staring at my hand, examining the tiny veins, until I'd finally passed out sometime close to sunrise.

Pulling my gaze away from the blood vessels at my wrist, I forced my brain to a problem I could actually do something about.

My stomach cinched tight as a zip-tie at the thought of another missed A.P. Bio class. The teacher loved to give pop quizzes, which I got zeroes on since I missed them. That, plus my twenty percent participation score, put my overall grade in the low seventies. Really, who ever heard of a participation grade in Biology? Pretty sure college professors didn't give participation grades.

Not a big deal. Unless the only thing you've ever wanted to do with your life is to be a geneticist. I never dreamed of living in a castle, or beautiful dresses, or princes, or ponies. Nope, my dolls always wore lab coats, graduated from the Biology program at MIT, and saved the world.

With a deep shudder from the frigid air, I pulled the metal door open. A gush of warm air filled with the scent of lunch cooking in the cafeteria washed over me. I sniffed, must be chili day. I knew I still needed to focus on school, but my brain wouldn't let go of the image of my cells lighting up, the burnt smell, and the look on Jax's face. Focus, focus, I'd have to break the news to my parents tonight, and we could decide what to do.

For now, I was a not-so-average student with average worries like getting into college. After the extreme amount of groveling and promises of improved attendance it took to get the extra credit lab, I was not looking forward to facing my teacher.

Just my luck. Who should I run into in my rush past the main office? My Bio teacher, Mr. Heckman, otherwise known as Mr. Hickey due to an unfortunate *curling iron* incident. He prefers Mr. H.

"Well, Miss. Foster. We missed you this morning."

I forced a smile and tried to sound out of breath. "Asthma. My mom should have called in for me."

He studied me for a moment, then nodded slowly.

"You missed a quiz. Another zero brings your

grade down to a D."

My stomach tightened more, and then compacted into a hard ball. My teeth ground together while I battled the urge to do a very, very bad thing to Mr. H. One thing my parents frowned upon was transforming my teachers into reptiles or bugs. What kill-joys, transforming was my one witch talent and they never let me use it.

The one time I did they spent the entire day cleaning up the mess. But my kindergarten teacher suffered no long lasting side-effects from her afternoon as a lizard. If you don't count the insatiable cravings for live bugs. Other than transformation all I could really do well was blow stuff up. Possibly even more so than we'd thought.

My mind raced through calculations of what a D would do to my GPA. Not a chance at MIT. I needed at least a B plus for a shot at my dream school, and some hope of life after witchcraft. I did my best impersonation of contrite, wide eyes and everything. "I have the lab done, and I'll write up and bring it to class tomorrow."

He rocked back and forth on his heels, a habit that drove me crazy during his lectures. "Not tomorrow. Bring it to me after school today, and I'll give you credit for the quizzes you missed. But don't expect me to keep letting you do extra credit to get your grade up. This is a college level class, not everyone can grasp the curriculum."

His condescending tone made me want to pull out my last test and shove the 98 percent up his nose, then ask if he thought I could handle the curriculum. I pushed my anger deep and kept my voice sincere. "I'll do my best. I think my biggest trouble is the participation grade. But I'll bring you the lab write-up after school."

Mr. H. contemplated the ceiling, and his generous brow pulled together like one long dust bunny creeping across his forehead. "I do have a few students in my Botany class that need tutoring. That could be considered participation. But don't expect it to help you on the AP test."

I nodded. "I have lunch hour fifth period. Just let me know who needs help."

"I'll tell you what I decide in class tomorrow." He gave me what I'm sure was supposed to be a meaningful stare then walked away with his nose thrust into the stratosphere. The bell rang and my classmates spilled into the hall.

I stalked to my locker, shoved my books inside, grabbed a piece of gum, and slammed the door. My next class was English, which I shared with my best friend Emma.

I slid into my seat and buried my face in The Odyssey. I could definitely relate to angry gods, torment, and monsters.

"Maddie," Emma said after she sat down behind me.

I rotated in my seat and put on my everything-is-great-face. "Hey, what's up?"

Her hand paused in its swipe through her blond curls. The cheery expression slid from her face like melted butter off pancakes. "Uh oh. What happened?"

The truth begged to jump off my tongue. Oh, not much, just some freaky reaction with my blood, could mean I'm even more screwed up than everyone thought. Which is hard to believe.

But even though Emma was my best friend, she didn't know that I was a witch. She couldn't know. No one could.

Instead I shrugged. "Lots of hoops to jump through. I have to meet Mr. H after school, and I probably have to start tutoring on my lunch hour."

Her lips parted, and the corners tugged down before she recovered herself and yanked them into a smile. Talk about puppy dog eyes. "I thought we were going to get coffee after school, and, you know, see if the rumors are true."

Crap, crap, crap. That put me being three places at once. Emma had lived next door to me all my life. We'd been friends from training wheels through training bras. I couldn't leave her hanging. I reached out a hand to place over hers. "Don't even think about leaving me out of the spy mission. Give me half an hour, then I'll be there."

She shook her head. "I can handle it."

"Not a chance." I gave her a wink.

Chapter Three

The rest of my classes passed in a blur. I continually forced thoughts of my burning blood and possible explosions out of my mind, and maybe a couple fantasies about a certain dark-haired jerk, while trying to take notes and surreptitiously write up a lab report without my teachers noticing.

I held off my irritation with my power-tripping Bio teacher until the final bell rang, and I headed to his office. After twenty minutes of forced gratitude and close to sincere assurances that I would love to tutor Botany students, I escaped with what little remained of my pride.

****

I got to the coffee shop ten minutes late. Emma's Toyota Prius sat beside the curb with a hunched figure in the driver's seat. Remind me to never suggest a career in the CIA. I parked around the corner then ran up and knocked on the window.

"Hey. Sorry I'm late. Any sign of him?" I asked. He'd have to be a complete moron not to spot Emma.

"Not yet. How did it go with Mr. H?"

"He wasn't exactly helpful. You might want to park in a less conspicuous spot. Don't want to scare off our prey."

Rumor had it Emma was being played by her boyfriend of two years. At first, we hadn't believed the stories, Nathan seemed like way less of a pig than most guys, but soon everyone was telling Emma they'd seen Nathan getting his flirt on with the chick from the coffee shop.

Her head whipped around. "Oh, how stupid. I'll be right back."

"Why don't I go snag a couch and get us some drinks. I'm in serious withdrawal."

The delicious aroma wafting out of the coffee shop was enough to make my mouth water. It had been hours since my last espresso, and a caffeine headache was building as my body slurped up the last of its reserves.

I went to the counter to get my caffeine fix and came face to face with a way too perky smile. An equally cheerful voice matched her sunny expression. "Can I get you a coffee?"

Looks like the tips weren't the only bonus with this job. All the coffee I could drink. I moaned. The place would go bankrupt if I worked here. "I'll have a triple shot espresso macchiato and a skinny chai latte."

Her eyebrows lifted. "A triple shot?"

"You got it."

"Ooookay." She nodded and turned to do her barista stuff.

Mere moments later I sipped my drink and made my way to the overstuffed leather seat. The liquid singed my tongue but I didn't care.

The couch in the far corner sat bathed in shadows. I plopped down and sipped. I could practically hear my exhausted cells cheering while they gobbled up the sugar and caffeine as quickly as it could get into my blood. All the magic my parents had me doing left me in a constant state of exhaustion. Most witches could keep up with their demands just fine, but I always seemed to use way too much of my energy with easy spells.

Emma walked through the door and scanned the room. I contemplated my fashion forward friend for a moment. The soft pink sweater hugged curves and complemented her coloring perfectly with leggings and awesome boots. We made quite the pair, her put together look in contrast to my own slouchy, whatever-was-on-the-floor-closest-to-my-bed style.

Her gaze slid over the dark corner twice before I called her name to get her attention. Her squinted eyes relaxed. She waved and wove her way through the tables to my dim hideaway.

I handed her the chai. "So what's this chick's name?"

She pointed out the perky barista. "That one."

I sized up the competition. So what if she could pull off a pixie cut and her legs looked great in her short shorts while she buzzed around making delicious caffeine-laden nirvana in a cup? I took another drink. Perfect. Actually, maybe I should start dating her.

I drained the last drop and glanced over at Emma. Her shaking cup seemed to be glued to her lips. I followed her wide eyes to the door where the guy in question had just walked in. Nathan.

He laughed with a couple football teammates while they strolled to the counter.

While we sank deeper into the corner, I grabbed Emma's hand and squeezed. Nathan brushed back his pretty boy hair and adjusted his letter jacket. The perky barista leaned over, flashing what cleavage she could manage from the mosquito bites on her chest. I shouldn't judge. She probably had half a cup size on me.

The two chatted at the counter, then the girl turned her attention to Nathan's teammates to take their orders.

"See, nothing to worry about." I whispered and nudged Emma's side. "Can't trust the rumor mill."

Emma watched the bland scene for a bit longer then a gale force sigh escaped her lips. "Maybe you're right."

"It has happened once or twice."

Before I could say any more, Nathan's coffee was ready. Instead of setting the cup on the counter, like any normal order, the barista beckoned him over with a crooked finger.

Uh oh.

After a quick glance around, probably to be sure her boss wasn't watching, she dipped a finger in the whip cream topping and dabbed the sweet foam on her lips.

Nathan smirked and leaned across the counter.

Emma's hand gripped mine like a vice.

They went in for a definitely not G-rated kiss.

I tore my eyes away from the love birds at the counter to see Emma fighting back tears. Her muscles tensed. I pulled her back as she tried to get up. "Don't. He's not worth it."

"I can't believe it. He swore to me it wasn't true." Her trembling tone reminded me of the day we sat on her front porch for six hours, waiting for her dad to show up and take her on a special birthday outing. He called the next day. Work emergency.

I hadn't been able to do anything to make it better then. I glared at Nathan, who was now holding a piping hot whip cream and sprinkle-covered grande. Likely a mocha. Wuss couldn't even drink real coffee. And to think I stuck up for him.

He took a seat with his buddies, not a care in the world. Call it my sense of injustice or whatever, but I couldn't stand to watch him sit and relax with a smile on his face.

My parents never let me perform magic in public. For obvious reasons. News stories tended to follow about suspected terrorist attacks, but really, that was only like once. Or twice.

My muscles tensed to get up and walk over to do something mundane like throw coffee in his face. I know, being a witch should be way cooler. But I had to do something.

Before I could stand up, the tiny lights of my blood cells flashed in my mind. I paused, I already had to have an uncomfortable talk with my parents about the burning blood. What was one more tiny problem?

I settled back into my seat. Across the room Nathan laughed and lifted his cup to blow on the steaming drink. I focused my aim, carefully using only a little of my energy to undo the electromagnetic bonds of the molecules in his cup.

It took all my attention. I'd only managed success with this particular spell a couple times and if my aim was the least bit off…Well, let's just say it wouldn't be pretty.

Chapter Four

The bottom of Nathan's cup blew out, and the contents covered his crotch in mocha napalm. My excess energy had superheated the coffee to a scalding temperature and sent chunks of the cup flying through the air. He sprang from his seat and fanned his pants while his wide-open mouth emitted a surprisingly high pitched shriek.

My hand slapped over my lips, my entire body shaking with enjoyment. A little overkill, maybe. Too bad my mom wasn't around to see me actually do a spell right.

Emma stared, stunned, then squeaked and fell into convulsions on my shoulder. The barista ran around the counter with a towel to help her now-falsetto boyfriend while most of his teammates busted up. I wondered if a couple might fall out of their chairs.

Part of me wanted to jump up and take a bow. To finally let everyone see what I was capable of, but I sat there like a good little witch and pretended to be just as shocked as the rest of the place.

Nathan grabbed a glass of water from the table and dumped the contents on his pants. Relief washed over his face. He stood, dripping, in the middle of the coffee shop. A few snickers spread through the crowd.

It took several seconds to regain my self-control. "I don't think he'll be enjoying any play time for a while."

Emma wiped tears from her eyes. "I love Karma."

She cleared her throat and strutted through the crowd to Nathan's table. The towel slipped from his hand when he spotted her cheery face, and he waved away the attention of the barista.

His voice sounded a bit high, and his eyes darted from her face to my glaring one. "Emma. How long have you been here?"

The laughter died out when everyone recognized Emma. With a hand on her hip, she gave him a slow once over, lingering on his pants. "Long enough."

The barista rose to her feet, obviously picking up on the change in Nathan. "Who's this?"

Emma turned her attention to the girl. "His girlfriend. Or should I say ex. You can have him. And don't worry about the damage." She motioned to his crotch. "There wasn't much there, and he sure didn't know how to use it."

The guys from the football team erupted into laughter. I glanced around, and my gaze settled on a face almost hidden in a corner. It wasn't so much his features that made my eyes rest on him. In a room bursting with energy he sat, surrounded by calm, almost like he was exuding peace from his pores. Kind of like a Tibetan Monk.

That and the massive tattoo made him impossible to miss. The swirling branches crept up from beneath the neck of his shirt and wove their way past his chin and around his ear into his hairline, which was shaved close except for on top.

While the calm and tattoo caught my attention that wasn't what kept it. All the eyes in the room were on Emma and Nathan. All eyes except for his. He stared at me. And the smirk on his lips said it all. He knew. He knew what I'd done.

I pulled on Emma's arm. "We should go."

We moved to the door, riding the laughter behind us like surfers on a wave. The strange tattooed guy stared until I walked through the door, the smirk never leaving his face. One thing was for sure, he wasn't a stuffy prim and proper council member. So, who the hell was he?

I already had a battle waiting for me at home over performing magic. I didn't need any more stress. I didn't have time to deal with some freaky, staring weirdo. As long as he didn't follow me.

Around the corner from the shop, we collapsed against the Prius, Emma's laughter infectious.

She blew out a breath. "I feel great. God, what a loser. Did you hear him scream?"

I nodded. "I wish we'd gotten it on video."

"Oh! That screech would make the best ringtone," she paused. "I'm so glad you were here with me. You're the best, best friend in the world."

I shrugged off the compliment. Most best friends weren't forced to constantly lie about who they really were.

Emma rolled her eyes at me then leaned in. "You know, if I'm being completely honest, I kind of feel sorry for her. He is the worst kisser. Like all tongue, you know?"

My lips pressed together, and I nodded while she continued her rant about tongues and spit and tonsils. I could only hope that my expression wouldn't give away my other dark secret. At this point I couldn't stand for her to find out the truth.

I didn't exactly lie. She made assumptions, and I didn't correct her.

"I mean, nibbling on someone's lip is one thing but you don't have to chew it off." Emma wrinkled her nose.

I could only nod again, my chest in an ever tightening vice. I had no idea what it was like to have someone nibble too hard.

I'd never kissed a guy. It was pathetic, really, a senior in high school and never been kissed.

I stared at the pavement near my feet. Jax's smoky copper eyes and smirk flashed in my mind for some inexplicable reason. A pinch tightened my stomach. What would I give to be normal? I would give up what little I could do with my powers in a second if it meant fitting into the real world.

Emma stopped her rant. "Are you listening to me?"

"Of course I am," I said. "Tongues, spit, gross."

She pushed off from the car. "I said we need to find you a boy."

I glared, but inside the vice loosened. We were off the kissing topic. "Do we really have to talk about this? Again?"

"Hear me out." Emma considered me for a moment. "I'd kill for your hair and your eyes are, like, seriously blue. Didn't that guy from Trig say you had nice hair last week?"

Personally, I'd always wished my hair would just pick a color and go with it instead of being in between blond and brown. Although, I had to admit it had great body so I let it grow out to my lower back. Plus, it made me feel less plain.

She picked up a lock of my hair and twisted it.

"Uh, if only you'd let me dress you!"

I crossed my arms. This was a way more complicated subject than she could know. Witches were a dying breed. In each generation our numbers grew smaller and the birth rate dwindled.

Sometime in the dark ages, like way before cell phones, arranged marriages were instilled to ensure that the couples had the genetic compatibility to produce offspring. Enter, Surfer Boy, as I called him, my betrothed who I had yet to meet. Yeah, I wouldn't mind putting off that meeting until, let's say, never. There's no point in dating if you can't pick who you end up with.

"What exactly is your point?" I asked.

She held her palms up. "Nothing, jeeze, just trying to help a girl out."

I heard the crack in my own voice. "Not today, please."

Her face fell. "What's the matter?"

I opened my mouth, but, for once, nothing came out. I stared at her furrowed brow over concerned eyes.

She reached a hand out to grip my arm. "If something's going on, you can tell me anything—you know."

I did know. I knew she wouldn't doubt me, even if I told her about being a witch. She'd do her best to understand and would help me through my fear about my blood boiling. I knew she'd be on my side and love me for who I was. But I also knew she'd end up dead.

Maybe not today, but someday in a freak accident or explainable fashion, knowing about witches would kill her. The council would be sure of it.

No. I wouldn't risk her, and for what? One person

who completely accepted me? All of me? I forced back the flood of words that begged to be spoken.

I pushed her shoulder and pasted on a smile while I stuffed my own upset to the deepest pit of my stomach. "Nothing's wrong. I just don't share your taste in falsetto males with overly aggressive tongues. No offense."

Her eyes went wide. "Oh, you. I can't believe you." She smacked my arm.

I dodged the next blow and laughed when her paper coffee cup hit the brick wall just over my head.

"I'll get you back for that," she called.

I waved and headed to my car. Time to face the music at home.

****

I knew the moment I walked into the kitchen that I had stepped into a battle zone. Mom sat with her hands clinched in front of her, only releasing them to repeatedly push her hair behind her ears. Dad sat across from her attempting to grade a paper from one of his students.

Parker pulled a disappearing act when I walked into the kitchen. Smart boy.

I set my bag on the floor and hoped for a clue as to which of my screw-ups they were upset about. Stoney faces met my gaze. Not a clue. Crap, might as well get it over with. "I have something really important to tell you."

"You mean that you willingly broke the only real rule that we have for you. We already know," Mom snapped.

Okay, so we're talking about the coffee incident first. "Look, I'm sorry I didn't come home to practice right after school. I had a meeting with my teacher then Emma really needed me to…help her."

Mom sat forward. "You mean help her kill her boyfriend?"

To keep me honest, my parents put a magic tracker spell on me, kind of a supernatural GPS that pinged if I performed a spell. The bigger the spell, the bigger the ping. It made me feel about as trusted and grown up as a five-year-old.

Dad set his red pen down. "Let's not get ahead of ourselves."

"She could have easily killed that boy. A few centimeters off or losing control of the energy and his intestines would be Jell-O," Mom insisted. "And then we would have had to clean up yet another of her messes."

It's not like I'd ever killed anyone before.

Dad nodded.

Although I knew she was right, I couldn't admit it. I licked my lips. Much as I hated to pour fuel on the fire, I knew I had to tell them. "You guys can punish me, or whatever, but will you please listen to me for a second?"

Mom got up and waved a finger in my face. "Don't try to change the subject. You're not getting out of this that easy. You performed a new spell out in public, risked killing someone, and you come in here acting like it isn't important."

Well, actually it wasn't really, compared to my other problem. Anger bubbled inside my chest. "I've done a demolecularization spell before. I was sure I wouldn't kill him."

Mom raised her eyebrows at me.

I rolled my eyes. "Okay, pretty sure."

Her hand swiped through her hair again. "Don't you take that flippant attitude with me. You were only considering yourself, not what would happen if you made a mistake." She got to her feet and pointed a finger at me. "Do you know where we were last night?" She paused, her eyes boring into me. "Begging the council to put off meeting your betrothed. Why are we even trying?"

Momentary shock froze my voice.

"This is the sixth time we've had to ask. You have no idea how hard we've tried to protect you," she ranted.

I knew I should count to ten or breathe deeply, anything to keep my mouth shut, but as usual my anger got the best of me. "Why bother? I don't even want these stupid powers anymore." I threw my arms to the side. "Call the council, they can fry my brain with lightning. Maybe I'd be less trouble to you if you let them turn me into a drone like Aunt Clara."

The blood drained from her face, and she took a step back. Dad stood up and placed himself between us. Maybe that wasn't the smartest thing to say.

The great family scandal, the name we never spoke, was Aunt Clara. She dared to go against our witch traditions and refused to marry her betrothed. She tried to run away with an ungifted boy but they caught her, of course, only an idiot would try to hide from the council.

I glanced over at a framed picture on the shelf. My mom and her sister, before, smiling at the camera. As a punishment the council *washed* her mind—meaning they took away her free will and made her into a drone.

Really, she was lucky to be alive, messing with someone's mind was hardly an exact science and more often than not the subject ended up dead. She now served to enforce our laws, punishment fitting the crime, they said.

Basically, she was one of the boogie men that parents warned their naughty children about to scare them into behaving, *Be good or Clara Stark will come for you.* Only, unlike other versions of the story, she actually did come take people away and kill them.

I glanced back to my mom. She'd never recovered from losing her little sister, nor had the family ever recovered from the financial and social hardships that went along with the scandal.

Mom's hands tightened into fists until her knuckles turned gray. "How can you be so ungrateful? All the hours we've spent, trying to help you get the basic spells, the searching through books to find any idea on how to improve your skills. We should have had the council remove your powers when you were two and we realized there was something wrong with you," her voice trembled.

"That's enough," my dad snapped.

Mom's mouth clamped shut.

I stared at her face and gripped the back of a chair, fighting the bile that climbed up my throat.

Her wide, blinking eyes mirrored my own shock.

The truth had finally come out. They'd always known something was wrong with me. They knew I was a Defect. Why couldn't I have been born a normal human? My anger bled out of me where her words drove a knife into my heart. What would she say if she knew the whole truth? That even my blood blew up.

My voice choked on the swelling in my throat, but I absolutely refused to let her see how much her words hurt. "I never asked for your help, and I don't want it."

"Everyone is upset. We can talk about this when we've all calmed down," Dad said.

Mom stepped closer and put a hand on my shoulder. "I'm sorry, I didn't mean that. Your father's right, we're all upset." She tried to meet my eyes. "Maddie, please, I'm sorry. It's just the thought of you ending up like Clara…"

She could claim she didn't mean it all she wanted, but I knew it was true. Words are like bullets—you can't really take them back. My body quivered, my teeth clinched. "I'm not upset. I'm fine."

"We both love you and are here to help you." Dad sighed and put his arms around Mom and me. "We're all under a lot of pressure, and we can't afford any mistakes right now, not with your magic finals coming up. Absolutely no spells unless you're studying. Do you understand?"

I nodded once, then spun on my heel and pounded upstairs. Time for a new plan. I'd be cleaning up my own messes from now on.

****

That night I spent a good hour sitting on the edge of my bed staring at a bare wall while thoughts raced around my head. I had to fix this myself. My stomach twisted into an Origami swan. I'd never been able to do anything right my entire life.

The kids at camp called me a Defect, worthless, a cosmic joke on my parents. The worst had been my camp counselor. One tiny explosion on the first day, and she hated me. Maybe because it covered her in pond slime? Or perhaps she didn't like the fish guts in her hair? The algae in her teeth? The entire camp saw me in action. I'd tried to warn her not to have me be her partner. She insisted.

I slammed my fist into my pillow. I might be a Defect as a witch but I still had a damn good brain. Take a breath, Maddie, think about it scientifically. First rule of science, never make assumptions.

Countless scientific breakthroughs came from proving the original hypotheses wrong. You have to follow the data. I'd made one major assumption. That the blood reacted and blew up because I was a Defect.

My jaw firmed. My decision solidified in my mind. My anger quieted the shouting voices of doubt to a whisper. First things first. I had some data to gather.

****

"Parker." I gently shook his shoulder.

"I'll bring him back when he quits barking mom," my brother said in a sleepy grumble.

I shook him harder. "Wake up."

He opened his eyes.

"Bring who back?"

Blink. Blink. "Uh, no one." He sat up. "What are you doing?"

I motioned for him to be quiet and sat in the chair at his desk. "I need your help. But you have to promise not to tell."

He leapt out of bed like there was a spring attached to his butt. "Cool, what do you want me to do?"

Ten minutes of explaining, plus the promise of letting him watch me practice a few times, sealed the deal. I stood in the middle of the room, dressed in black, with my backpack over my shoulder.

"Okay, I'm ready." I sucked in a deep breath. "See you in ten minutes."

He nodded, not a trace of smile on his lips. "Be careful, Maddie."

It felt like pressure built up inside me, then with a burst of air, almost like blowing a dandelion puff, I no longer had a body. For a split second my consciousness floated. Then with a rush of pressure my body rematerialized. This time in Professor Cho's Biology lab.

That's one way to beat a locked door. Have a little brother who's actually good at transportation.

Without wasting any time, I crept into the storage room, praying that Jax had put the vial back. I scanned row after row of compounds, all neatly labeled, Sodium, Hydrochloric Acid, Hydrazine, Acetone, no, no, no.

Three shelves later panic took hold. In only a couple more minutes Parker would pull me back, vial or not. I had a little bit riding on this experiment. Like my entire self-worth.

I reached the last shelve, nothing. My forehead banged the wood. Glassware rattled. Think. He might have put it somewhere in the lab.

I raced out of the storage room and froze. In my haste, I'd missed the small light on the far bench. And the lean, toned, figure softly snoring in a chair.

His pencil, still gripped in his hand, lay on a notebook in front of a microscope and a familiar brown vial. I glanced at my watch, 45 seconds until Parker pulled me back. Tip-toeing like a ninja, I raced across the room. Okay maybe it was more like a drunk prima ballerina.

I paused a few feet from Jax's chair. His notebook lay open, and chemical reactions and compounds filled the page. Shaking hands grabbed the vial then slipped the notebook from under his hand.

Five seconds left. I hefted the microscope from the bench and stepped away. As the pressure began to build inside me, Jax's tired eyes opened and focused on my face. Then I was gone.

****

Parker adamantly refused to go back to bed. Especially after I asked for a sample of his blood.

Whispering in my room we hovered around the stolen microscope. I put a few drops of Parker's blood on the slide.

"Ready?" I asked. The only way to be sure it was the defect in me that made my blood react was to test another witch. I put the slide on the stage, clipped it in, then brought my brother's blood cells into focus. Two drops of Jax's solution and the room lit up in a rosy glow.

The cells blazed instantaneously, faster than mine had lit up, but instead of maintaining the light, as my cells had, they flared up into fire-balls. Parker fell away and covered his face from the heat. The slide burst into glass shards and smoke wafted to the ceiling.

I waved my hand in front of my face and stifled a cough. The power of the explosion blew the fire out in only a few seconds, but my room was left filled with a choking smoke and burned smell. Good thing I'd thought to disable the smoke detector.

I jumped up and pushed the window open. Freezing air blasted into the room but cleared the smoke to a bearable level.

Parker and I stared at each other, wide eyed, over the remains of the slide.

"That was awesome! Let's do it again!" he said and reached for the needle to pierce his finger.

I held up a hand to hold off my over exuberant partner. The reaction with my blood had been a sputtering candle compared to the blazing bon fire of the reaction with Parker's blood. Well, that answered that question. It definitely wasn't a Defect thing. It was a witch thing.

****

The sound of Parker sleeping added background noise to my research. He kind of sounded like a cat, not really a snore but more of a purr. I smoothed down his hair and resettled on the floor next to my bed.

My computer sat open, mostly useless in this search, replaced by Jax's notes. From what he'd scribbled down I gathered that he knew what chemicals he'd put into the vial six months ago, at the beginning of school, when Professor Cho had asked him to mix up the solution. But now, well things had changed. The chemicals had reacted, probably several times, to form something completely different, an unknown.

Jax tested the properties, and we now had a large, possibly protein-like molecule, with hemotoxic properties. Yeah, you think? Which wasn't surprising considering that he'd started out with six different compounds that were all hemotoxic.

I flipped through the pages of the notebook. A photo that had been tucked in the back slipped out onto my lap. I held it up. A much younger Jax sat with his arm around a woman. The pallor of her skin and her skeletal frame left no doubt that she suffered from a serious illness. Two sets of molten copper eyes smiled sadly out from the photograph. It had to be Jax and his mom.

My heart squeezed tight. I hoped she'd survived whatever illness she had, but I doubted anyone would hang onto a sad picture like this unless it was one of the last. I gently tucked the photo back into the notebook.

****

The next morning, I stumbled down the stairs in my favorite pair of jeans and a stretchy long-sleeved T-shirt that was only slightly wrinkled, my hair pulled into a ponytail. No one knocked on my door in the wee hours to get me up to practice. Probably trying to make nice after our fight last night. Plus, Sparky, who miraculously returned to his yard the previous day, only woke me up twice with his incessant barking.

That left me two hours of sleep after our late-night theft and science experiments.

I didn't say a word but walked straight to the coffee pot. I stared out the window at the snow while I drained a mug, caffeine already sweeping cobwebs from my thoughts. I poured another and scooped lukewarm eggs onto my plate from the pan on the stove.

I sat down, careful to avoid looking in my mom's direction, and pulled some energy to zap the eggs with heat. Sparks danced on my fingertips. My dad cleared his throat.

"I was just going to heat them up a little," I said.

Dad held up a hand. "No spells. I mean it. You need to save your energy for practice."

I carefully reabsorbed the power into my tissues. Gives recycling a whole new meaning.

Parker sat opposite me, picking up plastic building blocks with his magic and building some sort of space ship. His magic came naturally. I was old enough to see my parents' relief when they realized he was normal.

I'd been relieved too.

I met his eyes and winked. He grinned at our shared secret.

I pointed at the ship. "I have to eat cold eggs, but he doesn't get in trouble for that?"

Dad didn't bother to look up but opened a folder of papers and began to sift through them. "You can use the microwave, and he's not going to make the blocks explode."

I leaned back and sipped the heaven in my mug. "Right."

Mom leaned over with her hand extended, energy on her fingertips. "Here, let me."

I jerked the plate away and walked to the microwave. "No, thanks, I'm good."

While the eggs heated I leaned against the counter.

My parents glanced at each other. "Maddie," Dad said. "You said you had something important to tell us last night."

Crap. I was as bad a liar as I was a witch. I rested my head on my hands so they couldn't see my face. "It's not important anymore." Not after what *she'd said* last night.

Mom rested a hand ever-so-lightly on my shoulder. "Honey, you can tell us anything."

Now they wanted to know? I needed a distraction, anything.

The microwave dinged, and I jerked the plate out and sat at the table again.

Mom resettled in her seat and waited. They weren't going to let this go easily.

The papers that my father had been reading, yellowed with age and protected by plastic sleeves, rested on the table next to me. The words in the elegant script came in to focus.

"…plants fail to thrive…"

"What is this talking about? Botany?" I asked, pointing at the reference.

Dad leaned forward, always ready to discuss history. "Yes, actually, it was a common hobby among the English nobility in the eighteenth century. This letter was actually from a distant ancestor of yours. A great-grandfather several times over from your mother's side. A duke even. You didn't know that you were descended from English nobility, did you?"

The suspicion in my mom's face kept me talking about the letter.

"Was there ever any doubt? I am pretty noble, I'm told." I let a sliver of a smile fall over my lips and scanned the rest of the paragraph. "What was he trying to grow?"

"He never mentioned the name of the plant. These are newly discovered letters so I haven't completed my analysis. He was a bit of an eccentric, so I'm not sure we'll get much out of his correspondence. Look at this part." He pointed to a line a few paragraphs below.

"'We are the children of cattle and rabbits'," I read aloud. "Yeah, I'd say eccentric is a nice way to put it. The duke had some issues. Let's hope those traits weren't hereditary."

"That would explain a lot about your grandmother," he said with a grin my mother's way.

I chuckled, my father and my grandmother had had an interesting relationship. She'd never been afraid to tell him what she thought, speak her mind, and that…caused a few problems.

"Can we leave my mother out of this?" Mom asked and forced a smile to her tense lips.

Dad scribbled a note in his worn leather journal, the place he wrote every thought and clue he found so he could leaf through it for inspiration. He shuffled through the yellowed documents and pointed out a few other lines of interest about my eccentric ancestor.

A knock at the door sent Parker flying out of his seat. "I'll get it."

My mom followed him, and my tensed muscles relaxed with the questions about last night averted. The shrill voice of our neighbor, Emma's mom, carried into the dining room. "I don't know how Sparky keeps getting out. He's a little Houdini."

Parker returned to his seat and became overly engrossed in his breakfast.

"We'll keep an eye out for him," Mom assured her.

The door closed, and she walked into the kitchen, her arms crossed. "Parker, did you transport the neighbor's dog again?"

Parker stuffed a large bite of toast into this mouth and gave her a wide-eyed shrug.

I bit my lips to keep from laughing. That dog woke me up almost every morning with its barking, not to mention distracting me from my spells. I wished he'd get rid of the thing for good.

"Parker Foster. You put him back immediately," Mom ordered.

He swallowed and slumped in the chair. "He woke

me up. Besides I'm trying to train him. If he barks he gets sent to time out."

"And where is time out?"

Parker squirmed. "Alaska."

"Parker! He could freeze, or be eaten by wolves," Mom exclaimed.

With an Oscar-worthy sigh, Parker slumped out of the room to return the dog from timeout in the frozen tundra.

A good time to put my plan into action. I got up and rinsed my plate in the sink. "By the way, I have to stay late at school so I won't be able to practice this week."

"We need you home to practice," Mom said. "We didn't want to worry you but…the council is sending your final tester sometime next week."

My stomach threatened to reject the coffee that tasted so wonderful only moments before. I couldn't possibly pass my finals next week. "Can't we put it off?"

Dad set his papers down and reached a hand out to squeeze mine. "We already used the extension."

I plopped onto the chair and resisted the urge to crawl back in bed and hide from the world. "I'm not ready."

"It's going to be okay," Mom said, in a voice that tried to hide a boatload of doubt. "You've made improvement on your spells."

Yeah, successful one in ten times instead of none. Great improvement. I focused on my breath, in and out, in and out, while I fought the very real temptation to run screaming from the room and the house. No, make that the state. This moved up my time frame.

****

I escaped to school, the one place I felt half way normal anymore. I coasted through my classes without a single piece of information penetrating my overloaded brain but managed to get hundreds on both my quizzes.

My lunch and off hour was thankfully busy, leaving me no time to freak out. Instead I had to focus on tutoring sophomores for Mr. H.

"I don't get it," my botany-challenged student, Lisa, complained. She looked like she wanted to throw the book across the room instead of reading it.

I turned the page back for the third time and tried to think of a new way to explain the difference between phloem and xylem cells in a plant stem. "Okay, so let's make it really simple, phloem transports food. Remember the 'f' sounds go together and xylem transports water."

"Oh, I can totally remember that," she said. Her previously slumped back straightened, and her chin came up. "Thanks for being so patient with me. I know this stuff is like so easy for you."

I nodded. "No worries. Botany is a bunch of memorization. Give it some time and it will click." *I wish my life were so simple.*

"Okay, next chapter. Toxic plants," I read the chapter title.

We went over the study sheet, taking notes and discussing any questions she had. I read the last study question aloud. "Give an example of a plant that is toxic to humans but not some animals."

"I remember seeing that," she said and flipped through the book. "Here it is. Deadly Nightshade, while lethal to humans, can be eaten by cattle and some smaller herbivores without any ill effects."

A memory sparked in the dark depths of my brain, something important. The thought wiggled into my subconscious like a worm in the dirt. I struggled to follow the trail, nada.

"Good job, Lisa."

She closed the book and packed up her notes. "Thanks for your help. I'll see you next week."

Yeah, I thought, if I still have a brain next week.

****

An unfamiliar blue Chevy sat across the street from my house when I pulled up. A dark figure lounged in the driver's seat.

Jax jumped out of his car the minute I cut the engine on mine. I should have known he'd find me.

He strode across the street, all smoky hot in his faded jeans. His black T-shirt hugged his biceps and hinted at a defined chest hidden beneath. The cold of the winter air didn't seem to faze him. Part of me was surprised he didn't melt all the snow in a five-foot radius.

I caught myself brushing my hand through my hair as I tried to remember if I'd even bothered with mascara this morning. Not that I cared what he thought, I reminded myself. He's a jerk. I needed to get rid of him.

He didn't give me a chance to talk. "I know you stole my research."

I crossed my arms. "Why would I waste my time on your 'research'?"

"Don't deny it. I saw you." He paused and glanced away, then firmed his lips and stared at me, daring me to deny it again.

It was cute really, watching his rational, scientific mind try to explain the impossibility of magic.

I shook my head. "You really need to work on your people skills. Accusing someone of theft is no way to ask for help."

I could see the scathing reply he held back. "Let's say for a second you didn't steal the vial and my notebook, and I was dreaming or something." He put his hands out palms up. "What happened with your blood could be one of the greatest breakthroughs in science in decades."

His enthusiasm made me pause. I was under a time crunch, what with witches coming to fry my brain at some point in the very near future. He could be helpful to figure out what the hell was going on under the microscope. My lips pressed together. I'd taken the research about as far as my bedroom lab would let me. I needed his equipment.

I schooled my expression to one of skepticism. "That seems a bit extreme."

He stepped even closer and reached out a hand to grip my upper arm. "This is big, I can feel it."

The warmth from his hand heated my skin in a most distracting way. I pointedly glanced to his grip on my arm.

He let go and took a step away. "All I need is another sample of your blood. I can remake the serum."

"You want me to just give you my blood?" I laughed out loud. "Besides," I remembered the notes in Jax's journal that I'd borrowed. "That vial sat around for six months reacting, you can't just whip up a new batch."

"I knew you took it. I need the notebook back. I

kept important things in there." He took a step toward me.

Guilt softened my expression. I knew he was talking about the picture and not his notes. I held up a hand. "We need some rules if we're going to work together and the first one is no questions."

"No way." He crossed his arms. "You need to tell me what the hell is going on."

I didn't flinch. "Like I said, no questions, or no deal."

His fists clinched, and his brow scrunched, while the scientist in him demanded answers and the realist in him told him to take the deal. "You give me back my stuff plus some blood, we'll call it even and work together. No questions."

I held out my hand. "Deal."

I brought Jax's notebook out to his car and pretended not to notice when he flipped to the back and checked to see if the picture of his mom was still there. He texted me his number and said he was headed straight for the lab after I handed over a vial of my blood. I insisted on meeting him there later.

I watched him drive away, wishing I could follow him immediately. I had to temper my excitement until after my nightly magical practice session. On the plus side, I managed to conjure ten out of the hundred tries. The grapes might have been more on the raisiny side but let's not be too picky, they didn't explode.

After my parents finally fell asleep I snuck out to meet Jax at the lab.

He met me at the door to let me in. He practically vibrated with excitement.

"This reaction is extremely exothermic," he said as

soon as I closed the door behind me.

"Yeah, I figured that out when my blood burned to a crisp." I rolled my eyes.

He stopped in the middle of the hallway. "No, it shouldn't even be possible to create this much energy from these molecules. I have no idea where the energy is coming from."

I grabbed the door to the lab and pushed it open. "Show me."

Jax was right. It shouldn't be possible. The reaction was along the lines of nuclear, without the radioactive fallout. But with nothing left at the end we didn't have any idea what was happening during the process.

The easy camaraderie we fell into in the lab both pleased and frightened me. I'd never worked so well with anyone. For the first time, I didn't need to explain my reasoning. He finished my thoughts before I could even start my sentence. He stuck by his promise and didn't push me for details or ask questions.

"Can you—" I started to ask, and then saw that he was holding out the solution I needed. I took the bottle from his hand. "Thanks."

He grinned, then lifted his hand to smooth back a stray lock of hair that had escaped my ponytail. His fingers brushed ever-so-lightly against my skin, just above my lab goggles.

I held completely still. My gaze found his behind his goggles and locked together. Even through two layers of plastic I could feel heat building from that molten copper gaze.

The timer on the Nuclear Magnetic Resonator beeped and results spit out of the machine. The moment between us cracked like glass.

Jax cleared his throat and grabbed the paper off the stand. He scanned down the results while I peered around his shoulder.

I pointed to the printout in his hand. "It has to be the extra−" I barely stopped myself from saying set of genes. My mouth snapped shut, and Jax just raised an eyebrow in his annoyingly hot way and waited.

"Never mind," I mumbled. But I wanted to tell him. I wanted to tell him everything about witches, about Defects, and about me. I shook my head and bit my tongue the rest of the time— frequently reminding myself that there could be no future with an ungifted. No future with Jax.

It didn't matter how many steamy glances we shared.

I left the lab at four in the morning to grab an hour of sleep, confused over my feelings and just as baffled over what was happening with my blood as when I arrived.

****

I jolted awake at the beeping of my alarm and considered chucking the annoying machine across the room. I slapped the snooze button and burrowed into the warmth of my covers for a few more blessed minutes of heaven.

Soft knocking at the door penetrated my haze, but I couldn't muster the strength to speak. The sound grew louder, accompanied by my mom's voice, "Maddie, can I come in?"

"Ugh," I called, which she took for a positive.

I didn't open my eyes but felt the bed shift with her weight. I could hear the swoosh of her hand through her hair, over and over. Uh, oh.

"I need you to wake up so I can talk to you," she said.

I rolled over and cracked an eye.

Her hand swiped through her hair again. "We got word late last night…"

I blinked. My heart labored to pump the suddenly sludge-like blood through my veins.

She took a breath and continued, "Your final test will be tomorrow."

Chapter Five

Any vestiges of exhaustion were gone, replaced by wide eyed hyper-alertness. Tomorrow.

"But they said next week," I sputtered.

"A tester became available so they scheduled it a few days early. It wouldn't be a problem for..." she stopped.

"A normal witch," I finished for her.

Her hand squeezed my shoulder. "No more practicing, you need to save your energy for the test."

"Mom, there's no way I'll pass. They're going to strip my powers." I was thankful she couldn't see the terror in my face in the dim light, but the crack in my voice gave me away.

She sucked in an unsteady breath. "Don't say that. You do your best..." A sob choked the rest of her sentence.

"I'm sorry I'm no good at being a witch," I said, and let out the breath I'd been holding.

Tears splashed onto my bed. Her shoulders quaked silently. "I tried so hard to find the answer for you. That is the whole reason I switched departments and began searching for the answer."

I sat up in bed. "What do you mean, what does this have to do with your work?"

"There were never...people like you, when the power of the earth could be accessed. They never had to burn out anyone's powers. After the secret was lost, records started showing children with your tendency to make things explode. Your father and I believe the problem was always there, but they somehow could fix it with the power. That's why we have tried so hard to find it...for you," she said.

"I always thought you wanted to clean the family name," I whispered.

She laughed without humor. Utter exhaustion saturated her voice. "I don't care about reputation or money. I couldn't stand to see you go through...that."

My lungs ceased to function at the thought of them burning out the part of my brain that made me a witch, leaving me incapable of manipulating energy anymore. Fear spread goosebumps over my skin like a cold wind.

If they did a good job no other brain function was affected, if not, well, I could end up anywhere from slightly deficient to a drooling vegetable to dead.

We were out of time. To save my powers, and my mind, I had to pass this test.

****

As if the imminent threat of someone frying my brain like a doughnut wasn't enough, I remembered I had a Bio test second period. With the possibility that all I would have left was my ability to do well in school, I couldn't fail Bio and destroy any chance of getting into college. If I could still formulate a sentence after they took my powers.

With ten minutes to go before class, I opened the text to cram some information into my brain and tried to compartmentalize. Evil witches are not coming to fry your brain, just another day at school.

Enzymes. Yeah, fun stuff. I could get into this. I

54

flipped to the quiz at the end of the chapter.

An enzyme cannot bind to a substrate if the enzyme has,

A. an attached substrate

B. a competitive inhibitor at its activation site

C. No brain function because their neurons have been fried by horrible witches.

Okay so maybe compartmentalizing wasn't my strong point.

I skimmed over the rest of the practice questions and forced my fear and worry into the deepest pit of my stomach where it clawed at my insides like a ravenous beast. Mr. H walked in and handed out the test.

He paused at my desk and spoke in a low tone. "I was pleased with the lab and report. I adjusted your grade."

I met his eyes and nodded, forcing a grateful smile. It may not matter anymore, I couldn't help but think.

I went through the test methodically, one question at a time, and finished before any of my classmates. If someone had asked me to tell them a single question I had just answered I'd have come up with nothing.

In English Emma surprised me with my favorite, a piping hot caramel latte.

"You have been pretty out of it lately so I figured you needed some love," she said, and handed the drink over.

I inhaled the burnt sugar and coffee bean aroma. "You're the best friend I ever had."

"I'm the only friend you ever had," she giggled. "Is it your parents again?"

I blew out a forced breath. "They're pretty

clueless."

She barely suppressed a laugh. "They do try though, remember the family vacation last year?"

If I rolled my eyes any harder they would stick to the back of my head. "A trip to Canada in the middle of January hardy counts as a family vacation. Come on, Mexico? Hawaii? Somewhere south? I think the most exciting part of the entire trip was going to get our picture taken for the passports."

"You have to give them credit for trying."

I took a sip of the steamy heaven and groaned. So yummy. "Your mom came over looking for Sparky again this morning."

She tucked a stray blond curl behind her ear. "I can't figure out how he gets in and out of the yard. We've done everything we can think of. I guess he just really loves chasing squirrels or something. He's always barking at the ones in your trees."

"Crazy." I nodded. Yep, loads of squirrels on our trees, no witches around here. "I'm sure he'll come home, he always does."

Unless an Alaskan grizzly bear decided he'd make a tasty treat.

"I hope so. Last time he had these weird scratches on his side, my poor baby." she said with a shake of her head.

The rest of the day I watched the clock, counting down the hours until my *Final*. Twenty-six hours to go.

****

I plopped on the couch and let my head fall back against the cushion. With my parents still on campus and my brother playing outside I tried to relax in the silence. Swirling suns spun by my closed eyes. Maybe I should blow off my final and run away, I thought.

The only thing that stopped that train of thought was my stubborn pride. I wanted more than anything to prove them all wrong. I wasn't a Defect, sure maybe a little different from your typical witch, but different didn't have to be bad. If you needed something blown up I was your girl.

I took out my phone and stared at Jax's number, barely resisting the impulse to call him. The desire to talk to him nearly overwhelmed the danger I would put both of us in. Even his snarky remarks would be a needed distraction. My finger hovered over the green button.

Sparky's high-pitched yap penetrated my staring contest with the phone. I pressed my lips together and momentarily considered practicing my transportation one more time. Forcing my muscles into action, I went to the door to quiet the bark-alarm the old-fashioned way. Bribery.

I walked out on to the porch, hot dog in hand, just in time to see Sparky float over the fence. With a final yip he spun through the air. His body shrank as it spun, a white blur of fur growing smaller and smaller until the spinning stopped and a white kitten sank into Parker's outstretched palm.

"Meow."

Parker grinned and rubbed Sparky the cat's soft fur.

"Parker," I said in my best imitation of our mother's angry voice. "Mom specifically told you not to use magic on the dog anymore. And you're never supposed to do it outside."

He met my eyes and beamed. "No, she told me not to transport him to Alaska anymore. She didn't say anything about transforming him." He held the little fluff ball out to me. "Besides isn't he way cuter this way?"

I couldn't resist the big blue eyes and velvety fur. I stroked the kitten, who let out a soft and bewildered mew. "Okay, maybe he is a ton cuter. But you have to change him back before Mom and Dad get home."

Parker's grin spread. "Deal."

His hand shook slightly. Transforming took more energy than most spells. Probably why it was easier for me. No need to hold back so much.

"Get a snack, I don't need you passing out on me."

I turned to go in the house. And met the round eyed, drop mouthed gaze of a very flabbergasted Jax.

Electricity zapped through my tired body at the sight of him. My initial joy was quickly doused by the look on his face, the fear in his eyes.

He stood in my front yard, with a clear view of the scene over the four-foot fence. It was obvious from the huge eyes, and chalk-white face that he had witnessed every bit of it. The easy camaraderie we'd had in the lab was gone, replaced by distrust.

A tight burning sensation like heartburn spread through my chest, something that happened when I screwed up—so, frequently. Let's just say that antacids were a staple in my diet.

I stuffed my hurt deep. I had to keep Parker safe, even if that meant pushing Jax away. My eyes searched the rest of the houses and cars, thankfully no one else was around to have seen my brother's magic. Only one problem to deal with.

I raised my hands and realized that I was still holding the hot dog. Letting my hand fall quickly to my side, I stepped slightly in front of Parker and the kitten to block his view. "What are you doing here?"

He blinked, opened his mouth, closed it, and blinked again. "I…um…I…called in a favor from a guy in the physics department."

He stopped when the kitten meowed behind me.

"What could the physics department do?" I prompted.

He refocused on me and raised a finger aimed at the kitten. "How…"

I stepped forward. "Physics?"

"Right, I wanted to test a crazy theory…that the energy was coming from somewhere else. So I put the reaction in an experimental isolation container."

"And?"

He shook his head. "Normal, just like my blood."

Interesting, no reaction. I'd have to think about the ramifications once I made sure Jax wouldn't get Parker in trouble. Without my parents' help I couldn't take the memories from Jax's head, well, not without blowing up said head. Good old-fashioned tactics would have to suffice. I tried for a glare and pretended that my brother hadn't transformed a dog into a kitten right in front of him. "Okay thanks for letting me know. Call next time."

Jax stared at Parker like he'd sprouted whiskers himself. "That's it? No explanation? How did he do that?"

I stepped fully in front of my brother. "What are you talking about?"

Jax weakly gestured to the kitten. "The dog…"

I scrunched up my brow. "That's a cat. Geez, how many chemicals have you been sniffing?"

Blazing eyes snapped to my face. He took a step back. "You know exactly what I'm talking about. Don't act like I'm a nut or something. First, I see you disappear and you convince me I was dreaming. Now…"

"I think you better leave."

He pointed an accusing finger at me. "You knew why your blood lit up. You're … you're, like him."

I refused to let the pain in my chest weaken me as I struck the killing blow to our fledgling relationship.

I stepped to the edge of the porch. "Try telling anyone what you think you saw and see how long it takes for them to kick you out of school for using drugs. Like I said, you better leave before he decides he'd like a friend for his new kitten."

Jax stepped back then spun and rushed to his car.

Behind me Parker snuggled the kitten. "Do you think he's going to cause trouble?"

I watched Jax speed away while my heart shriveled and died inside my chest, my bravado gone. It doesn't matter, I told myself. "Let's deal with one problem at a time. If he causes trouble just remember to say that it was me who performed magic in front of a human, not you. There isn't much more the council can do to me."

"What do you think the blood not reacting means?"

With one last ruffle of Sparky's fur I walked to the back door. "The energy is coming from somewhere else."

The lightbulb finally blazed on. Energy from outside ourselves. The power of the earth. We'd found a clue to the power of the earth.

It had to happen the day before my final? I find a clue with almost no time to pursue it?

I went inside to eat a bottle of antacids.

Chapter Six

The power of the earth. I couldn't believe we'd found a clue. It only took a couple hours sifting through chemical and pharmaceutical companies before I spotted a reference to snake venom and finally had an epiphany. I fully blamed the sleep deprivation for my new lack of mental prowess.

I thumped my head on the wooden edge of my desk a couple times. My ancestors would hardly have been able to walk to the corner drug store to get a prescription of whatever had reacted with my blood. It would only have been available from a natural source, like an animal or plant. The initial discovery was likely a complete accident, like getting bitten by a snake.

I spent the next hour listing all the natural sources of each compound. The list consisted mostly of plants, hemlock, evening primrose, lily of the valley, and about ten others I'd never heard of. The last few were found in venom like the Brown Recluse spider, Rattlesnake, Poison Dart Frog, and Lionfish.

Now I just had to pass my final so I could continue the research. Easier said than done. Much easier.

****

Two hours to go. I couldn't remember a thing about my classes. I did recall Emma asking me if everything was okay before she left me alone. Being my friend for over twelve years, she was used to my moods.

Walking out to the parking lot, I discovered a new hood ornament on my car. An extremely hot, incredibly sexy, and awfully angry, hood ornament who was drawing a ton of stares from girls—while he lounged on the old Ford like it was a Corvette. The sight of Jax sent blood throbbing through my vessels and brought heat to my face.

Much as I'd tried to convince myself that I didn't care I'd never see him again and that he hated me, the dreamer inside me was doing an awkward happy-dance while the pragmatist was swearing like a sailor. He was a distraction that I couldn't afford, and one I'd already wasted too much time on. I gave myself a mental slap.

"What are you doing here?" I demanded and ignored the looks from my classmates.

He crossed his arms and watched me walk toward him, a laser-like glare never leaving my face.

I stopped in front of him. "You need to leave me alone. The deal is off."

He pushed off the car and walked around to the passenger door, his hand on the handle.

I glanced at my watch. One hour forty-five minutes. I didn't have time to babysit a freaked-out jerk who hated me. With a sigh, I unlocked both locks and opened my door.

Jax climbed in and closed the door. I put the key in the ignition but didn't turn the engine over.

He pivoted to face me. "Don't even try to deny your brother turned that dog into a cat. I saw him."

"Okay. So you saw."

"And you were in the lab. You disappeared."

"You caught me. What else do you want from

me?"

"I want you to tell me what the hell is going on." His raised voice reverberated and amplified in the confines of my car. "Are you some kind of witch too? I must have missed the warts and green skin."

My eyes narrowed. "Don't forget the broom and caldron."

His jaw clinched. "Are you going to deny it?"

A major rule, like even bigger than no death rituals, was never to tell an ungifted about us. "I can't. I can't tell you anything."

"I'm not giving up. I won't leave this alone," he said.

I heard the determination in his voice. "Do you want to know the truth?"

"Yes," he confirmed without pause. Anger deflated from him like helium from a balloon.

I let myself stare at his eyes. My voice was almost a whisper. "Even if it's dangerous? I mean, could kill you dangerous?"

He rested his hand over mine. "I have to know."

Everything about him radiated *trust me*. He felt... solid. Unlike the rest of my life, and I couldn't muster the energy to deny the truth anymore. "I'm a witch."

Jax's hand disappeared from mine. He turned and stared out the window.

The moment broke. The illusion of safety vanished and panic twisted my stomach. What the hell had I just done?

The parking lot emptied around us. He shook his head and continued my inquisition. "Is that why your blood lit up?"

I rested my head against my seat and wished I

could take back my confession. It was selfish. If Jax was hurt because of me, I'd never forgive myself. "If I knew the answer to that, I wouldn't have to put up with you."

"Why don't you just wiggle your nose and find out the answer yourself?"

I spared him a glare. "It doesn't work that way." Not to mention that most of my spells ended up making things explode.

I could practically see the gears churning in his brain. Flying around with possibilities and excitement. I wanted to smack him, not the first time I'd had the urge, or shake some sense into him. He was in danger now because of me.

Jax stared at me for another moment. "Could you cure disease? Make food for starving children? Your powers could be used for good. Why hide them?"

"There are still a lot more ungifted than us and history has told us that revealing our powers never ends well, even when we had good intentions."

He raised one eyebrow. "That sounds like a cop out if I've ever heard one."

I glanced at my watch. One hour thirty minutes. "Well, you go get burned at the stake and see if you have a change of heart. You're missing the bigger problem here. If they find you, you'll end up dead. I shouldn't have involved you."

"I was in this the minute your blood lit up," he said, his voice firm but with an edge of uncertainty.

"Now that you know the truth, you can't pass the truth spells. They'll torture you, rip the truth from your mind. And you'll end up thinking aliens abducted you and experimented on you. If you survive."

"Okay, so what can we do about it?" he asked.

I shook my head and put a hand on my forehead. Everything spun through my brain, Jax, the test, my powers. I needed a plan, some way to keep Jax safe.

"One thing at a time." I blew out a breath. "We need to destroy your notes, the research, anything that would indicate you were doing more than helping me with my lab for school."

"Destroy everything? No way. That serum is valuable." He shook his head. "I can't throw it all away."

I grabbed his arm. "Forget breakthroughs. Research credit is useless if you're dead."

He gritted his teeth but didn't protest.

"No one else knows, right? You didn't tell anyone?" I asked.

He glanced away momentarily.

"What did you do?" I pushed.

"I'm not stupid enough to tell anyone. They'd try to steal it anyway." He paused. "I recorded the reaction a couple times."

On film? Shit. I held out my hand. "Give me your phone."

He shook his head. "Not on my phone, the camera broke like a year ago, I borrowed my roommate's digital recorder. I was going to upload it to my PC."

"Shit. You didn't erase it?"

"Not yet. He's a film major. I figured he wouldn't steal my research."

I leaned forward. "You have to erase it, break the memory card, whatever, that information can't get out."

He put his hand on the handle but didn't open the door. "I'll take care of it. Just give me a little time."

I turned over the engine and gestured to the door. "Unfortunately, time is what I don't have."

****

One hour. I didn't remember the drive home, but suddenly I was sitting in front of my house. I walked inside and sat at the kitchen table like a zombie. Mom handed me a sandwich, and I tried to force it down my parchment paper throat into my cement lined stomach.

I pushed the worry and guilt over telling Jax out of my mind as much as I could. The best thing I could do for him right now was pass my final and get the council's attention off of me.

My parents sat silently across from me. Every time I looked their way I got an encouraging smile. I couldn't muster one in return.

They'd sent Parker to a friend's house, no need to traumatize the poor boy. I had to pass this test, no way around it. Against my better judgment I calculated the chances of my completing all the spells without incident. So…I had two tenths of one percent chance, rounding up of course, of completing all the spells successfully at the same time.

I closed my eyes and blew out a breath. No sweat.

The doorbell sent my mother and father out of their seats like they had springs in their backsides. I found my muscles unable to respond to the simplest command. The half-eaten sandwich paused in it's ascent to my mouth.

Dad plucked the bread from my hand and took the plate to the sink. Mom led a professionally dressed woman into the living room. Recognition set in. Cramps tightened my abdomen and my stomach threatened to reject the sandwich. My camp counselor stood in the living room. A woman who had tormented me every summer of my childhood until the gods smiled on me, and she got married.

My mother's voice was smooth, but I could detect the strain. "Maddie, you remember Miss. Castings—or should I say Mrs. Muller now—from camp?"

My head jerked in a pantomime of a cordial nod.

Mrs. Muller's grin reminded me of the cat who had the mouse in its sights. "So nice to see you again, Maddie. I can't wait to see the progress you've made since camp."

Maybe I could transport her and we'd see how it went. I pasted a smile on my lips and took up the mental armor I'd worn to survive camp. The kids had been bad enough, but she'd more than encouraged the bullying.

"Let's get started then," she said, obviously anticipating my failure.

Per the rules of the council, my parents had to stay upstairs, to ensure no cheating. I led the way downstairs to our practice room, which shown like the inside of laboratory clean room thanks to Mom's efforts. No evidence remained of my many follies.

She pulled an iPad out of her bag and tapped on the screen to open a form. I took the opportunity to get my bearings. All the necessary items I would need for the spells rested on a small table in the center of the room. A cricket scurried around a glass cage for the transformation spell, a bare plate for the conjuring spell, and an orange for the transference spell. I had slightly better luck with oranges than grapes. Next to the first sat a second orange for the levitation spell, and a simple bean seed for the plant aging.

I ran my hands through my hair and restrained it in a ponytail to keep it out of the way. I'd never understood the point of the plant aging spell, but it had been a part of the final test for witches for a thousand years. Kind of a throwback to the old days, I guessed. I had to take a seed and sprout the plant then take it through the flowering stage of development.

"I've wondered about you many times over the last few years," Mrs. Muller said. "When I saw your name on the upcoming tests I requested to be your Procter."

More like she wanted to see the Defect in action and be the one to fail me. I met her gaze but didn't reply then yanked the ponytail out of my hair and let it fall over my shoulders.

She motioned to the table. "No need to drag this out. If at any time you fail a spell the test will be over, and I will report to the council that you have failed. You will then have a day before your powers are permanently removed."

Wow, so she didn't think this would take long. I slipped the elastic hairband from my wrist one more time and pulled my hair back again. Despite the irritation on my proctor's face I took a moment to breathe deeply, do a neck roll, and shake out my hands.

"Are you ready?" she asked, her lips pursed in a sour face.

I nodded and turned my attention to the table before me. My chest tightened like a corset around my ribs, and my thoughts sputtered to a halt. This was it. I sucked in a breath. As the testee, I had the right to choose the order in which I performed the spells. To get warmed up I started with one of my better spells. Levitation.

Energy from my body channeled through the region of my brain that made me a witch, an extra set of neurons that normal humans don't possess but the mutations in us created. The energy focused and took the shape I demanded of it. Kind of like molding smoke with your hands.

You have to be bossy with energy. Never show it your weakness. It tended to have a mind of its own, as the many deceased fruits that had crossed my path could attest. I formed a layer of energy under the orange and gently pushed upward.

Not too much energy, save some for the other spells. I heard my mom's advice in my mind.

The orange trembled on the table and then slowly rose through the air to hover about twelve inches above the table top. I released the breath I'd been holding and lowered the fruit to its original position. One out of the way.

Mrs. Muller tapped on her iPad. "Shaky but successful. I'm surprised, I remember the poor fish you tried to levitate back into the lake at camp. I'll never think of sushi the same way."

I pushed the image of the exploded fish I'd tried to save back into the recesses of my mind. The laughter and taunts of the other kids echoed in my ears. For a split second I was that terrified, embarrassed child again. Focus on the now. My fingers tingled with the gathered energy I pushed at the empty plate.

I pictured a delicious frosted brownie then sent out runners to find the elements needed to conjure one. If you're going to get covered in chunks of something might as well be tasty. Although, if I wasn't careful I might get too much carbon in there and it would taste like charcoal. But what the hell.

I pulled, gently, then swirled the threads together. Handling my magic energy kind of felt like trying to manipulate small objects with huge gloves on my hands. I was the bull in the china shop for sure.

A few of the threads caught, as if tangled on some invisible object in space. I pulled slightly harder, too hard and, well, I'd be covered in brownie. Then lose my powers.

The threads refused to give. The swirling mixture in front of me flickered. Panic rolled over me like ice while sweat erupted from my brow. My parents' hopeful faces flashed in my mind.

I couldn't hold it much longer. A couple seconds at most then I'd lose control. In sheer desperation I yanked on the threads. The elements rushed into the mixture with too much force, pushing the precarious balance I'd established.

A bead of sweat ran down my face. Several threads escaped, and the mixture looked like a sparkler on the Fourth of July, ready to ignite. Unable to do anything else, I sent a controlled burst of energy into the mix in a last-ditch effort to save the spell.

A light shimmered on the plate, pale blue. The elements settled into the order my mind demanded. A dessert took shape and, with a *pop*, a large frosted double chocolate brownie appeared. Air burst from my lungs, and I leaned forward to rest my hands on my knees.

Maybe it wasn't quite square, and the edges were smashed in. Or was it inside out? I didn't care, I resisted the urge to jump up and down in place and screech with joy. Two spells down. I chanced a glance at Mrs. Muller.

Her brow scrunched together like a fuzzy caterpillar crawling across her forehead. "Well, that may be one of the most unappetizing brownies I've ever seen. I was sure you were going to lose it for a minute, but you passed."

With a smirk I walked over and took a huge bite. Frosting smeared across my face, but I didn't mind. Chocolaty yumminess, with a hint of cheesecake. And only a dash of charcoal.

My Proctor rolled her eyes, and with her voice brimming with irritation she asked, "Are you ready to continue or do you need a glass of milk?"

I swallowed. "No, I'm good."

Hope uncurled, tender and new, inside my chest. With one last lick of chocolate frosting from my lips I stared at the table. Three spells left. Should I do the sure thing or save that one for last?

Her snide voice over my shoulder broke into my thoughts. "You know, I still tell the story about you at the end of season talent show. Everyone in the first row ended up covered in tree sap. It gets laughs every time."

That made up my mind for me. I held up my hand to the cricket in the cage. I could transform it into whatever I chose, the end product just had to still be alive and functioning. No problem.

Transformation took the most energy of any of our spells, so I didn't have to worry about holding back so much. My hand vibrated with energy. The image of the creature I chose solidified in my mind.

Inside the cage the cricket glowed green and trembled. The body spun while it changed shape, legs moving, swelling until the confines of the cage were too small. The glass cracked, then shattered.

Behind me Mrs. Muller gasped. I grinned and continued to pour energy into the spell. The swirling slowed.

A twelve-inch-wide, striped brown, hairy Goliath Tarantula came to a stop on the floor next to the table.

I watched Mrs. Muller's face bleach white, and her eyes grew as wide as the spider on the floor. She wasn't the only one who remembered things from camp. Her arachnophobia was well known to all the campers.

Mrs. Muller's mouth opened in a silent scream. Tarantulas rarely bit humans, and their venom was not harmful, but I kept those facts to myself.

My fuzzy friend moved with surprising speed to the left. Screams erupted from the Proctor like a tornado siren. She scurried up the stairs faster than a gazelle being chased by a lion.

I doubled over and held my quaking stomach while I struggled to stay on my feet. A ruckus began upstairs and spilled down with my parents pounding footsteps.

"Maddie, what is going on in here?" my mother demanded.

I pushed myself upright using the wall and gestured to the spider crouched in the corner. "I did a transformation. Who knew she was afraid of spiders?"

Dad chuckled. Tension drained from his face. "Have you done any other spells?"

Wiping tears from my eyes I nodded. "Only two more to go."

Mom's mouth dropped open in utter shock. "Oh honey, that's wonderful. Let's get rid of this," she gestured to the tarantula. "So you can finish."

She changed the spider back into a cricket, scooped

it up, then cleaned the broken glass to remove any reminder of the upset for Mrs. Muller. With a quick squeeze of my shoulders, she went upstairs to get my Proctor.

I couldn't keep the slight upturn from my lips when a shaky legged Mrs. Muller crept downstairs. Her eyes darted from corner to corner. She picked up the iPad she'd dropped on the floor, good thing it had a Life-Proof case.

With shaking hands she entered the test result in her notes. "I'd forgotten there was a spell you could actually do. But I guess being able to transform is the typical Defect pattern."

I continued to grin and returned to the remaining items on the table. The seed would be next. My energy reserves were getting slightly deteriorated. I used more of my power just trying to keep the spell under control than actually doing it. Most witches could control with no effort.

Deep breath in and I began. I sensed the spark of life inside the bean seed and poured my own energy in to it. The growth process started in fast forward. The seed split, and a tendril of green showed. Then the dicot leaves sprouted and pushed toward the ceiling and spread to reveal larger heart shaped leaves. The stem elongated, and on the third branch a bud appeared.

The plant usually exploded at this point if it was going to. Hold it, almost there.

I held back the flood of energy that wanted to rush through the bond. A single white flower pushed its way out of the bud and spread its petals into the most beautiful flower I'd ever seen. Pure white, perfectly formed petals surrounded a bright yellow center.

Perfect.

A slight tremor began in the muscles of my arm, fatigue setting in. I squeezed my hand into a fist and refused to show Mrs. Muller any weakness.

Tap, tap, tap on her screen. A bead of sweat trickled down her face. "Well, I must say I didn't expect you to get this far. One test left. The Council will be… surprised."

Fragile tendrils of hope spread over my chest like warm sunshine. One test left. I'd gone from a one in one thousand chance of passing to a one in ten. I imagined for a moment the expression on her face and everyone else's if I passed.

The tremor in my arm stopped, now if I could just stop my knees from shaking.

Her voice reeked with irritation. "Whenever you're ready. Let's get this over with."

The orange loomed before me. At least I almost always got the demolecularization part right, it was putting it back together that posed a problem. The orange disappeared with an audible popping noise. The molecules needed to disperse but keep their memory so I could reassemble them. I held out my hand.

Loud coughing from behind me pulled my attention away from the spell at the most sensitive moment. My attention was momentarily focused on the area over my shoulder where Mrs. Muller stood, hacking for no apparent reason, instead of on my palm like it should be. Like I said, energy could have a mind of its own, the slightest chance and it would run wild.

The molecules of the orange followed my focus and the orange materialized in the space directly in front of Mrs. Muller's face. Because of my distraction, the molecular bonds that formed inside the orange weren't stable. They didn't hold.

Chapter Seven

The fruit exploded with the force of an M-80 firework. Juice and rind shrapnel pelted my proctor's entire front side, dripping from her chin and hair.

I stood, my hands limp at my sides and stared. One thought played on repeat through my mind. I'd had it.

She wiped juice from her eyes and glared at me.

Like it was my fault.

"You failed."

Anger poured out of me like boiling water. "You distracted me on purpose."

She continued to shake off remnants of orange. "It doesn't matter. You still fail."

She didn't even deny it. No one would care that she had coughed to try and distract me at the weakest moment. This was a pass/fail test, no exceptions. "Why would you do that?"

"I never thought you had any chance of making it to the last test. Everyone knows you're a Defect. I can't have you running around blowing things up and have it on your record that I passed you." She grabbed her soaked bag. "Accept it, you're a Defect. You should never have had powers in the first place."

I tried to speak but couldn't get enough air out of my lifeless lungs. I may have made flippant comments to my parents about being stripped, but I'd hoped…hoped I'd pass…somehow. I stared for a moment, unable to grasp that my worst fear had actually come true.

"Tomorrow your powers will be stripped," she said. "I'm sure it will be a huge relief to your parents. Defects are nature's mistakes. And don't be stupid and try to run. Everyone gets caught if they try to run."

The black tar of rage that I'd kept packed away for years came to the surface like a geyser. Years of torment and festering hurt overtook my senses and my tongue. "I may be a Defect but my brain got me closer to the secret to the power of the earth than you and all your powers ever will."

Her wide eyes clued me into the massive mistake I'd made. My brain caught up with my mouth. Shit.

Her hand stilled in its attempt to clear debris from her hair. She stepped toward me. "What do you mean? What did you find?"

I hurried to the bottom of the stairs. "Nothing. I'm just a Defect, remember."

"Maddie, wait, we can talk about this," she called after me.

I rushed past my parents and out the door. They knew from the look on my face that I'd failed, and if that didn't clue them in, the walking Orange Julius chasing me would.

My eyes only saw what was right in front of me, my ears didn't register anything around me, only the words *you failed.* I stumbled out the front door, to the curb, and walked right into a wall of lean muscle and heat. Jax.

He wore a close-fitting long-sleeved T-shirt that clung to his muscles like shrink wrap. My stomach tightened. His scent hit my nostrils—clean and…spicy, almost like a cedar chest filled with peppercorns. Yum.

His hands gripped my arms in a reflex to keep me from falling. I jerked my head up and met his surprised gaze. His copper eyes glistened like liquid metal, daring me to jump in. My eyes moved to his lips for a second, and suddenly a strong urge to kiss him swept over me. I blinked and pulled away. The cold shocked my skin where his warmth had just been.

"What are you doing here?" I demanded.

He returned one hand to my arm. "Are you all right?"

"I'm fine. You need to stay away from me. It's too dangerous," I snapped.

"I just wanted to tell you that I got everything out of the lab, but my roommate's camera is locked up in the film lab," he said.

I closed my eyes and struggled for a breath. "You have to get it and stay away from me. I screwed up, you're in more danger."

The front door opened, and the dripping Proctor stepped out onto the porch. Her eyes settled on me, then Jax.

My parents followed closely behind, their features twisted with grief. I couldn't stand their pain. Pain I'd inflicted.

I opened the door to my car. "You have to get out of here. Now."

Jax stared at the wet, dripping, Proctor. "Did you do that?"

I shoved him toward his car. "You need to go."

The urgency in my voice penetrated his thick skull. He jogged a couple houses down and hopped into his car. I slammed my own door and cranked the engine over to drown out the sound of the Proctor's voice.

I pulled the car out and floored it. Two houses down, I caught sight of a figure perched on the hood of a sedan watching me drive by. A figure with a branching tattoo on his neck.

****

I sipped the steaming latte and wrapped my hands around the cup.

Jax sat next to me in the driver's seat of his car, his drink untouched in his hand, while he absorbed the overload of information I'd told him. I'd given in to meeting with him after about a hundred texts and threats to go back to my house and wait for me there.

He needed to understand the danger he was in if the council thought he could help find the answer to the power of the earth. At least, that was what I told myself, it wasn't that I needed someone to talk to. Maybe a little of both.

"So what are you going to do?"

"The first thing we have to worry about is that camera. It has to be destroyed," I said.

He brushed it off. "You have bigger things on your plate. I can handle the camera."

"How? It's locked in a storage cage in a locked room."

"I got it. Trust me. We need a plan for you."

I attempted to make my tense muscles relax to no avail. "Well, I can either sit around and wait for them to fry my brain and torture me for information about the secret, or I can find it myself and fix my problem."

He nodded slowly. "So you're going to sit on your butt and wait?"

A halfhearted grin spread across my lips. "Definitely. Who needs a brain anyway?"

"So when do we leave?"

"Jax, I've already put you in danger. I can't ask you to help me anymore."

"Oh, yeah, so leave me here to be tortured while you go off to discover the answer to the biggest secret that man doesn't even know about. Count me in. Plus, I'm still hoping to get a free ride to grad school out of this somehow."

"I should have known that was your plan."

He shrugged. "No one else is looking out for me, someone's got to."

"What about your parents?"

He contemplated his hands, and his voice softened. "My mom died when I was twelve." He cleared his throat. "And my dad is too busy with his new wife and kids to give a damn about my life."

The pain in his voice pulled the empathy strings on my heart. The image from the picture of a twelve-year-old Jax with his arm around his dying mother flashed in my mind and tightened my throat.

The usual cockiness returned to his voice. "Besides, you think they're going to sell airplane tickets to a minor?"

My gaze narrowed but my lips turned up. "I'm sure I could have figured something out. But now that you mention it, that would be great if you could buy the tickets. They'll be watching me, so I can't exactly walk out of my house carrying a suitcase."

He chuckled. "Admit it, you need me."

"Tell yourself whatever your fragile male ego needs."

An ultra-cocky grin spread across his lips. "So, where are we going?"

I sat up from my slumped position in the seat. "I hope you have a passport. We're going to England."

****

My parents pounced on me the moment my foot crossed the threshold. The relief in their faces spread guilt through my stomach. I should have at least told them what happened.

Mom wrapped her arms around me and squeezed. "Are you all right?"

My wilted arms rose to return the embrace. "I'm okay."

"The Proctor told us you nearly made it," she said.

Bet she didn't tell anyone that she purposely distracted me. It didn't matter at this point. "Almost."

Dad, who had hung back quietly until this point, spoke up. "She was very interested in a comment you made about a clue to the secret."

I met his eyes and held them. I'd decided the less they knew the less danger they would be in. Plausible deniability. Plus, then they could pass the truth spell. "I was just blowing off some steam. I wanted to shut her up."

He nodded, slowly. "If there was something you wanted to tell us, you know we would listen."

I threw my hands to the side. "She coughed right as I was reconfiguring the orange. That's why I failed. I was pissed off."

Mom gasped. "Why would she do something like that?"

"Because they don't want Defects running around blowing things up. It doesn't matter," I said.

Dad's hands clinched into knots, along with his jaw. "They can't do this."

"It's not right. It's just not right," Mom sobbed.

Strong arms wrapped around us. Dad held us close, our heads bent together.

They had tried to fight the council when my aunt had gotten caught. Their attempts to help only made it worse for her. That was how she ended up as a drone, doing the council's bidding, instead of being stripped. The council experimented on her and ended up with a magical terminator.

Mom patted my shoulder. "We took the tracker off of you."

I blinked. So I was free to perform magic for the last twenty-four hours of my powers.

"Can you get the weird guy with the tattoo to quit following me too?" I asked.

"Someone has been following you? Maybe the council sent them?"

The fabric of Dad's sleeve muffled my voice. "I don't know. It's some dude with a massive tattoo on his neck. I'm probably imagining it."

"That doesn't sound like the council. They have strict codes. I'm going to have to look into it," Dad said.

He finally released us and put a hand on my shoulder. "Tomorrow we'll deal with all of this and the procedure together."

The *procedure,* what a nice way to say frying a chunk of your brain.

****

I left my parents downstairs and went up to my room. Their hovering only made things worse, plus, fleeing the country took preparation. Thanks to my parents' so-called family vacation to Canada, my passport was up-to-date. Really who goes north in January? Even birds knew better.

My duffel bag filled quickly. I didn't have any idea how long I would be gone. Possibly forever. I restricted myself to necessities and not sentimental possessions. Clean underwear trumped family photos. But the one thing I couldn't part with was my Grandmother's locket. The gold oval was a bit thicker than normal lockets and held an unusually deep pocket, almost too big for pictures. On the outside, a five-petaled red flower had been engraved. The petals came to points, almost like a sun. The simple piece of jewelry was all I had left of my grandmother. The one person who thought I was perfect just the way I was.

Doubt poured over me. I couldn't really do this. I was probably wrong about the clue and the plants anyway. I'd been a failure, a disappointment, my entire life. What would make this any different?

I clutched the cool metal in my hand. Behind my closed lids, the sweet, smiling face of my grandmother appeared. Wavy brown hair gone gray, bright blue eyes that never lost their enthusiasm, and a mischievous grin that never aged. I could hear her voice telling me, as she often had, that no matter what anyone said, I was perfect to her. Tears welled up behind my closed lids. My chest ached with the void her death had left.

With the locket firmly clasped around my neck, I yanked the zipper shut on the duffel bag, and sat down to wait. I'd texted Emma earlier and told her I had a weird favor. My phone chimed with her response.

You're what? Who is this guy?

I rolled my eyes and texted back. *A friend, just a friend, can you help?*

Of course. Throw it over and I'll meet you there.

You're the best.

Sometime after midnight the house sat quiet, except for my parents' hushed voices in their room. I'd waited for as long as I dared for them to fall asleep. I had to chance it. I snuck down the stairs with my duffle bag.

A loud squeak underfoot made me wince. I waited and listened.

My parents' door opened. "Maddie?"

I silently swore. "Yeah?"

"Honey, are you okay?" Mom asked.

"I was going to get a snack," I lied. "Sorry if I woke you."

The floor creaked with her steps.

Damn. I dropped the duffel bag over the rail with a soft thud as her head appeared above me.

"Let me make you something," she said.

"No," I said too fast. "I can make it myself. Besides, I have some stuff to think about."

The hurt in her expression tightened my throat.

"Oh, okay. If you need anything come get me," she said with a forced smile.

I nodded and went to the kitchen where I made a point to make noise getting coffee started. I couldn't catch a break. Evil proctors, weird tattooed stalkers, and squeaky stairs. What was next? After a few minutes of clanging around I crept outside where yapping Sparky made my attempts at silence seem useless. Where was Parker when I really needed him? I crunched through the snow and tossed the bag over the fence into Emma's yard. One mission accomplished.

A moment later my phone chimed. *The eagle has landed. Package in hand.*

You are a serious dork. I texted.

Back inside the house, I turned on the water in the sink then carefully avoided the creaky parts of the floor and made my way into my parents' study. The two-hundred-year-old letters rested in the safe, where I knew they would be, along with several other original documents, my father's journal and a few thousand dollars cash.

I took the original documents, the journal, and half the cash. In their place I left another letter, this one in a sealed envelope with *Do not read until after you are questioned by the council* written in bold print.

The creaking of the stairs stopped me.

The bolt of the safe hit home, and I delicately slid the letters into a messenger bag that wasn't much bigger than a purse.

I crept around the corner and through the door to the kitchen, dropped the bag in a chair, just in time to grab a mug of coffee as Dad rounded the corner across the kitchen.

Dad sat at the kitchen table. "Couldn't sleep either?"

I glared at him through slits for eyes. "Not really."

His gaze rested on my messenger bag then darted to the door leading to the study.

I busied myself with cream and sugar so I didn't have to look him in the face.

"You know, I was cleaning out the attic last week," he said.

"Okay?" I crossed my arms and took a sip of

coffee. He wanted to make small talk? Today?

"Yeah. Several things up there we didn't need. So I took them to a pawn shop. Good to have extra cash around." He let an envelope fall to the table then rose from his chair and wrapped his arms around me. "We'll stall them as long as we can. If you need anything, call me."

I looked up into his face. "Thank you. But this is enough. I can't put you in anymore danger than I already have." My voice broke. "Parker needs you."

He squeezed me again then released me and walked to the door. "I'm going back to bed. I won't come to wake you for a few hours." He glanced back with shiny eyes. "Stay safe."

I nodded and couldn't stop myself from giving him one last squeeze before I grabbed my messenger bag.

At the front door, I paused and soaked in every detail of the only home I'd ever known. My trembling hand tightened on the doorknob. I opened the door and stepped out.

****

Jax's unmistakably well-defined shoulders and back, along with his wavy brown hair, were easy to pick out in the thinning crowd at O'Hare. I licked my lips and smoothed my wrinkled shirt.

Tingling warmth spread through my abdomen in a most distracting way. Completely annoyed with my physical response to the mere sight of Jax, I tapped his arm—maybe a tad harder than necessary.

He spun and glared. "About time you got here."

"Some of us have parents in the house," I snapped.

His copper eyes darkened to more of a bronze, and his lips pressed together in a firm line.

Immediately, I regretted my choice of words. Although I hadn't meant to I'd obviously struck an understandably sore spot. "I mean, not all of us live in a dorm. Besides, I had to slip my tail. Hopefully, they are still waiting outside the coffee shop for me."

His mouth relaxed a bit but the storms continued in his eyes. "Right, I just didn't want to miss the flight. This is the only direct flight leaving this morning."

Still feeling like a jerk, I reached out and lightly touched his arm. "I'm sorry, that came out totally wrong."

"No big deal. I got over it a long time ago," he stated in a voice that said the complete opposite.

"Is the camera problem fixed?" I changed the subject.

"Memory card destroyed."

"How did you get in?"

"I charmed a lonely female guard with my good looks. Let's go."

I rolled my eyes for his benefit.

"We can head to the gate as soon as I find Emma," I said and searched the crowd.

"Emma?"

"Yeah, she has my bag. Like I said, I could hardly walk out of the house with a suitcase."

Emma's blond curls bounced into view. She jogged through the crowd in high-heeled boots. I wondered for a moment how she didn't break her ankle in those things. She bounded up to us and dropped the duffle bag on the ground. "Sorry I'm late, I had to—"

Her voice stopped when her eyes zeroed in on Jax. She stared and stared and blinked.

"Emma," I said and nudged her arm. "This is Jax."

She blinked again and broke out of her shock. "So nice to meet you. Maddie hasn't told me a thing about you." She turned wide eyes on me. "You have so been holding out on me."

Jax raised one eyebrow my way and chuckled. "She has a way of keeping secrets, doesn't she?"

I rolled my eyes and pulled Emma a couple steps to the side. "Okay, now you have to get out of here. No one can know you helped me. I mean no one, not my parents or anyone. Understand?"

"Oh, this is so romantic," she gushed. "I wouldn't have been late, but I had to help out your wardrobe a little. But, you are going to be happy I did. He is hot."

"What do you mean you had to help my wardrobe?" I demanded. Emma was forever trying to dress me and give me a makeover. To date I had been able to withstand her efforts. The thought of her packing my bag sent tendrils of panic over my skin. I was stressed, I needed my comfy jeans and stretchy shirts. Fashion be dammed.

"Don't worry, I took care of you." She grinned evilly and hugged me.

"Just remember to get home and act like nothing has happened."

She nodded. "Have fun." She sent me a private wink. "And be safe."

I watched her walk away. Her last comment brought my eyes to the bag again, oh god… I'd better unpack in private.

The departure board showed our flight to London. The status showed Boarding.

Jax fell in beside me. I saw his shoes out of the corner of my eye. His steps matched my own exactly.

Without thinking, I sped up.

"Where's the race?" he asked.

I glanced up and saw an unusually large suit clad man in his forties rush through the door I'd just come in. Not so strange in a busy airport except that when he spotted me his expression reminded me of a lion with a gazelle in his sights. He changed course and made a B-line for me and Jax.

I grabbed Jax's arm. "They found me."

Chapter Eight

Jax's eyes followed mine and settled on the huge man. "Shit."

He half dragged me through the crowd and around the corner.

"Is he one of you?" he asked, as we ducked around another corner.

"Most likely. They wouldn't send a human to drag someone back to be stripped."

Our follower appeared behind us. A good six inches taller than the crowd, he had a definite advantage. With so many eyes around they couldn't use their magic to zap us with Witch Lightning or anything. They would need to stick to subtle and hopefully less painful magic.

"Give me my ticket and meet me on the plane." I held out my hand.

He shook his head. "I don't think it's a good idea to split up."

Frustration, and maybe a bit of fear, hardened my voice. "Would you for once not argue with me? He'll follow me, and I have an idea."

Jax handed me my ticket, and I darted away from him through the crowd. One glance over my shoulder confirmed that the man stuck to me. If Jax got caught, he could claim he was just helping me get away. Maybe.

I spotted what I needed and slowed to be sure the man saw me round the corner of the women's restroom. Once inside, I hurried my pace and walked past the long line of sinks. At the same time, I ripped off my cream-colored hoodie and turned it inside out so the blue liner showed.

Although my hair tickled my neck, I left it tucked down the back of my jacket to disguise the length. I passed a wall of mirrors and straight out the other entrance. It opened to the corridor about twenty feet from where I'd gone in.

I fell in behind a large woman with an oversized carry-on bag, then merged to the edge of a group of college students. I headed the opposite direction from Jax and our friend, who I nicknamed Igor.

With a glance over my shoulder I saw my stalker hadn't left his post. He stood with his back to me while he watched the women's restroom.

I stayed with the crowd and moved in the direction of Terminal Three for international departures. The airport was laid out like a huge hexagon with four terminals branching off and the fifth for international arrivals on one side and accessible by the airport transit. Without a ticket, a person could only access the inner hexagon. To get to the terminal and Concourse G, I had to get through the security lines without the thug on our trail seeing me.

Once I got to the other side of the metal detectors, he wouldn't be able to follow unless he took the time to buy a ticket or used magic, a big no-no with so many witnesses. I picked up my pace as much as I dared without drawing attention to myself. I passed security for Terminal Two after five minutes of walking. The game would certainly be up by now.

When I reached security for Terminal Three, my breath came in pants. Rows of corded-off aisles filled with travelers spread before me. I groaned and scanned the crowd for the shortest line while I dug my passport and ticket out of my pocket.

A figure pushed off from a column to the side of the room, not even ten feet from me. I stood and stared at my tattooed stalker.

It might be time to blow something up. I gritted my teeth, strode over, and stood directly in front of him.

"Did the council send you?" I demanded.

He chuckled, all calm and annoyingly Zen.

"No, let us just say you have allies that would see you escape what the council has planned," he said with an accent.

"What's that supposed to mean?"

"We will help you when we can," he explained. With a nod, he disappeared into the crowd.

Great, I have a friend. Could they help me, like now, with this council goon? No, be all Zen-monk-like and walk away. I clenched my fist and returned my attention to getting myself out of this mess.

The first-class line stretched half-way down one isle, a good third shorter than the rest. Lucky for me Jax went all out and got first class seats, hopefully it didn't drain his savings.

I hopped in line and glanced around for anyone on my tail. Coast was clear. The line crept forward while security officers checked ID and passports.

I recognized Jax well ahead of me in the security line. He now wore a baseball cap over his brown waves, and a plain white T-shirt instead of his jacket. Great minds.

I politely tapped the shoulder of the man next in line. He turned around to face me.

"Excuse me," I said. "That's my boyfriend." The word felt awkward on my tongue. I pointed to Jax. "Could I possibly cut in front of you?"

The man nodded. "Sure, go ahead."

I repeated the exercise with the next ten people in line. Jax overheard the last exchange and turned to greet me with a cat-that-got-the-mouse-grin on his face. His eyes sparkled with mischief.

"There you are, honey," he exclaimed in a voice I'd never heard out of him before. "I was getting worried."

His arm reached around my back to pull me chest to chest with him. My nerves went into overdrive at the sensation of his firm-in-all-the-right-places body against my own. Before I could recover he bent and pressed his warm, soft, and oh-so-luscious lips against mine. He tasted salty, yet sweet. The peck of a kiss was over before my befuddled brain had time to react.

My wide eyes met his merry ones then he turned to the couple behind us. "Thanks for letting her through."

They waved off his thanks. "Can't keep young love apart."

I faced forward in line and snapped my still-open mouth shut.

Wonderful warm sensations got stomped out by anger and embarrassment. I whispered through clinched teeth. "I can't believe you did that."

He tightened the arm still wrapped around my lower back and spoke into my hair. "You said I was your boyfriend. I was selling the story."

I refused to meet his eyes. My face burned, and I knew it must be hot-tamale red, which made the situation even worse.

"What's the big deal? It's not like it's the first time a guy kissed you," Jax said.

My mortified expression gave away the truth. My first kiss, a joke.

Jax paused and chuckled. "I'd have tried harder if I'd known. Next time."

Anger broke through my embarrassment. "Dream on."

With my neurons on speaking terms again, I remembered the danger following us and surreptitiously scanned the room. On the balcony overhead Igor stuck out like a fox in the chicken coop. He leaned over the rail to get a better view of the room below.

I blinked. My insides dissolved into liquid. Two couples stood in front of us waiting to get through security. Even with our changed appearances he would spot us before we could get through the line. The crowd gave a bit of protection but not enough. There was plenty of magic they could throw at us without anyone being the wiser.

I may not be a great witch but there were still a few things I could do. I gathered my power and sent out the tendrils, grabbed and yanked.

A woman walking behind Igor tripped and lost her grip on the iPhone in her hand. It flew through the air and cracked on the tile. I sent an extra spurt of energy to be sure the screen shattered. Blowing things up was my specialty, after all.

Igor jumped at the shriek and crash behind him. I choked on my laughter as I watched the woman pick up her phone and gasp over the damage but knew it wouldn't buy much time.

Forcing a human to do something was strictly forbidden, but there were no rules against the power of suggestion. With a silent apology, I planted a few choice thoughts, and a few violent urges that may have been my own, in the woman's head. Her glare could have melted the Polar Ice Caps.

She turned on Igor. "You tripped me," she sputtered.

I could hear her rant over the murmur of the crowd all the way below.

"My phone's broken," she said, and thrust the now useless rectangle in his face.

The scene drew enough attention that Igor had to play it cool while the woman continued to verbally assault him. Then her purse started swinging. Pure joy shot through me when the heavy Coach bag connected with Igor's skull. Sick, I know.

I tore my attention away from the scene above and met Jax's gaze. He knew I'd manufactured the diversion. I couldn't tell how he felt about my use of magic.

His brow scrunched, and his gaze darted from me to the angry woman. "Is she hormonal or did you mess with her head?"

I chewed on my bottom lip. "I just gave her a gentle push."

"Why not mess with his head?" he asked and pointed to Igor.

"I can't. It doesn't work on us."

He took another look at the screaming woman. "We need some ground rules. Number one. No messing with my head. Got it?"

I nodded. "Got it."

The security guard waved me forward. Tension drained out of my shoulders after we cleared security. I peeked one more time at the upper level, where Igor was having a serious issue, before we hurried to the gate.

The flight attendant took my first-class ticket with a sugary smile. "We've already called First Class, so you can go right on through and let an attendant know if you need anything."

I collapsed in the leather seat wide enough to fit at least two of me, maybe three. *I'd made it.* Except my body wouldn't relax even in the lush cushions. Jax settled into the aisle seat next to me and craned his neck around to watch the entrance. I followed his gaze and ordered myself to relax, but my attention remained on the entryway. Waiting.

Twenty minutes later, the flight attendant locked the door, and I held up my hand for a high five. "England here we come."

****

After a couple hours of dozing, my internal alarm went off. Still exhausted, I kept my eyes closed, but the motorboat sound coming from Jax's seat kept me awake. I gave up any hope of resting, raised my seat, turned on the reading light, and spent most of the flight going over my father's research one more time. I needed to know exactly what I was looking for in case we didn't have much time with the records.

The storehouse in England for our historical research was hidden in plain sight, so to speak. The professor in charge of the History Department at

97

Cambridge University was one of us. My father's English counterpart.

The letters I'd borrowed from the safe were yellowed and fragile. I kept them in their plastic covers to protect them from the natural oils on my skin. The duke that my father focused in on as a possible council member seemed to have a lecherous eye. In every letter he mentioned beautiful ladies at least once. Pig.

The duke had disappeared on a trip to Paris during one of the most unstable periods of the French Revolution. Who knows, maybe he was one of the thousands of victims of the guillotine.

Any talk of plants or his horticulture interests, my father and his colleagues disregarded as an irrelevant scientific hobby. Now those paragraphs were the ones that held my attention.

Next to me, Jax stretched and contemplated the tray the flight attendant dropped off. Although to us it was eleven in the morning, once we landed in England it would be late afternoon.

"Here, you need this more than I do." Jax held out his espresso.

I blinked the sting out of my eyes and took the cup. "That bad?"

He chuckled.

With the sun looming over the horizon outside the window, I restacked the papers and carefully put them into my messenger bag. I combed my fingers through my tangled locks and wrapped my cardigan tighter around my chest. "You try sleeping next to a chainsaw."

He responded by calling a flight attendant over to ask for three more espressos, all for me. A trip to the bathroom to tame my hair and splash water on my face helped. I'd at least lost the gape-mouthed-drooling-with-a-blank-stare zombie façade. I know, it's amazing more guys weren't lining up to have a chance with me.

I shook out my hair and stuffed my hair-tie in my pocket. My fingers brushed against a piece of paper. I pulled the folded slip out, frowning.

Avoid the walkway. Go out the unlocked door and down the stairs. Follow the yellow bag to the exit to get a vehicle.

So this was the help the monk mentioned.

When I got back to my seat I showed the message to Jax and told him about the monk.

"Follow the yellow bag?" He arched an eyebrow. "Is that like the yellow brick road? Do you think we can trust him?"

"I'm not sure of anything right now, but if they're against the council that makes them our ally."

"I guess we don't get off the plane with the rest of the passengers then."

The ocean spread outside the window with no land in sight. I settled into my seat and picked at the eggs, bacon, sausage, and toast.

"Are you going to eat that?" Jax pointed at the sausage links with his fork.

I pushed my plate toward him. "Go for it."

He stabbed the links and munched away. "So, what exactly are we searching for in this top-secret warehouse?"

I pulled the documents out. "They always thought they were looking for a spell or a book. Something like that. So everything that had to do with science or hobbies they disregarded."

I pointed to the letters and references to new plants the duke grew in his greenhouse. "So they thought this was just a botany hobby that was popular with nobles in eighteenth-century England. They painted plants, grew plants, made tea out of plants, brought back exotic species for their greenhouses. No one ever paid much attention."

I pointed to the entry I'd found in my father's journal. He'd written *Botany?* then scribbled it out.

Jax flipped through the journal. "But they kept all of this extraneous stuff in this storehouse in Cambridge?"

"Historians never throw anything away. Trust me, my parents still have the paper I first wrote my name on, backward of course." I said.

"Backward?" he asked.

I shrugged. "I never seem to do things the *right way*."

"But they saved the paper. My mom used to be that way," Jax commented.

After not just putting my foot in my mouth at the airport but shoving it all the way down to my stomach, I didn't trust myself to say anything.

Jax took one of the letters from my hand and gave it a quick read. "What's with him saying he has some beautiful ladies for his friend to meet?"

I snorted. "Maybe he was a noble pimp. He mentioned them several times."

Jax chuckled. "There are a couple of mentions in here about plants. How could they never consider the possibility this was important?"

"Science is considered the ungifted way of trying to reproduce our powers. Scientists manipulate their environment the way witches do with our energy. Any interest in science is looked down upon," I explained.

He shot me a raised eyebrow. "So you're taking AP science classes?"

I shrugged. "Yeah, like I said, my parents aren't exactly proud of me but they try to support me."

"My dad wanted me to be a lawyer, like him. After I told him that wasn't happening, he couldn't care less what I majored in. So long as I stay away."

"He doesn't think science is a good major? Wow, I thought my parents were the only ones with that bias."

Jax stared at the letter. "He said I'm more like my mom than him." He picked up the second letter and pointed to a line. "What about this, 'I have a wonderful new tincture for you to try, it has helped Eleanor with her pains immensely.' A tincture could be what we're looking for."

I nodded and leaned over the armrest to point out another line from the third letter. "Look at this one. 'Eleanor has deteriorated in the last few weeks. I have been testing out new remedies but was wondering if you might have a suggestion. If you could find time for a visit, I would appreciate it. I need your help to complete my work.' If she was sick and he had access to the power, why didn't he use it to cure her? Maybe he needed an ingredient?"

Jax's warm breath swooshed through my hair. "That sounds possible."

I turned my head and realized that leaning over him put my face only inches from his. My eyes darted to his mouth while our quick kiss replayed in my brain of its own volition. Tingles shot over my lips at the memory.

His hand reached up and gently pushed my hair

behind my ear. "Did you want me to move over?"

I retreated into my own seat and cleared my throat. All sarcastic, clever responses forgotten. I picked up the papers and put them away while I recovered myself.

"So, they've never even looked into how this mutation works or how you all are different?" he asked.

I didn't need any encouragement to change the conversation. "Not really. We know that the mutation gave us an extra set of neurons in a part of the brain that ungifted don't have. It also messed up our hormones, which is why our numbers have been dwindling down to only a few thousand. And the reason behind the arranged marriages."

Jax blinked a few times. "Wait a minute, so you have like a fiancé or something?"

Had I forgotten to mention that? I waved it off. "Not anymore. I guess one perk of flunking my final is no more Surfer Boy."

"Surfer Boy?" Jax asked.

The laugh that came out of my mouth sounded way too much like a giggle. "I never met him so I gave him that nickname since he was from California.

He nodded, slowly. "Okay. If the mutation messed with your hormones, it could definitely have some other effects you don't even know about."

The excitement over finally having someone to share my theory with zapped my nervous energy. I straightened. "I know. That's exactly what I was thinking. The reaction with your serum gave me some ideas. What if the compound my blood reacted with was a cofactor for an enzyme the mutation produced? It's not found in our bodies, but if we ingest it, the reaction is catalyzed."

He contemplated the back of the seat in front of him while he thought. "That could be entirely possible. The enzyme would sit there doing nothing until the cofactor activated it."

I folded my legs under me in the seat, no trace of my tiredness left. A part of me had been longing to talk about this with someone who would listen. And Jax not only listened, as we talked, I realized that his smooth, cocky exterior covered an amazingly sharp and analytical mind.

The rest of the flight time flew by while we discussed various possibilities. Jax had his own theories about the cell dynamics, cell biology being his major, that I never thought of myself.

"It's an interesting theory. But a toxin? I'm not sure it's possible," Jax pointed out.

"How can you say it's not possible?" I exclaimed and waved my hands around to make my point. "Haven't you ever seen the bacteria that live around volcanoes? Or in highly acidic water where nothing should survive? For the compound to be a toxin isn't that farfetched."

He sat and grinned, watching my tirade. "I know I just wanted to get a rise out of you."

My cheeks grew hotter than a straightening iron. I slapped his arm. "You jerk."

The captain came on the intercom and announced our descent into Heathrow Airport. With the eight-hour flight plus, the time change, we would arrive about 6:30pm.

The laughter faded. "We have to get out of the airport fast and get to the storeroom. Even if the monk does help, we won't have much time."

Jax's jaw firmed. "We'll have to outsmart them to keep ahead of them."

Chapter Nine

We followed the instructions on the note. At the top of the gangway, we stepped to the side while I pretended to have a problem with my bag. Passengers filed past us. Jax tested the knob of the usually locked door off to the side of the Jet way. Sure enough it turned easily in his hand.

I glanced down the gangway, half expecting to see council thugs pounding upstream.

"Let's hope this monk knows what he's doing," Jax said, and pushed the door open.

We slipped through and ran down the outdoor steps to the tarmac. Miles of concrete spread around us.

I glanced up to the windows that lined the building next to where the Jet-way attached to the gate. Rows of airport seats and exiting passengers from our flight were visible through the glass. Leaning against a pillar, with his back to the window, was a huge man in a gray suit. My breath quickened and my muscles twitched. We were way too exposed.

I grabbed Jax's arm and pointed to Igor.

"Holy shit. How could he have gotten here before us?" he asked.

"Private jet probably. We need to move, fast. Find a yellow bag," I said.

A luggage cart drove past pulling five carts of bags.

"You mean like that one," Jax said and pointed to the last cart.

A neon yellow suitcase sat atop the pile in the final rack.

Grateful to have some cover, we ducked behind the cart and ran alongside into the luggage area. The machines clanked and clattered, sorting and distributing bags. The cart stopped and the driver, clad in green coveralls like the other workers, hopped out. She turned and stared our way.

My muscles tightened, waiting for her to demand to know what we were doing there.

She lifted her shoulder length hair to reveal a scrolling tattoo on her neck, this one even more intricate, with flowers and leaves coming off the branches. She dropped her hair and waved for us to follow.

Jax gave me a nudge in the back, and we followed her into a doorway marked Exit.

Several doorways and long corridors later we popped out on a sidewalk in front of a long row of taxis and rental car booths.

"Guess we get to skip the long lines at customs," Jax whispered.

"We have taken care of transportation for you." She held out a key fob and spoke in that same Zen-like tone. As if she hadn't just broken a dozen laws by sneaking us past customs and security. "The silver Mercedes at the curb is for your use."

A thousand questions pounded in my brain to ask her but the thought of Igor in the airport, so close, stopped me. "Thank you."

I reached for the keys, but Jax grabbed them before

me. "Better let me drive."

"Really?"

He grinned like a kid with a new Christmas toy. "You want to get out of here fast, right?"

I threw my bag in the back and climbed in the passenger seat.

Jax put the key into the ignition, and turned it over. He rubbed his hands together in what looked like glee as the engine roared to life. I watched the exit door from the airport in the side mirror, my heart still pounding in my ears. "That was too close."

My heart rate didn't slow down until we were on our way out of the city. Around every corner I expected to see our way blocked by the council. I crumpled in the seat and watched for anyone trailing us. The historic landmarks and beautiful countryside were wasted on me.

"I don't see any one, do you?" Jax asked from the driver seat.

A voice in my head warned me that this was too easy. "Guess we can trust the monk. We're still ahead of them. The question is for how long."

I turned my attention to navigating the confusing streets of London. Jax did quite well with driving on the wrong side of the road, but I didn't say anything. Better not pump up his ego any further.

London buildings gave way to a countryside covered in snow.

"The dean of the History department's name is Talbot. He and my dad have been friends for years," I explained, as the historic stone buildings of Cambridge came into view.

Jax kept his eyes on the curves of the road. "Do

you think we can trust him?"

"No way. And even if he did want to help us we'd put him in danger."

"So what's the plan?"

"We need to scope out the library before it closes, then find a hotel. Tomorrow we get to brush up our breaking and entering skills," I answered.

Jax parked on a street next to a modern building almost completely covered in reflective glass windows.

The library was anything but an ancient stuffy building full of dusty books. We stood in a huge pavilion full of reading tables and nooks with a four-story vaulted ceiling. The two interior walls we faced had windows to the four floors and showed row upon row of bookshelves. The ceiling high above us was completely made of skylights which allowed natural light in and gave a wonderful warmth to the space.

I walked over to one of the few empty tables in the back. The place was rockin' for a Wednesday night. I set my backpack down, my stealthy student cover story, and spoke quietly. "Now we need to figure out where the basement is."

Jax stood close enough to whisper, his own backpack on his shoulder. "And a place to hide."

A student one table over sent us a curious look. I put what I hoped was a pleasant mask on my face and busied myself taking my research papers out of my backpack. She returned her attention to reading.

"I'm gonna take a walk around," I said.

Jax wandered over to a reference shelf and selected a book to sift through. I strolled behind the main desk and glanced around for any sign of a stairwell or elevator.

My father told me years ago about a sublevel, accessible only to our special personnel, that housed all the documents and possessions historians collected from any estates with suspected council members from Europe. My father served as the caretaker for the American records. Fun, exciting job, yeah.

I spotted the signs for the bathrooms across from an elevator and made a pit stop to scope out any possible hiding places. The thought of balancing, crouched on a toilet, for an hour while the library closed sounded about as fun as getting a swirlie.

I walked through the swinging door and went down a side hall, on the lookout for any maintenance closets.

Several doors lined the deserted corridor. I tested the knobs on the first three and found them locked. The last one, however, twisted in my hand. I cracked the door and peered in. Mop, broom, cleaning supplies, plus just enough room to hold two juvenile delinquents. If they stood close together.

I strode through the hallway as if I belonged there, rounded the corner, and ran straight into a firm and familiar chest and set of defined arms. I gripped Jax's sides to keep from falling on my butt.

"What's the matter?" I whispered.

"The library is closing. Did you find anything?"

I put some space between us, although I admit I had been enjoying the feel of being pressed together a little too much. "I have a couple ideas where to hide, but I haven't found the entrance yet."

We packed up and headed out to find a hotel for the night. Then we could make plans and decide on somewhere to eat. I still didn't know how we were going to get into the storage area. Frustration tightened my stomach into something that resembled a Celtic knot.

The council already knew what flight we'd been on. The one thing we had going was they would want to keep me to themselves. Any clue to the secret was valuable information that would be guarded and shared with only those absolutely necessary. So it would only be a few powerful witches after us, better than all of them.

I tried a deep breath to release the knot in my chest.

The historic hotel we'd checked into had been wasted on me. We could have stayed at a seedy highway motel for all I cared. Although, I noticed a predominance of portraits of stuffy English lords and ladies throughout the décor. And it did have a wonderful bed which had me dosing off moments after my head touched the pillow.

Jax came out of the bathroom and woke me from my jet-lag induced nap. We'd decided to share to conserve funds, and he volunteered to take the pull out couch. "Why don't we find something to eat and we can make a plan for tomorrow. Or would it be better to stay in the room? Out of sight?"

"Actually, it will be harder for them to do anything to us in a crowd. We'd have a shot at getting away since they'd be limited on their magic and would need to physically catch us." I knew they weren't far behind us.

He nodded, and his brown hair fell in perfectly tousled strands to frame his face—longer in the front but trimmed around his collar. Even with the jet lag and only a few hours of sleep he looked fresh and steamy. Leave it to a guy to make faded jeans and a T-shirt high fashion.

With a glance at my rumpled shirt and shorts I grabbed my travel tote. "Give me a sec to freshen up."

In the bathroom, I steeled myself against my worst fears and opened the duffel bag. Soft pastel pink and blue fuzzy sweaters peaked out at me. I groaned and pulled them out onto the floor hoping some of my own clothes would be underneath. No such luck.

Make-up, leggings, boots, sweaters, denim jackets, even a skirt surrounded me in heaps. Only one single article of my own clothes had made it past Emma's inspection, a pair of jeans.

I resisted the urge to scream. What the hell was I going to do with a pencil skirt and high-heeled boots? If we all survived this I was going to have to kill her.

"Everything okay in there?" Jax asked through the door.

"Fine," I called back. "Almost ready."

My stomach twisted. I held up one shirt after another, and they were all form fitting, mostly v-necks. How could Emma have done this to me? I stood and contemplated the baggy shirt I'd worn all day. Wrinkles creased the fabric and there was a coffee stain on the arm. Dirty, grimy homeless look or exposing curves for all to see?

I steadied myself on the counter and assessed the options: stay in here for the rest of my life, go out with a hot, hot Jax looking like a dirty laundry bag, go out naked, or put on something Emma had sent.

It was close.

At least I could wear my own jeans. That much settled, I tried on a couple of the tops. With the powder blue sweater on I examined my reflection in the mirror.

The v-neck clung to what little curves I had and accentuated them. The bumps from my jeans were visible under the sweater and I guessed that you were supposed to wear it with leggings but not a chance of that happening. I tugged at the hem, wishing it would grow more fabric. The color did match my eyes perfectly.

Frustrated and still considering putting back on my dirty shirt, I glanced at the make-up. No way.

I shoved the clothes back in the bag and put on my old running shoes again, no boots for this girl.

Jax stood in the room, cell phone in hand, when I finally got the nerve to open the door. I forced myself not to cross my arms over my chest while his eyes lingered on the fitted sweater I'd chosen.

"Ready?"

"Let's go," I answered and bolted in front of him. I had no idea how I was going to get through this trip with what Emma had packed. It wasn't like I had time to go shopping with crazy witches on our tail.

The smells coming from the pub around the corner promised a good supper. We settled into a booth and scanned the room. No witch thugs. I opened the menu. I caught Jax's raised eyebrow over the rim of the menu. "Really? We're in England. You have to order fish'n'chips."

I wrinkled my nose. "I've never been much for fish."

He leaned over the narrow table, his copper eyes held mine like a vice. "Come on, live dangerously."

My heart jumped up the pace a bit. I couldn't stop my lips from pulling up. "Fish'n'chips is considered dangerous is it?"

He settled into the seat and nodded. "Definitely."

The waitress came and took our order. Two fish'n'chips.

Rowdy rugby players from the university took up half the establishment and made conversation difficult. I gathered that they had come home victorious from their Jamboree. Judging from the bruises and dried blood on their faces it had been quite the battle.

Jax turned his head to watch the television news clips on the screen to his side.

He motioned to the story on the screen about yet another famine in a third world country. "See what I mean? Couldn't you guys fix stuff like that? Send rain or make crops grow better?"

My heart went out to the skeletal children on the screen. "I would help, but the only thing I could do is blow stuff up." My one in ten success rate with spells hardly inspired confidence. I moved my gaze away from the starving children. "We've tried to help before, many times, each time thousands of witches died for their efforts."

His brow wrinkled. "When did they intervene?"

"Think of any time there were witch trials and go back a few years. There was always a crisis that we averted but after the problem was solved the gratitude turned to fear and witch trials began."

"I don't know. That excuse seems a bit thin to me. There must be more to it," he said with a shake of his head.

My eyes studied his profile. Hair fell across his forehead in disheveled waves. Waves that would take less genetically fortunate people hours to manufacture. His entire attitude, arm thrown over the back of the

113

booth, knee bent and relaxed on the seat, even the angle of his jaw exuded strength and assurance.

Warm tendrils uncurled in the pit of my stomach and grew like weeds to my chest and extremities. The memory of our kiss flashed unbidden through my mind and brought more heat rushing through my system. The unfamiliar feeling set off conflicting emotions in my over-rational brain.

The news ended and he returned his attention to my face. "You okay?"

I cleared my throat and wrapped my hand around the cold water glass. "Yeah, just a bit hot in here."

The eyebrow lifted again. "What? Do you have a thing for Rugby players or something?" He glanced over his shoulder at the group behind us.

I shifted my gaze to the men. One of the players grinned at me, a black space where his front tooth should be, and flexed his extremely well-built arms. I tugged at the too-tight-for-my-comfort sweater and wished for a baggy sweatshirt.

"I think he may like you," Jax laughed.

My gaze shot away, and I centered it on my folded hands. "Not really my type."

His face took on a neutral expression. "So what's your type? Someone with powers, like you?"

I'd always assumed I'd marry my intended, and I never let myself picture anyone else. For a moment I tried to imagine myself in a relationship. A dark and steamy guy that bore a striking resemblance to Jax took shape in my mind.

My eyes darted to his face. When in doubt, bluff. "Blond, of course, and tan, clean-cut, kind of GQ."

Whatever my expression gave away widened his

smile. "Sounds like a schmuck."

"I assume you'd go for the typical chesty model type?"

He shrugged. "I don't know. I kind of like a girl that can pull off geeky."

"Hm, I can see the geek allure." I took a drink and recovered my scattered nerves. "Not that it matters. I never had a choice."

His smile faded. "Yeah, your fiancé. So is that still on?" He fiddled with his own glass. "I mean with the test and everything."

The confused warm fuzzies in my stomach grew horns and spiked tails at the mention of the test. My hand clinched around the glass. "There is a spell that is supposed to connect us. I assume they've broken the engagement and the spell, but I haven't noticed anything different."

"So you could still be engaged and not even know it?"

I stared at my drink, anywhere but his face. "Trust me no one would want to marry a Defect, much less one that ran away."

His forehead wrinkled. "Defect? If what you did in the airport was defective I missed that."

I watched a bead of condensation run down my glass instead of meeting his eyes.

"So what about you? You getting married someday?" The question came out of my mouth before I really thought about the connotations.

His relaxed position tightened, and he found something interesting across the room to stare at. "No. I'll never get married or have kids. I don't want to screw them up."

The conviction in his voice gave me pause, but my tongue once again got ahead of my brain. "Why would you screw them up?"

He shrugged but I wasn't buying the nonchalant attitude. "Isn't that what parents do? Have kids then get divorced or die and leave the kids. Last thing the world needs is more messed up people."

"I'm sure she wouldn't have left you if she'd had a choice," I said.

He nodded. "No, she fought for two years. I watched her deteriorate into a different person before the Tay-Sachs finally killed her."

My brow wrinkled. "Tay-Sachs? I thought that only affected infants."

"That's what everyone thinks. The late onset is much more rare. She didn't show symptoms until she was thirty-two. Then they misdiagnosed her for a year, saying it was ALS. It was there all those years, if someone had been able to find it, to fix the mutation she could have survived." His voice cracked, and he coughed to cover it up.

I reached across and put my hand over his. "Jax, I'm so sorry."

He let my hand rest on his for a moment then shifted positions. The aloof mask fell over his features. "Yeah, well life sucks sometimes."

The emphatic reaction he had to my mutation leading to cures made more sense to me, as did his major. I'd thought he was in it for the money. Maybe I was wrong.

The waitress appeared with piping hot fish'n'chips and a bottle of malt vinegar. Jax, seemingly, fully recovered and back to his confident self, doused his food liberally with the vinegar then held the bottle out to me.

I made a face and reached for the ketchup.

"Come on, if you're going to eat it do it right," he said.

I rolled my eyes for his benefit and dumped the vinegar on a few fries. After a bite I had to admit it was a different but pleasing taste and covered the rest of my food.

We finished our meal with the topic of conversation on a much more interesting subject than marriage—cell mitosis and mitochondria. With all the dishes cleared and the check paid I chewed the last of my ice.

Jax picked up his empty glass then put it down. "I guess we should go."

I considered suggesting some dessert but then grabbed my bag. "Yeah we have a lot to do."

Time to return to the hotel to plan for my first foray into the criminal world.

****

Papers spread out on the bed in front of me. Jax sat on the ottoman, pulled alongside the bed, and his hand cupped his chin while he stared at the document in front of him.

"What do you—"

A knock at the door cut me short. My wide eyes darted from the door to Jax and back. My insides turned to liquid and threatened to spill over.

We simultaneously grabbed up the papers and documents, then stuffed them into my bag.

"What do you think? Out the window?" Jax asked.

I pondered the options. For all I knew it was the

maid service on the other side of that door. Or it could be council thugs ready to torture us.

I swallowed past the boulder in my throat. "Let me see who it is."

Jax watched me creep to the door and stretch up to peer through the peep hole. A single figure stood outside the door, and he definitely wasn't here to turn down the bed. Unless they hired models for the turn down service. Not a bad idea, I'd definitely stay here again.

I turned and lifted a shoulder to Jax. I hesitated then flipped the latch and unlocked the deadbolt. With the door opened a crack, I peeped out. "Can I help you?"

A blazing smile greeted me. "I think it's me that can help you, Maddie."

My muscles jumped in reflex, jerking the door with them. "How do you know my name?"

"I've known your name since I was ten and they told me who I was going to marry."

Sun streaked blond hair topped a well-tanned chiseled face, the epitome of a California native. Oh my God. Surfer Boy.

Chapter Ten

I blinked a few times, then a few more. "Alex?"

He raised both eyebrows and nodded. "If you let me in, I can explain."

I held the door fast. "What are you doing here?"

He glanced around the hallway. "I'd rather not explain it out here, and we're on a bit of a time constraint. I'm not more than a few hours ahead of the council."

The mention of the council set my blood searing through my veins and shot my pressure up enough to cause an aneurysm. I released the handle and let the door swing open. "Come in."

Alex strolled across the threshold and paused when he spotted Jax standing in the center of the room with his arms crossed, and what I could only describe as an angry pit-bull expression on his face.

Barely missing a beat Alex extended his hand. "Alex Warner and you are?"

Jax glanced at the extended hand but kept his arms crossed. "Jax."

"Well, a pleasure to meet you," Alex said, and dropped his arm but kept the pleasant smile on his face.

After a quick peek into the empty hallway, I closed the door and threw the dead bolt as well as the safety latch. It wouldn't stop witches but the act made me feel better.

The boys eyed one another like two alpha males sizing each other up for a fight. Alex stood a couple inches taller than Jax, at least six foot two, lean but wiry. Jax may not have the height advantage, but his well-toned body radiated confidence and menace from every pore. While Jax was the epitome of the dark bad boy, Alex was his opposite in the golden haired angelic category. Even Alex's designer jeans contrasted with Jax's worn and faded ones. And it didn't escape me, or likely escape Jax, that Alex was exactly what I described in the pub as my perfect guy. Great.

"What do you want?" I demanded.

His sky blue eyes turned to me. "Well first of all we need to deactivate the tracker spell they have on you. They'll catch up in a couple hours, tops."

My blood pressure topped two hundred again. "Tracker spell? But my parents wouldn't—"

"Not your parents. The council put one on you when you failed your test."

He nodded and held out a hand to me. "Here give me your hand."

Jax sprang forward to stand between us. "Don't touch her," he growled, then spoke in a low voice over his shoulder. "How do we know we can trust him not to spell you or something?"

Alex leaned against the wall and laughed. "I assure you, if I'd wanted to hurt you, it would already be done."

I put a hand on Jax's arm. "He doesn't have to touch me to put a spell on me. It's okay. I think we have to trust him. For now."

The glare that passed between the two was not lost on me.

I took Alex's hand. Warm strong fingers gripped my own.

He held my gaze. "Watch and you'll see."

He closed his eyes, and I felt the energy pass from my hand into his, not a large current but a tingling trickle. Around me the room took on a red shimmer. My skin glowed like a firefly. I was a beacon clearly visible with the witch energy.

I blew out a breath. "So they've been tracking me the entire time."

"I don't believe it. They would have caught us at the airport in Chicago if they were tracking you," Jax said. "Couldn't he have just put that on you?"

I paused. Jax could be right.

"They were hoping to catch you at the airport when you got off the plane. No one's quite sure how you avoided them." He waited for me to answer.

I stared blankly back. No way was I ratting out the monk. "Is that how you found me? The tracker spell?"

"That and a little information I gathered once I got past a few firewalls."

"You're a hacker?" I'd never heard of a witch using such mundane techniques. Not when you could rip the information out of someone's mind.

"It's a hobby." Alex closed his eyes again. "I'll need to use both of our energies to break the tracker."

Witches could share energy, if both were willing. After a moment's hesitation, I didn't put up any resistance to the gentle tug on my power. Even if he was lying, the spell still needed to be broken.

I felt him manipulate my energy, intertwining it with his own, and wrapping it around me like a blanket. More energy poured from both of us until the energy supplying the tracker spell was blocked by ours. He held the shield there for a minute, until the tracker spell sputtered like a candle without oxygen, and the glow faded from my body.

He opened his eyes. "Done."

The muscles in my legs trembled, and I sat in the nearest chair. I understood why he wanted to use both our energy. That spell would have wiped out one person.

Jax stepped forward. "Are you okay?"

Alex was already on his way to the mini fridge. "She'll be fine, just needs a little sugar and time."

He brought me back a soda, the lid already opened, and carried one for himself in his other hand.

I accepted the cold can and downed a big gulp.

Jax shifted his weight from foot-to-foot then sat on the edge of the bed and waved a hand Alex's way. "So this is Surfer Boy?"

Hot blood rushed to my cheeks. I glared at Jax before turning to Alex. "Um, yeah, sorry. It was a nickname I gave you since you're from California."

Alex laughed. "Not a problem. I do like to surf."

"So they can't track us anymore?" I asked after another gulp of soda.

He shook his head. "No, but we should move tonight because they probably had a pretty good idea of where you were when we turned it off."

Jax nodded. "Great. You can leave now."

Alex didn't shift from his seat and looked my way when he spoke. "You're going to need a lot more of my help before this is over."

Jax didn't let me get a word in. "Why should she trust you? Just because you broke a tracker spell?" He stuffed his hands in his jean pockets and mumbled, "Didn't look that hard."

While his protective attitude might have been endearing to some, it only grated on my already freaked-out nerves. But I did share the suspicion of this stranger's intentions. I doubted he flew across the Atlantic Ocean out of the kindness of his heart to help someone he'd never met and risk his standing with the council—not to mention his life.

Alex opened his mouth to answer Jax, but I held up my hand to stop him. "You need to tell me why you're really here. I appreciate your help with the tracker, but that hardly proves your intentions."

He shifted in his chair. "Not a problem. I'm not here to help you because you're my fiancée, although that doesn't hurt matters."

Jax rolled his eyes.

"My parents wanted me to find out what really happened. They haven't trusted the council for years. When your test results came in and they saw how you were sabotaged, then the scandal with you running away, well, it raised some questions, like why is the Council so interested in you?"

I met Jax's eyes. He gave me a tiny shake of his head.

"Then we heard the rumor that you had a clue to the secret," Alex continued. "My parents know that the council cannot be in control of the secret. I came to help you and keep the answer safe from the council."

I tried to get a read on him, to see past the eye-pleasing, seemingly sincere, face. Up front he could very well be telling the truth, but my rational side knew there had to be more he wasn't telling us. "In other words, your parents want the answer for themselves and so they sent you to see if I really knew anything."

"That would be one way to see it, I suppose." He leaned back in the chair. "You're not the only one who has lost someone you care about to this council. They made an example out of your aunt, but they've hurt many more that no one ever found out about. So I guess you have to decide—who would be worse to control the secret? The council who wash people's brains and strip powers to exert their control, or my family and their supporters who have been working against a corrupt council for centuries."

"Who did you lose?"

Alex's face lost any trace of a smile. His features slackened, and his eyes closed for a moment. "My brother and my grandmother. They didn't make it through the stripping of their powers."

My stomach performed unpleasant acrobatics that threatened to bring the fish'n'chips up for an encore performance. "Were they like me? Not good at witchcraft?"

He stared at his hands. "Not exactly, my grandmother voiced strong opinions to the wrong people, and my brother wouldn't blow anything up. He had a problem with creating wind storms whenever he tried to perform a spell. He failed his final test." His voice trembled. "They made sure he did. Sound familiar?"

He looked up and blinked away the moisture in his eyes.

The sincere loss in his voice rang true. I believed him.

"Okay, say I believe you. What happens if I don't

know anything?"

"Then I still want to help you because I don't want to see you stripped of your powers or washed. You can tell me the truth, Maddie. I'm here to help either way," he answered.

"I don't really have a clue," I tried to force sincerity into my voice, and maybe a bit of vulnerability. I couldn't detect any dishonesty in his story, but I needed time to think, and talk to Jax. "I thought I did...but it was a dead end."

Alex held my gaze for a beat then nodded sharply. "Then we need to get you out of here and hidden."

A smoky darkness clouded his eyes. But it cleared before I could be sure I even saw it.

Jax rose to his feet. "And what if we don't want your help?"

Alex took an envelope from his jacket pocket. "I understand. Here's something to help you, and I'll be on my way."

I opened the envelope and flipped through a stack of crisp English pounds. The inky smell of the money hit my nose. I'd never seen so much cash in my life.

He also held out a card with only a number printed on the front. "If you need help call this number, and we'll do what we can."

I stared at the card and cash in my hands, then raised my eyes to Jax.

He shook his head. "We don't need him."

"We're being hunted by powerful witches. I didn't even know there was a tracker on me, much less how to deactivate it. Let's face it, one defective witch up against a horde of witches, the odds are hardly in our favor," I exclaimed.

"Our chances are better on our own than with someone we don't know we can trust," Jax argued.

Alex paused at the door.

"I believe he's telling the truth about his brother," I said.

Letting someone who could actually perform spells and wanted to help us walk away felt like an idiotic move, even if I wasn't sure I could trust him. "Wait."

Jax's glare bore into me but I ignored it. "I think we could use your help."

Alex straightened his shoulders. "All right then. Let's get you out of here."

I rose on unsteady feet to gather my things. Jax jumped to help me, then went into the bathroom to grab everything out of there, his body tense.

Alex pointed his jaw Jax's way. "Interesting character. Boyfriend?"

I paused in my packing. "No, he's just helping me out."

"But you told him about our powers," he pressed.

I turned and put a hand on my hip. "If you want to talk about all the rules I've broken, we're going to be here for a while."

He held up his palms in surrender. "Just asking."

I lifted the duffel bag, which seemed a million times heavier than it had been, to the bed.

Jax came out of the bathroom and grabbed his bag then lifted the duffel from my grasp.

"Need help with that?" Alex asked.

Jax strode past him to the door. "I've got it."

****

Our rental car pulled up in front of a London hotel near the airport. Alex parked his rental in the spot next to ours. Safety in numbers being our new strategy. With the break-in still only half planned, I had to make a decision fast on how much to trust Alex with. My decision to let him stay had been a spur of the moment, go with your gut, kind of thing. Now I had to deal with the ramifications, like Jax barely speaking to me the entire drive. What I did get out of him was sarcastic and snippy.

I blew out a breath and made my decision. In for a penny in for a pound, to go with a British saying. "I'm going to tell him."

Jax paused, the car off but the keys still in the ignition. "I don't think we can trust this guy."

"I don't completely trust him either, but we could use the help," I answered.

Jax yanked the keys from the slot and grabbed the door handle. "Whatever. It's your show. I'm just along for the ride, and the rights to any medical discoveries. No skin off my back if you lose your powers."

I flinched at the bite in his voice, taken back by the anger. My nerves recovered, however, and I fired some bullets of my own. "Let's not pretend that you were ever in this for anything other than yourself. You want your free ride to grad school? You have to earn it."

I stalked from the car and didn't glance back to see if he followed.

The room arrangements were done by the time I got to the lobby, thanks to Alex. He sprang for three rooms which gave me some much needed space from Jax. I liked him a little more.

The key card slid into the slot, and I glanced over to my supposed fiancé, his room being right next to mine. If he'd wanted to take us in he could have done it a hundred times already. Either he was working for the council or he wasn't and could actually help us. "We need to talk."

He let his hand fall from the handle and moved to my door. "I'm ready when you are."

Jax ignored us and closed his own door. With more force than necessary.

Inside the room I spread the documents and my father's journal out before Alex and began to explain my theory. "So for years we've been ignoring any references to so-called hobbies of the nobility in England, like Botany and Horticulture."

He leaned over the documents and listened without comment until I paused.

"So you think they were growing some sort of plant that allowed them to access the power because of all these references in the letters, even before the hobby was popular?" he asked.

"I actually wonder if they're the ones that made botany popular in the first place. But yes, that and the fact that my blood lit up like a mag light when we mixed it with a chemical compound."

He blinked, his forehead wrinkled. "What?"

I had to dumb the science down a little, but I gave him the Cliff Notes version.

The bed shifted under his weight. He stared at a blank spot on the wall. "All these years and we have been on the wrong track entirely."

I gathered up the documents. "Only if I'm right."

"You have to be. And tomorrow we're going to break into the storage at Cambridge and prove it."

****

"We need to find Talbot. He's the Dean of the

History department here and is the keeper of the records, basically the English version of my father," I explained when we pulled into the lot on campus the next day.

Jax played the role of my silent driver, still bent that I'd told Alex everything.

"If he goes into the vault in the library it will show us where the entrance is, and then we wait until closing time and break in," I continued. "The problem is how to get him into the vault. We don't have the time to sit around and wait for him to get an order and go get a document."

Alex spoke up from the back seat. "Leave that to me." He pulled his computer from its case and typed for a minute. "Taken care of. He just got an urgent request from a high up council member."

Turns out Alex was a closet computer geek, and the hottest computer geek I'd ever seen. His major was, of course, History, since Computer Science was for those who couldn't perform magic, but his hobby was hacking. Not a skill set I possessed. So he already made a valuable addition to the team.

I pulled up a picture of Talbot and my father on my phone from dad's trip to England last year and showed it to the boys. The stick-thin middle-aged man in glasses and thinning mouse brown hair shouldn't be too difficult to spot.

We entered the Sealy Library and took up observation points around the room. We didn't have to wait long.

Jax meandered over to my isle of books. "Talbot just came in. He walked right by my table."

I nodded and continued to page through the book in

my hand. "Where is he?"

"He went in the bathroom."

I peeked around the corner. The hallway outside the bathrooms was empty. I gestured for Jax to follow me. We wogged across an open area to a high bookshelf and positioned ourselves on the side opposite the bathrooms.

"We need to see where he goes," I said. I selected another book at random and pretended to skim through it.

Jax took up his usual pose of leaning on one shoulder and flipped through another volume. The ding of the elevator made me jump, almost dropping my book.

He raised an eyebrow.

I glared, then turned my attention to a group of students filing out of the elevator from the upper floors. Their smooth English accents floated to my ears. I momentarily wished I sounded that cultured and cool.

The door to the bathroom opened, and Talbot strode out. He headed to the closing elevator, paused, and glanced around, then pulled a white plastic security card from his pocket. He swiped the card through a slot next to the elevator call button.

The doors opened, and he stepped inside.

Jax touched my arm then pointed to the numbers above the elevator. The B lit up then went dark.

I blew out a breath. "It must be one floor below the basement."

"Would the stairs go to it?" Jax asked.

I slapped the unread book shut and gritted my teeth. "No. Dad said they have a single entrance. Damn, we aren't going to be able to get in."

Jax replaced his cover volume, his brow together. "Why can't you just use magic?"

I collared my frustration and kept it on a tight leash to avoid the rabid beast biting him for the innocent question. "They have alarms that will sense the slightest use of magic anywhere in this building. One spell and we're done."

I know being a witch should have been way cooler than it really was. I pulled out my new burner phone to text Alex.

"Time for some old-fashioned delinquency to save the day," Jax said.

Racing fingers paused over the screen of my phone. My gaze jerked to his face, and my forehead scrunched.

He shot me a devious smirk. "Stay here. Watch and learn."

He strode across the pavilion to our table and motioned to Alex to stay hidden. With the backpack slung over his shoulder, he made his way back to the corridor and leaned against the wall around the corner from the elevator.

He pulled his cell phone out of his pocket. A moment later my forgotten phone buzzed in my hand. The screen showed Jax's face.

I hit the button. *Summer camp pays off.*

I crinkled my brow. The crowd in the library had thinned over the last twenty minutes. I could only hope that Talbot didn't take his sweet time in the records room.

Ten minutes ticked by. I shifted my position down the row and pretended to scan the shelf.

A librarian approached me. "The library closes in

five minutes, dear."

I smiled and nodded. We wouldn't get another chance at this. The Council could find us at any time. I realized I was pacing up and down the aisle and forced my feet to stop.

The elevator dinged.

I held my breath and watched the doors part. The professor stepped out with a bundle of whatever goose chase Alex had sent him on tucked under his arm.

I nodded to Jax who pushed off the wall. The moment Talbot hurried around the corner, Jax stepped into his path. The two collided. For anyone watching, it appeared that Talbot had plowed into an unsuspecting Jax, not the other way around.

Jax stumbled back. He dropped his cell phone and fell into the wall.

"Oh, I say. So sorry," Talbot said, obviously flustered. He bent over to give Jax a hand up. Jax grasped the offered hand and climbed to his feet with a slight wobble.

Professor Talbot gripped Jax by the shoulder. "You okay?"

Jax nodded and bent to retrieve his phone.

Talbot stepped back and adjusted the bowtie at his neck. "So sorry, completely my fault, in a bit of a rush don't you know."

"No worries," Jax said quietly and waved away his concern.

Talbot turned and rushed out of the library, still straightening his tie.

Jax watched him leave then strolled to my hiding place, his hands in his pockets and a gleam in his eye. "I forgot to ask what my reward would be."

"You got it?" I asked, shocked, impressed, and maybe a little turned on all at the same time.

He held his hands out. "You doubted me?"

I rolled my eyes then motioned for Alex to follow us. "Save your ego trip for later. Let's hope he doesn't miss his card. We have to hide."

The storage closet was anything but roomy. I stood between the two boys. The space had just enough room for us to stand shoulder to shoulder, if the boys angled their bodies slightly in front of me. We stayed in our claustrophobic semicircle for half an hour listening to the librarians checking the rooms, chatting in their English accents the entire time.

Alex had flipped the lock on the door after we stepped in, and I'd had a serious problem controlling the urge to scream. Visions of not being able to get out flashed through my mind. But his foresight saved us. The handle rattled about forty minutes later. That would have been awkward. Hello, Mrs. Librarian. No of course we weren't having a threesome in your closet...we were just going to steal some documents...

Stuffy moisture gathered in the closed space, a side effect of breathing in the same air ten times over. Nasty. Sweat rivulets ran down my neck and tickled my back.

Jax's fingers gripped mine and squeezed. "I think they're gone."

Heat spread up my arm to my stomach from the places Jax's skin touched mine.

"Let's give it one more minute," Alex urged.

I waited about thirty seconds. Complete silence, and much more breathable air, waited for us on the other side of the door. I pulled my hand from Jax's grip. "Good enough. Let's go."

Alex opened the door, and light spilled in, blinding my unprepared retinas.

I held my hand out to Jax. "The card?"

"We'll talk about that reward later," he said quietly and dropped the thin plastic in my palm.

My mouth dropped. He'd gone from barely speaking to me to flirting. What the hell? I started to ask him if he'd forgotten his bi-polar meds, but for once stopped myself before I said something I regretted and walked to the elevator instead.

I inserted the card into the strip and swiped. A ding sounded, and the doors slid open.

We filed in and waited for the doors to close. Finally, the shiny metal sheets slid into place.

"Now what?" Alex asked.

I shrugged. "We couldn't exactly see through the door. Look for a button or another place to swipe the card."

There was no magnetic strip reader on the panel inside the elevator, only buttons for the floors, and a red emergency button. We crouched and examined every inch of the panel and the other surfaces in the elevator. I jammed the card into any suspicious gap with no success. After a couple minutes, I straightened and ran my hand through my hair.

Alex relaxed against the wall, his eyes on the panel. "What about the emergency button?"

"You mean the one that sets the alarms off?" I asked.

He pointed to the panel. "Look how it's arranged."

The open and close buttons sat at the top corners. Below them, the numbers one through four lined up in a vertical row with the B on the bottom and the red emergency button directly below in the line.

"It almost seems like that should be the floor below the basement," Jax said.

I held up my hand. "If you're wrong and we push it, we're going to have the fire department here in five minutes."

Alex shrugged. "Do you have a better suggestion?"

"I say we try it," Jax urged.

I blew out a breath. "Just give me a minute."

I reexamined the panel, then crouched on the floor, and ran my hands along the carpet while the boys watched.

"Push the damn thing," I growled.

Jax punched the red emergency button. I squinted my eyes and waited for the wail of sirens.

Chapter Eleven

The elevator lurched and began its descent.

Alex put his hands behind his head. "It's good to be a genius."

I snorted and leaned against the rail of the elevator. He'd been right after all.

The doors slid open to reveal a plain carpeted hallway with a single door at the end. The walls were painted and bare of pictures or decorations. I twisted the handle. Locked. The smooth cream-colored paint on the walls left no space to insert the card.

I bit my lip and reminded myself successfully breaking in had been a long shot. My hand tightened around the white plastic card. "Anyone know how to pick locks?"

Jax moved in front of me. "Let me have a look at it."

"Another skill you picked up at summer camp?" I asked.

He bent to examine the lock. "No, it's what got me sent there in the first place."

Jax took a multi-tool out of his pocket and pulled a thin strip of metal out of one end. From the other end he pulled out a slightly thicker and shorter strip. Both slid into the key hole of the lock.

Alex and I watched over his shoulder. He gently jiggled the two pieces of metal this way and that. For some inexplicable reason I found his long and very talented fingers entrancing.

Jax kept his attention on his task. "You know, breathing down my neck won't speed this up."

"Oh, sorry," I said, and moved away.

Alex also stepped back. "So why would you learn to pick locks?"

He shrugged. "When I first came to live with them, my stepmom used to lock me in my room. I wanted to get out."

I stared at the mess of waves on the back of his head, glad he couldn't see the shocked expression on my face. Sympathy welled up at the thought of a twelve-year-old Jax locked in a room. Who in the world would lock a grieving child in their bed room?

Jax continued. "After that it was mostly to annoy my dad. He sent me to summer camp for troubled kids to teach me a lesson. I did learn a lot, just not what he expected."

A soft click sounded. Jax removed his tools and stood, swinging the door open with a quick bow.

"That's how you got the camera from the school," I said.

He grinned at me. "I said I could handle it."

Alex leaned against the wall behind me. "Not bad for a delinquent."

"My delinquent skills have been more help than your magic, Surfer Boy," Jax shot back.

Their gazes locked in a silent battle until I stepped between them into the room.

I flipped on the lights. Strips of florescent bulbs lit up in a cascade into the darkness, like a wave of light moving through the warehouse. The room before us had to be at least the size of a football field with hundreds of rows of shelves and filing cabinets.

"Let's hope he's as anal about organizing the records as he is about his bowtie being straight," Alex said.

I nodded. "We need to split up."

Jax took the filing cabinets while I went to the computer to see if I could cross reference plants or medicinal teas with anything in the warehouse.

The computer was password protected. I blew out a breath.

"Need some help?" Alex said from over my shoulder.

I vacated the seat and watched his fingers race over the keyboard. He broke the password in less than a minute. The searches for plants yielded multiple hits. Within half an hour I'd jotted down the locations of the documents and personal belongings. Alex wiped the search history so there would be no breadcrumbs for the goons to follow. Then I ran to find Jax.

With no real idea what we were searching for, I had accumulated quite the list. I found Jax combing through a filing cabinet about fifty yards down the center aisle.

"Here, this may help," I said, and pushed the list into his hand.

We grabbed a variety of objects and documents that had anything to do with plants or Botany. Stacks on the table included letters, contracts, paintings, and journals.

The first two turned out to be recipes for tinctures for headaches. I set them aside while the boys searched for the rest of the items on the list and looked over a contract the Duke of Bristol, my ancestor, signed for the purchase of a plot of land adjacent to his own fields in western England.

I wiped a bead of cold sweat from my brow. Historians had these same documents for years without finding anything, and I had only minutes or hours to figure out the answer. I'd just opened a leather portfolio and yanked out a stack of paintings when Jax arrived with a large bundle of documents and dumped them on the table.

My eyes raced over the top picture, a landscape, for any clues. There had to be at least fifty in the stack. I checked my watch, we'd already been in here for almost an hour. "We can't stay here much longer. Should we take all of it and go over them at the hotel?"

Alex plopped down a heavy box then turned to Jax. "You want to help me with the rest?"

"Sure," Jax answered.

I eyed the overfull box, and worried, my lip between my teeth. We'd be here all night, and the Council could get here any minute. With only one way in and out this room was the perfect trap. I began quickly scanning the watercolors and pencil sketches and separating them into two piles *possible* and *unlikely*.

Jax returned with another large box, and Alex stayed close on his heels with his arms full.

I didn't look up. "Do you guys want to start on the boxes? I'm separating stuff into piles to take with us or leave here."

They each took a box and went over each item, ranging from hair combs to snuff boxes. Alex pulled out a leather-bound volume and opened the cover.

"This may be interesting. It's a journal with poems and references to a botany hobby."

The worn leather volume reminded me of my dad's journal, the one I'd stolen when I left. He'd kept every clue he'd discovered, every idea inside its cover. I flipped to the first page. Annabel was written in neat scrip in the middle of the title page. I skimmed the pages, lots of poems, another popular hobby of the day, and several references to growing plants in her green house. "Definitely take it. We can read it later."

I reached the last ten pictures and straightened in my chair. The watercolors depicted detailed portraits of plants, the common names with genus and species along with details on how to grow them written in a careful hand in the lower corner.

The hobby was common enough for that time, but my heart beat faster in my chest. I read the inscriptions: English Rose, Lily of the Valley, Flat Leafed Parsley, and so on. I flipped the last page and stared at the beautifully rendered watercolor of a Chrysanthemum.

As I laid the stack aside, my eyes focused on a carefully printed recipe on the back of the paper. I snatched the pile up and shuffled through it again. Most in the stack bore similar inscriptions. I read through the ingredients and instructions.

Most of the recipes included the plant portrayed in the painting, so that made some sense, but three did not include the plant in the corresponding picture.

My gaze raced over the pages, and I sucked in a gulp of air. This could be what we were searching for. A tea would include the natural chemical compounds and be an easy way of ingesting them. One or a combination of these plants could very well contain the chemical compound that reacted with my blood.

The plant aging spell in the witch final finally made some sense to me. The test seemed a bit off the wall, but if the secret had to do with plants, well, maybe my ancestors weren't nuts after all.

"There was one more box, I'll go back and get it," Alex said and jogged down the isle.

I kept my attention on the documents in front of me. The sound of a door closing directly behind us broke through my concentration and spun me around on my heel. Talbot stood just inside the entry way, his beady eyes narrowed and a gun in his hand. The barrel pointed steadily at my heart, judging from my estimate of the trajectory.

"I had a feeling something was off about that request. Not often do I get them from High Council members." He sneered and leveled the gun at Jax. "Then when my card came up missing I knew."

I held up my hands. "If you'll let me explain, we didn't want to break in."

He snorted. "Let's dispense with the pretense. I know who you are. The worthless Defect that ran away."

The disgust in his voice when he said Defect smacked me across the face. I couldn't get a word past my swelling throat.

"She's better than you'll ever be," Jax growled. "You're just some lackey for the council. Do you pick up their dry cleaning too?"

"Jax stop," I said, and edged closer to him.

Jax's face stained red. He waved his hands around. "Here you have had the clues all these years and you were too blind to see what was right in front of your face."

Talbot's eyes widened. "What are you talking about?"

"Nothing. Jax shut up."

"Tell me what you found," he said.

"You're so smart, figure it out yourself," Jax piped up.

With a shrug, Talbot reached into his pocket and pulled out his phone. "Time for a little family reunion. How long has it been since you last saw your aunt?"

My lungs locked while my mouth turned into the Sahara Desert. They'd sent my aunt after me.

Without taking his eyes off of me, he hit the screen and held the phone up to his ear. "This is Talbot. I found Madison Foster breaking into my stores warehouse." He paused and listened. "Yes, I can hold them."

He hit a button and pocketed the phone. "Well, we have some time to chat while we wait. They only care about you." He swung the gun Jax's way. "Your irritating friend here is expendable. Why don't we play a bit of a game, you answer my questions or I'll start shooting? Let's begin with his knees."

A shadow moved behind Talbot and detached itself from the shelves. Alex. I held up my palms and nodded. "Okay, okay I'll tell you whatever you want to know. Don't hurt him."

A satisfied smile creased Talbot's thin face, but he kept the gun on Jax.

I forced my gaze away from Alex. He crept along a set of shelves. "It's been here all along. We just didn't know what we were looking for."

"Maddie, don't tell him," Jax protested.

"It's in the contracts." I held up the land contract bearing the Duke's signature. "The amounts are a code. That's why Jax is here."

Jax raised one eyebrow my way while Talbot examined him with renewed interest.

"He's a math genius. He broke the code," I said. "So, I wouldn't kill him if I were you— since he's the only one who can figure it out."

He aimed the gun at me again. Talk about indecisive. "Too bad for you. That makes you expendable. The council will thank me for killing a Defect before you can cause any more trouble."

Alex appeared behind Talbot, again, an antique metal fire poker poised above his shoulder like a baseball bat. He swung in a perfect arc that would have knocked Talbot's skull out of the park, if it hadn't been attached.

The gun dropped to floor with a metallic clatter. Talbot slithered down in a boneless puddle. Alex stared at the inert form at his feet for a moment then dropped the poker.

A smirk pulled up one side of my lips. "That's what you get for calling me expendable."

"Nice swing," Jax added. "For a Surfer Boy."

****

The box of documents slid down my leg to the floor with a thud. Jax and Alex set their burdens on the table in the hotel room. We'd frantically sorted through the documents and paintings, taking anything with a recipe on it or anything we thought could prove useful and leaving the rest. On Jax's suggestion I also grabbed any contracts or documents containing numbers as well, to throw off the thugs. Hopefully they'd believe the goose chase I'd started Talbot on with my math genius lie.

Talbot lay unconscious on the floor of the storage room. I didn't envy him the headache he'd have when he came to but at least he'd wake up. Probably.

I slumped into the wing-back chair and closed my eyes. The clock read well past two in the morning.

"I would suggest we move to a different hotel as soon as possible," Alex said from the bed.

I cracked an eye open and groaned—my muscles screaming at the movement. "Did you have someplace in mind?"

He nodded. "I stayed at The Rosewood with my family once. It was a little more upscale than this, and I don't think they would expect you to have the resources that I have access to."

I huffed. "You mean they expect me to be almost broke by now."

"Well, I was trying to put it delicately." Alex shrugged.

Exhaustion sapped away my ability to care. "Whatever. So should we move now or in the morning?"

"I would say the sooner the better. I'll go gather my things and check us out if you both want to meet me in the parking lot."

He stood up, and Jax stepped in his path. "Just because you took a swing at Talbot doesn't prove we can trust you. I'm still watching you."

"Let's not forget I could have waited another minute until after Talbot took a shot but I didn't." Alex held his stare for a couple of seconds, and then grinned.

"Doesn't prove anything." Jax's glare didn't

change.

Alex nodded slowly. "Right."

I slapped my hand against my forehead and rolled my eyes behind closed lids. "Next thing you know you'll be puffing out your chests and circling each other."

Jax's glare shifted to me, but he stepped out of Alex's path.

"I'll see you guys in a few minutes." Alex strode from the room.

I stuffed my clothes into my backpack and set my father's journal on top. The sight of the leather binding brought the journal we'd found in the storehouse to mind. I zipped the backpack shut and began sifting through the box of papers we'd borrowed. "Jax did you grab that journal that had the plant references?"

"Everything we took is in that box. Did we leave out something important?"

I chewed on the inside of my cheek. "Probably not. I was just curious. I think the paintings are what we needed."

I swung my pack onto my back and pushed away the feeling that we had left something significant behind. We'd have to do without whatever it was. Going back to the library now would definitely be suicide.

****

The exterior of The Rosewood Hotel in downtown London was made up of ornate cream-colored stone bricks that prepared me for an interior filled with paintings of old stuffy English lords and even older ornate outdated furnishings. When we walked into the hotel, I breathed a sigh of relief. Sleek modern furnishings filled the space with elegant décor.

I wandered around my room despite the exhaustion permeating my limbs. My fingers grazed the polished glass tabletops while I took in the nearly bare white walls. Bold striped carpet added to the modern feel that continued into the luxurious bathroom. I glanced in the mirror then turned away.

The stone of the bathroom floor felt cool against my bare feet. Gray and white marble covered almost every surface. In the middle of the room a colossal solid marble tub made my jaw drop.

Our suite was more like a two-bedroom apartment than a hotel. Jax was sleeping on the pull-out-couch in the adjoining living area while Alex claimed the other bedroom. The suite also sported a full kitchen.

I had to admit, the council would probably never think to look for us here. Without Alex we would be counting our pennies and staying in more of a hostel than upscale hotel. While doubts still lingered in my mind over where his loyalties lay I still thought it was better to keep him around, for more than his money, but to also keep an eye on him. He could be a formidable enemy all on his own.

My gaze lingered on the enormous soaker tub. At three thirty in the morning I knew the smart thing would be to go to bed, but the tub called my name with promises of a steaming bubble bath. Yet, I turned to the down-covered bed and crawled under the comforter. With one last glance at the piles of documents on the striped carpet, a stipulation I'd insisted upon when Alex offered to keep them in his room, I closed my eyes and met oblivion.

****

The wonderful aroma of brewing coffee coaxed me from my slumber. I opened an eye and spotted a steaming mug on the bedside table. The sound of paper shuffling drew my attention to Jax, who sat with his feet on the small table going through a stack of documents.

"I thought I'd get started on these," he said, his focus still on the papers.

I blinked, my eyelids like sandpaper over the surface of my eyes. "Alex?"

Jax met my bleary gaze. "Not in his room."

Chapter Twelve

Adrenaline infused energy spurted into my muscles. I sat up. "Where the hell did he go?"

He set the papers on the table. "I didn't realize I was supposed to be spying on him. You're the one who wanted to trust him."

"If you'll remember, I said, 'keep your enemies close, not, he's my new bestie.'" I threw the covers back and swung my legs over the edge.

"I thought it was the blond hair and tan that you liked, not to mention the cash." Jax dropped his feet to the floor, his jaw clenched tightly.

I grabbed my clothes and stomped to the bathroom. "Yeah, because if they catch me and kill me I'll totally be needing a Sugar Daddy."

The marble soaker tub no longer held any allure, I couldn't sit still long enough to fill it up much less lounge in the bath. What a creep, to insinuate that I let Alex's looks interfere with my judgment. I jerked the brush through my tangled mane and twisted it up into a bun.

I sorted through the various articles of clothing that Emma had replaced mine with, hoping some of the tight clothes had gotten together and made some baggy shirt and comfy jean babies. No such luck. The same clothes as before spread out before me. A skintight pink sweater, was she serious? More leggings, a miniskirt?

Oh my God, kill me now. I threw one item after another onto the floor and eyed the jeans I'd worn yesterday. Maybe I could use the bathtub to do some laundry.

Muttering a few choice words, I sifted through the pile of clean clothes again and came up with a pair of thicker leggings, a stretchy skirt, and a fitted white sweater. I yanked the sweater over my head and forced my legs into the leggings while I cursed Emma under my breath. Not an outfit I would have considered before but everything fit well, and I had to admit, was unexpectedly comfortable. I critiqued my reflection in the mirror to decide if I dared to be seen. A few tendrils of hair had already escaped the bun and framed my face, which appeared surprisingly tan next to the white turtle-neck sweater. Not nearly as bad as I expected.

I opened the bathroom door. Although I was covered from neck to toe, I still felt overly exposed. After a couple steps into the room I paused.

Jax glanced up from the document in his hand. His eyes widened, then raced down my torso and legs, lingering for a moment.

Warmth spread over my skin, and heat rushed to my cheeks. He was checking me out. His eyes returned to my face, and he cleared his throat.

I couldn't help the slight upturn of my lips, or the squishy, yummy feeling that bloomed in my stomach. Maybe Emma had been right about my clothes after all. But I was still mad at Jax for the Alex comment—I reminded myself.

Jax stood up and shoved a stack of paintings and documents at me, all business again. "These are all the ones we found that have recipes. We need to make a list of the ingredients."

His copper eyes bore into mine. I matched his fire with my own. We stood, the papers between us, locked in a silent battle.

I couldn't believe it when his eyes wandered to my lips. His gaze seemed to bring more heat rushing to my skin. My tongue slid over my lower lip, and my own gaze found his totally kissable mouth. I knew I shouldn't. I knew this would lead to nothing but trouble. But all I wanted to know about was what those lips would taste like.

Our kiss at the airport had been anything but hot, hardly the first kiss a girl dreams about. I wondered if the second one could be better.

Something about Jax made me melt inside, warm and gooey, like a fresh cinnamon roll. When he wasn't making me want to kill him.

He took a step and closed the distance between us. His hand reached around and settled on my back. Tingles moved over my torso, emanating from Jax's fingers on my skin. His eyes met mine once again, all the fire still there but now something new as well. A silent question. Then he jerked me to his chest.

My hand went up in reflex and grabbed his shirt. Our torsos pressed together. His arms tightened around my back. Our mouths met. No timidity or tenderness here. Just heat.

The documents scattered on the floor around us. All I could do was press myself closer to his firm body. My self-consciousness fell away, replaced by warm, tender happiness and a sense of rightness.

His hands frantically explored my back, slipping under the sweater, while mine searched his muscular chest and arms. All the while our lips moved over each other. He tasted sweet, with a dash of salt, and a coffee finish. Yummy.

Forget the peck at the airport. This was my first kiss. Anything but the shy portrayals in the movies. Perfect.

The sound of the door to the living room closing sent us leaping apart like oppositely charged magnets. My hand covered my mouth. I bit my bottom lip and failed in my attempt to suck a breath into my tight ribcage.

Jax brushed a hand through his hair then held up one finger.

My already rapid heartbeat kicked it up a notch or three. What if Alex had turned us in? My brain quickly calculated what I could make explode to give us a chance at escape.

"Hey are you guys up yet?" Alex called from the door to my room.

"Yeah, come in," I said in my best impression of an everything-is-normal voice.

The door opened and revealed Alex, his arms loaded with bundles of plants.

He paused in the doorway. His eyes roved around the room.

I glanced at the documents on the floor and rushed to pick them up, hiding my hot face from his keen gaze. "I had a little accident."

"I guess so. If I'm interrupting something, I can give you two a minute," Alex said, still in the doorway.

Jax smirked in a way that made me want to smack him. Hard. Really hard.

"Well, actually—" Jax began.

"No, you're fine," I cut him off. "So where did you

go so early this morning?"

I hoped that the glare I sent Jax conveyed my shut-up-or-I'll-kill-you mood, but he only shrugged and grabbed a handful of papers from the floor. Obviously, Alex brought out the jerk in him.

Alex held out the plants. "I thought we should get started on testing the recipes we found."

I stood and licked my tender lips. "We were going to make a list of the ingredients, but I guess you beat us to it."

Alex moved into the room and set the bundles on the table. "Yeah, I snapped pictures of a few recipes last night so I had a copy."

I bit my tongue and kept my suspicions to myself. Maybe I should lock my door from here on out. Instead of demanding answers to the questions I had, I pasted a smile on my face. "I guess we should get started. Tea anyone?"

****

Jax paced the room like a tiger in a cage. No, I thought and watched his brooding, dark-haired, lithe form move back and forth in front of me, a panther, a black panther.

I stifled a burp with my hand and groaned at the herby taste in my throat. I let my head roll back onto the cushion and contemplated the tiny spider across the room on the ceiling. "I don't think this one is working either." I glanced at Alex, who sat across from me on the sleek cream-colored couch in the living room of our hotel suite. "What about you?"

"How do you know that you'll feel any different?" Jax asked, his fingers laced behind his head while he walked back and forth. "I mean, unless you do a spell or something."

I bit my lip, contemplating. "You're right. Maybe we need to perform magic to access the power." I held out my hand to try a spell. "Good idea."

"Maddie, be careful," Alex said and jumped forward. "Let me try."

My jaw clenched, and I blinked several times before I poured energy into the little spider. Its body grew and spun, falling to the floor with a soft thud, then continued to grow.

Jax paused in his pacing, watching my spell unfold while Alex ducked behind the couch.

I poured energy into the spell. The spider came to a stop on the hardwood floor. A forked tongue darted out of the large mouth of a two-foot-long iguana.

"That's awesome." Jax rounded the couch to approach the lizard.

Alex peeked over the back of the couch. "Oh, good job."

"There is actually a spell I can do quite well," I said, and glared his way.

"Yeah, you did great. Just in case, I thought I'd get out of the way," he said, and climbed to his feet. "Did you feel any extra power?"

"No," I admitted and relaxed into the couch, my muscles feeling the fatigue of the spell.

"I'll go start the next batch."

I let my face fall to the cushion. My stomach cramped at the thought of more tea. "I don't think I can drink any more unless I get something in my stomach. Something heavy, like French Fries."

He grabbed a clove of garlic, a handful of rosemary, as well as a leaf of Lily of the Valley. We'd saved the more poisonous plants for last. Lily of the Valley could produce abdominal pain, vomiting, and reduced heart rate, though it had been used for centuries in folk remedies and by herbalists. Lucky for us, the tea only called for a small amount. I already felt like puking.

"I can drink this one if you don't feel up to it," Alex offered, his attention focused on the cutting board.

No way I was letting him possibly gain access to the power by himself. He'd already suggested we split the recipes up and each try different ones to speed the process. I forced myself to sit up straight and swallowed the bile rising in my throat at the smell of the cut leaves. "No. I feel fine."

Jax stopped feeding the iguana chunks of fruit, grabbed the room phone and punched two buttons. "Yeah, Room Service, I need an order of French Fries sent up and a side of ranch."

I met his eyes. "Thank you."

He nodded, the phone still in his hand. "Then can I get four double cheeseburgers, a couple vanilla milkshakes and a tall stack of pancakes." He paused and looked at Alex. "Did you want anything?"

Alex shrugged. "That sounds good."

"Double that order," Jax said, and hung up.

Our lizard friend scurried to a corner and tried to climb up the wall. The inch-long talons did nothing to give him purchase, and he settled for hiding behind a potted plant. I felt sorry for the confused reptile. "I'll change you back in a few minutes."

Jax went to the kitchen to bird-dog Alex in his preparation of the tea recipe. After watching with his arms crossed, he circled the counter and scanned the recipe. "How much Lily of the Valley are you putting in there? That's almost twice what it calls for."

Alex paused. "It said half a leaf in each cup. That's what I'm doing." Irritation permeated his voice.

Jax reached over and yanked the cup away and dumped it in the sink. "It says half of a two-inch leaf. The one you used is at least four inches wide and six long. What? Are you trying to kill her? This stuff is poisonous."

The muscle on the side of Alex's jaw bulged, and his nostrils flared a bit. "I was going to drink it as well."

Jax snorted, his focus on the plants in front of him. "Why don't you let me do the preparation now that we're getting into the dangerous stuff?"

I watched the battle play out in silence. All Alex would have to do is leave some tea in the bottom of his cup. I'd be unconscious, and he'd be ill but fine. I examined his face for a clue to his motives. His furrowed brow and gritted teeth could easily be explained by Jax's arrogance, not necessarily being caught.

Alex met my watchful eyes and blew out a breath then spoke in a much calmer voice, "I guess I'll have to trust you not to kill me."

Jax kept his focus on the tea and only grunted a response.

It could have been an honest mistake. Alex didn't have a science background and may not have understood the importance of exact measurement in chemical reactions.

A few minutes later my heavenly, piping hot *American* Fries and ranch arrived. I gobbled down the basket and watched the boys demolish the rest of the food. Jax brought over the cups of tea, the aroma spicy and garlicy. Not a bad combination with fries.

Alex took a sip, and his face scrunched up. "Maybe I'll put some sugar or cream in mine."

Jax threw up his hands and fell into a chair.

"What?" Alex asked.

I sent Jax a be-good look. "If you add anything it could impact the reaction in the ingredients. Even something as simple as sugar could change the conditions of the solution and make a reaction stop."

Alex rolled his eyes and took another drink.

An hour later, I felt very relaxed, and, maybe a bit drowsy but couldn't sense any power now accessible to me. "I'm calling it. It's not the one."

Alex nodded. "I agree, nothing here."

Jax glanced up from his laptop. "Well, judging from the information I gathered, you'll be happy to know that with the various ingredients you drank today you shouldn't have any headache, nausea, muscle fatigue, flatulence, menstrual cramps, or constipation for the next few days."

****

The next day went much the same, more nauseating tea, more waiting, no results. After I changed the lizard back to a spider I'd let Alex perform the spells. Transforming took more energy than most spells. I leaned my cheek against the cushion of the couch and groaned. "If I ever see another cup of herbal tea again, I'm going to throw myself off the roof."

Alex nodded. "Yeah, I've had enough."

Jax examined the list we'd made of all the recipes. "That was the last one."

My stomach churned even more as my heart sank

into its acidic juices and dissolved. I was wrong all along. "I was so sure I was right."

Alex roused himself from the chair and grabbed a box of papers from the Cambridge storeroom. "Let's start from the beginning again."

I curled up around a pillow and buried my face in the softness.

When I felt Jax's hand on my shoulder, I raised my head.

"Come on. We can still figure this out," he said gently.

I hid in the softness of the pillow again. "I should never have dragged you on this stupid wild goose chase."

He cleared his throat. "If I remember right, I insisted. And I still think you are on to something. Come on, one setback and you're giving up?"

I refused to look up or answer. After a minute, I heard him move away and then rustling papers cued me in to what he was doing. Bleak heaviness kept me glued to the couch, curled in the fetal position. One word kept running through my mind, Defect.

If Jax thought this was the first setback I'd faced he was wrong. My entire life had been a series of setbacks. People pushing me down, people putting roadblocks in my path, telling me I would never be good enough. Their voices rang in my ears, kids at camp, counselors, teachers, even my own family.

I'd accepted a long time ago that I would be nothing but a disappointment to them. Or had I? Why did I come on this trip? Did I risk everything only to give up and prove them right? The thought of all those jerks being validated sent new energy to my muscles, angry energy.

I sucked in a breath and forced myself to rise from the couch. I reached for the phone. "If we're going to do this, then we are going to need some food."

Many hours and a lot of room service later, I slumped in a chair in front of the table, nibbling on a cold piece of pizza.

Jax chuckled around the bite in his mouth.

"What?" I asked.

He gestured to the letters in his hand, the ones I'd borrowed from my dad that were written by a far distant ancestor. "I just can't get over it. Man, these nobles had the life. Travel around and see beautiful ladies. This has to be the fifth time he's mentioned beautiful women in his letters."

"To think I'm related to that." I snorted. "What a perv. I feel sorry for his wife."

Alex shrugged but kept his focus on the page in front of him. "Maybe she had her own paramour. It was likely an arranged marriage."

I blinked, my hand suspended in mid-air as I reached for another document. This was the guy I'd been betrothed to? His nonchalance hit a nerve. If he thought that I'd be okay with him having affairs…Thank God the wedding was off.

Jax's attention settled on my face.

It took Alex a full minute to look up and realize that I was shooting daggers in his direction. "Well, I only meant to say that it was a different time." He rushed on when I raised my eyebrows. "If we got married I would never, I mean…"

A huge grin spread over Jax's face while Alex floundered and sputtered. He leaned back to enjoy the show.

Finally, I held up my hand. "Whatever. It doesn't matter anyway because we are never getting married."

Alex buried his crimson face in the papers and stayed quiet. Smart decision, extremely smart.

I forced myself to read the documents in front of me, although, I had to go back and reread a few paragraphs. A letter from a previous curator at the Oxford storehouse grabbed my attention. It listed twenty different paintings that had been donated to the Royal Botanic Gardens before the historians could get their hands on them. In an addendum, it stated that later historians had arranged to examine the paintings and found nothing of great interest, only a few recipes.

I gripped the page. In my gut I felt the answer had to be a recipe of some concoction of plants. We'd missed some.

My stomach pinched at the thought of drinking more tea. But what choice was there? The council goons, led by my aunt, could close in on us at any time. We'd been lucky so far. But my luck was known to run out.

I sat up and handed the letters to Jax. Our fingers brushed together. The nerves in my fingers sent way more signals to the brain than the simple touch called for. I forced my eyes away from his mouth, and my thoughts away from our heated kiss. His molten eyes met mine.

I cleared my throat and pointed to the second paragraph on the letter.

Jax scanned the page. His sky-high eye brows told me when he got to the good part.

He grinned. "Field trip?"

Chapter Thirteen

We entered the gardens through the Elizabeth Gate. Jax grabbed a map and guide. He opened the folded pages and began to flip through. The crowd, already there, thickened and slowed our progress. I heard a variety of languages. Quite the tourist attraction apparently.

The Royal Botanic Gardens in London, also known as Kew Gardens, sported the largest collection of living plants in the world. The three hundred acres sat right in the middle of downtown London. I glanced at a sign that pointed out various attractions. It included not only gardens of living plants and greenhouses, but also an enormous library and a herbarium which housed more than seven million preserved plants, as well as an extensive art collection of paintings and drawings of various plants.

The art collection was the draw for us. Some of the artwork of known witch nobles had ended up in the museum. I needed to get my hands on the recipes hidden on the backs of the paintings.

"Here's something I bet Alex would like to see." Jax pointed to the map in his brochure.

I looked over and read the label. "Europe's largest compost pile."

"What?" Alex's brow wrinkled.

Jax met his questioning look and sneered. "I

figured you'd want to see it. Seeing as how you're full of–"

"Jax," I cut him off before he could be any more insulting.

Alex's jaw tightened but he didn't comment.

I pointed to the distant building that housed the nearly two-hundred-thousand piece art collection, and we turned on the path to the left. The chilly moisture in the air quickly seeped through my jacket and leggings to the thin sweater and my skin. I shivered in response. Emma and her clothes hadn't accounted for the weather on our trip. Being rumpled and warm sounded way better than being fashionable and freezing.

Alex frowned my way. "Cold?"

I shrugged and upped my pace. "I'll be fine. Let's walk a bit faster."

He waved toward the building we were passing. "Why don't we just duck in here for a minute to let you warm up?"

The building housed the herbarium and all its thousands of preserved plants. Might be cool to see but we weren't on vacation.

"Come on," he said and took my elbow. "We have time."

I hesitated. "Getting the painting is more important than my being comfortable."

"The last thing we need is you getting sick." He steered me to the entrance.

The welcome warmth washed over me as soon as we walked through the doors. I flexed my chilled fingers. The displays of plants caught my interest, and I wandered over to examine the preserved specimens. Three rows later, I'd recovered from the chilly temperatures but wasn't ready to leave.

Exploring the plants was the first semi-normal thing I'd done in a week. Tense muscles in my neck and back loosened, and my mind finally stopped racing every minute. The rhythm soothed me—read one description then go on to the next, read one, go on.

I walked to the next specimen with Jax close by my side. Under the glass a rose stem rested. One branch ended in a bright red flower while the branch next to it ended in a purplish blue flower.

I cocked my head to the side. "That's weird. I've never seen two different colored flowers on the same plant."

Jax pointed to the description and read the second paragraph. "'A Chimera is the phenomenon of a genetic mutation causing a different color to be present on two different branches of the same plant. It is fairly common in roses.'"

Anything that had to do with genetic mutations had always sparked my interest.

"You do not have much time." A deep voice spoke from beside me.

I flinched. While the face was new to me, I immediately recognized the scrollwork tattoo branching up his neck. This one was even more intricate with blue and red flowers blooming at the ends of the many scrolls.

"This the monk?" Jax whispered.

"One of them, I guess."

"Cool, thanks for your help at the airport," Jax said.

The man inclined his head in Jax's direction in response.

Jax and I scanned the room for a sign of council members. "Are they coming?"

He nodded and his dark chin length hair, shaved on the sides and long on the top of his head, swung before his face. "They are on their way."

"Why are you helping me?"

A serene smile spread his lips.

More Zen. All these guys must do Yoga or something.

"You are our task."

"What the hell does that mean?" I demanded.

He held up a hand. "You must hurry."

Without another word he walked away.

"Let's get moving," I said.

I glanced around and realized that Alex was nowhere in the vicinity. "Where did he go?"

"It's not my day to watch him." Jax frowned but moved quickly to scan the room.

"Not funny." I bit my lip.

We rounded a corner and I spotted Alex, his phone to his ear, across the room. He hung up and turned to see us staring at him.

"Checking in with my dad," he said, when we approached. "He's not sure how much time we have before they figure out that we are still in London so we should probably get a move on."

"Yeah, we need to get what we came for and get out of here fast."

By some unspoken understanding neither Jax nor I mentioned the surprise visit or warning to Alex. We did however up our speed and urgency.

The extensive art collection could have taken an entire day to view, but we knew what we were searching for. The room dedicated to historic watercolors done by nobility in the 1700s took half an hour to locate. I took the list of names from my pocket and glanced at the first.

Within a few minutes, my guts twisted up into a Celtic knot of organs. We were in trouble. There had to be at least twenty paintings by the various nobles in the collection, and the recipes were all on the back of the paintings. We couldn't see them with the paintings under glass.

Jax glanced up at the security cameras then shifted his eyes away. "I don't know if I'm going to be much help with those cameras. It would take me at least thirty seconds to pick the locks on the cases, and they may have tamper-proof sensors."

"Take it easy," Alex spoke in what could only be called a smug voice. "We won't need your delinquent skills here. I think transporting would be the better option."

Jax's jaw ground together while he stared bullets at Alex, but he kept quiet.

I nodded. If we, and by we, I obviously meant Alex, used magic to transport the paintings from under the glass there would be no need to pick any locks. "But what about the cameras?"

Alex pulled his iPad from his backpack. His fingers whizzed over the surface. "Leave those to me as well." He glanced up and met Jax's gaze with a smirk. "You can probably wait outside if you want."

I dragged a fuming Jax away and circled the room again while Alex worked on hacking the cameras or whatever he was doing. We still had a major problem. There was no way he could transport all the paintings before someone noticed. And if I tried, it was more than likely I would burn the painting to ashes. Not much use.

"What are you thinking?" Jax bit out, anger still coloring his voice.

I crossed my arms. "We're going to have to figure out the most likely ones. He can maybe get ten out of the twenty if we're lucky."

We moved in front of one painting after another looking for any indicator that it was different from the multitude of others we'd seen.

"I don't see anything," I said. With a tight rein on my frustration, I moved onto the next.

The watercolor portrayed Deadly Nightshade, one of the top five deadliest plants in the world. Ingesting even a small amount of any part of the plant would cause heart palpitations and death.

I read the scientific name under the common name. "Bella Donna."

Jax nodded. "Yeah, it's French for beautiful woman."

As the words left his lips, we both sucked in a breath.

My own stare met his wide eyes. "Are you thinking what I'm thinking?"

A crooked grin pulled one side of his mouth up in a way that sent tingles to some very interesting parts of my anatomy. "The perv."

A laugh spilled from my throat. "He wasn't talking about real women. It has to be a reference to the plant."

I restrained the urge to jump up and down, but instead threw my arms around Jax's neck and squeezed. His arms circled me. I reveled in the spicy cedar sent of his hair and skin.

Alex approached and cleared his throat.

I released Jax and bit my lip to keep from shouting. This had to be the answer.

A frown creased Alex's brow while his eyes went back and forth between our excited faces. "Something you want to share? Or do you two need some privacy?"

I gestured to the case behind us. "It's Bella Donna." I paused, then continued when the frown stayed on his face. "Beautiful Woman, like in all the letters."

Understanding dawned, and he turned his full attention to the watercolor. "You've got to be kidding."

I gestured to the iPad. "Did you get the cameras taken care of?"

He nodded. "No problem, they're on a loop. It should only take me a minute to get one out."

I chewed on my inner cheek and contemplated. "I still think we should take several in case they figure out it was us."

He glanced around the room. "All right. Can you make some sort of distraction? Keep the crowd's eyes on you so I can transport the paintings?"

"I think we can figure something out."

Alex leaned close as Jax walked past him. "I guess you are useful after all. Think you can handle it?"

Jax spun on his heel to face Alex. I grabbed him and whispered, "Make a distraction with me not him." I tugged on his arm to move him away from Alex. "We need to make this a huge scene so no one looks his way. Be a complete jerk."

We walked across the room, past a buxom redhead. Jax's gaze trailed her path.

I raised my voice and smacked his chest, hard.

"Oh, my God. You were checking her out."

Jax threw his arms to his sides. His still angry eyes settled on me. "What? No, I wasn't."

I got right in his face and jabbed my pointed finger in his pecs. "Don't even try to lie to me. I saw you. You pig."

People in the quiet gallery turned toward our loud scene and surreptitiously watched. I crossed my arms and tried to muster some tears.

"You know, I'm getting really sick of your insecurities." His chin thrust higher into the air. "Constantly paying attention to you is getting seriously boring."

Several bystanders openly stared at the developing battle. No one was giving Alex any notice.

"I am not insecure. And if you're so bored you can leave at any time," I spat back.

He laughed. "Not insecure? Are you kidding?" He scrunched his face up like a bulldog and spouted a high-pitched imitation of my voice, which sounded like a hamster that had huffed helium. "I need help. Do you think I'm pretty? Do I look fat in this? Were you checking her out? Am I a good kisser?" He let his voice return to its normal tone. "The answer to the last one, by the way, is a definite no."

Several onlookers gasped, and a woman glared daggers at Jax.

I didn't have to fake my shock. My jaw dropped. The feel of us kissing, his body pressed against mine, flashed through my brain. I'd enjoyed it—too much. But with nothing to compare it to...that old familiar doubt crept into my mind.

He raised one eyebrow. His ripped jeans and tight

black T-shirt fit with this portrayal of the rude bad boy. Everything from his body language to the tone of his voice screamed patronizing annoyance.

I covered my shock with real irritation. "I can't believe I ever even liked you."

"Hey, no skin off my back, sweetheart," he shot back.

If he was playing along, he deserved an Oscar. Alex was at the end of the row of paintings, almost done. I had to keep the crowd focused on us, but my mind drew a complete blank. One more comment like that and I'd have to physically assault Jax. Not that the idea sounded like a bad one. I put a hand over my face and choked out a pretend sob.

Jax waited for me to make a comeback.

The people around us shifted uncomfortably.

His brow furrowed for a moment then he went on. "Why don't you give me a call in a few years when you can at least kiss decently."

That should be long enough for Alex. Time to end this melodrama. I hurried away with my hands over my mouth, rushed past Alex, who had a strange bulge under his jacket, and out the door.

I leaned against a pillar, out of sight. I realized my hands were shaking and sucked in a choppy breath. The fight may have been fake, but real emotion muddled my thoughts. His comments about my kissing stuck. I'd told him to be a jerk. I'd got what I'd asked for and more.

I pressed my palms against my closed eyes but couldn't shake the anger or insecurity his comments brought out. I pushed the memory of our kiss away. After I'd recovered myself enough to be sure I wouldn't blow Jax to bits *accidentally*, I went to find the boys.

Jax's messy locks and copper eyes appeared around the corner of a hedge. "There you are. What happened?"

"What do you mean?" Forcing myself to meet his steady gaze, I pulled my chest up and cocked my head to the side.

"I was only kidding, you know, I mean about the kissing and stuff. I was just worried that it came off a little harsh." His eyes rested on me.

I gave him my most convincing have-you-gone-crazy look. "Yeah. We were having a pretend fight."

"I thought you seemed upset." He watched me intently.

I laughed and rolled my eyes. "That was kind of the entire point. You didn't actually think I was mad, did you?"

He blew out a breath. "Naw, I mean, just checking. Should we go make sure the Surfer Boy doesn't run off with the painting?"

"You gave Alex the chance to take off with the clue just to come and make sure I wasn't mad at you?" Considering you don't trust him that was a pretty stupid move."

I walked off before Jax could comment.

****

The bulge in Alex's jacket had gone down significantly. He flashed me the now organized, thick, roll of yellowed papers.

After a meaningful glare at Jax for doubting Alex, I turned my back to him, not particularly wanting to see him at the moment. "How many did you get?"

"Twelve," he said with a satisfied smile.

I held back my celebration. "And the Bella Donna?"

"But, of course." He bent forward in a theatrical bow.

I released the breath that had been stagnating in my lungs. The beautiful gardens and amazing collections surrounding us lost their allure. "Let's get out of here."

We wove through a sea of tourists toward the Elizabeth Gate. The flower beds gave way to tall trees as we entered another section of the gardens. I could barely contain my urge to rip the stolen painting out of Alex's jacket and examine it in the middle of the pathway. Nervous energy zinged through my body. My pace quickened to almost a jog.

Faces blurred together in the crowd, a collage of eyes, noses, and chins. Then out of the mish-mash a familiar set of features emerged.

My eyes settled on the face coming toward us. My steps faltered. I blinked several times to refocus, but my hand began to shake. The tremor spread up my arm until my entire torso quivered.

A hundred feet in front of us was our friend from the airport—Igor, along with another Council goon.

And my aunt.

Chapter Fourteen

My aunt's face was slack, expressionless, except for her eyes. They swept through the tourists like a shark stalking its prey.

I knew I should be running, but my feet seemed to be stuck to the path like they'd grown roots of their own. The crowd parted around me and rejoined like a stream around a rock. Of the many thoughts that raced through my completely freaked out brain one stuck out. I couldn't let her catch us.

Jax nearly walked into me. "What's wrong?"

I spun in a one-eighty and scanned the wide-open paths around us. No cover anywhere—no place to hide. A set of wooden stairs reached up into the trees ten feet behind us. With no better option to get away I shoved Jax toward the stairs.

Jax stumbled into Alex. "What the hell?"

"That way. Quick." I could hear the panic in my own voice. I forced myself not to attract attention by running but kept pace with the group around us.

Alex spotted the deadly trio coming our way, and his eyes widened. "You heard her. Up the stairs."

I rounded the first flight, integrated into a tour group, and couldn't help but glance down. I met my aunt's eyes from under her drawn brows. They locked on mine like a terminator zeroing in on its target.

Forget blending in now. I pushed Jax up the second

flight. "Run."

We pounded up the steps, weaving in between surprised tourists caught in our race. By the fifth flight my legs burned, but still I ran.

Jax and Alex reached the top before me. We sprinted along a five-foot wide wood and metal walkway that towered at least sixty feet in the air. The distant ground showed clearly through the metal mesh floor of the elevated path. Every ten feet circular overlooks stuck out from the narrow path on either side. Halfway around, directly opposite the stairs, a triangular platform jutted out into the trees.

The treetops fanned out around us in what was likely a beautiful scene if you weren't running for your life. The thunder of our feet on the metal mesh parted the groups in front of us.

The audible pounding of the trio on our tails urged my feet to go faster.

Jax slowed his pace in front of me. "It's a circle."

"What?" I gasped.

He pointed along the treetop walkway. "It's a circle."

I followed his direction. The walkway made a large oval in the treetops, leading to the same set of stairs we'd just climbed. One way up and one way down. All our pursuers had to do was send one of their group back to the stairs, and we would be cornered with no way down.

I'd led us to the perfect trap.

My mind raced for another escape while we continued to run. Every ten feet, huge metal support beams reached up from the ground and met the path beneath the semi-circle overlooks. The smooth metal of the beams would give no purchase, no way to climb down. No escape.

Our only hope was that they would stay together and we could outrun them. I chanced a peek over my shoulder. The three jogged along, almost in unison, not even breathing heavy and steadily gaining ground.

The Council always gave their goons the advantage by setting up permanent spells for endurance, strength, and other such skills. At least that was the rumor.

Without any choice, we pounded forward almost to the half-way point and the triangular overlook. Our chances of outrunning the goons sputtered like a dying candle. We sprinted past staring and some glaring tourists. They cleared a path and pressed against the waist high safety rail.

I pushed forward and was rewarded by seeing the distance that separated us from my aunt increase. I sucked in a deep breath and gasped, "Keep going."

The tingle of magic raised the hairs on my arms. Over the thunder of the metal, I caught the sound of my aunt's voice. The words were lost in the cacophony around us, but my insides twisted upon themselves. Magic.

The air in front of us shimmered, only visible to mine and Alex's expanded witch vision. I grabbed Jax's arm and dragged him to a stop. I gasped through the strain in my lungs. "Watch out."

He stared at the seemingly empty air. His brow furrowed.

"Dammit," Alex cursed. He pointed a couple feet in front of us. "They put up a wall. It would be like running into solid brick."

A group of tourists passed through the spell with

no problem, glancing back at us with puzzled and slightly annoyed expressions. Jax stretched his hand out and pressed it into the barrier. His wide-eyed, drop-mouthed expression told me he felt it. He stood for a moment with his hand on the invisible surface much like a mime in a pretend box. Only to the three of us this wall, though invisible, was as solid and real as the mesh that kept us from plummeting to the ground below.

With death closing in, we turned to face our pursuers. The trio slowed to a walk, so as not to draw attention to the situation.

"Can't you do your thing and stop them?" Jax asked.

I shook my head. "If Alex attacks them in front of so many witnesses he'll be in just as much trouble as I am."

"There isn't much choice," Alex said.

I grabbed his arm. "You can't. They'll kill you if we get caught."

A wry smile twisted his lips, and he shrugged. "I guess we can't get caught then."

Alex gathered his energy to throw a spell and attack the lethal trio. Lightning, a spell I'd only dreamed of doing, shot from his hands at the goons. His aim was on point. I might lead us to a dead end but maybe Alex could get us out of it safely.

Tourists screamed and ducked for cover. Electrical shocks arced through the air. Smaller bolts branched off the main line to energize the metal mesh under our feet. Parents grabbed their children and dragged them away from the lightning.

A few feet from my aunt, Alex's fiery energy

dissipated into the atmosphere without slowing the pace of the trio one bit. They had defenses. To stop the trio Alex would have to first disable their shield.

A stampede of sightseers shoved us into the rails, and that did slow the progress of my aunt. The screaming crowd raced for the safety of the stairway and the ground below.

Aunt Clara met my gaze, her face a duplicate of an expressionless mannequin. She pushed through the frantic crowd. Not one indication of our family relationship shown in her face, only her mission. She steadily closed in, now fifty feet away.

Alex threw bolt after bolt of lightning in an attempt to burn through their shield. Each time the energy simply vanished into the air like smoke on the wind.

He gritted his teeth. "I've never seen this kind of spell before. I can't even touch them."

I shifted from foot to foot, unable to be the least bit of help to Alex. I'd only ever seen such powerful magic performed. With my ineptitude at witchcraft, my parents focused on the basics, which obviously hadn't worked out so well either.

Our only possibility of getting out of this situation was for Alex to break through the defenses then battle three magically enhanced powerful witches. Not great odds.

The walkway sat empty. All the tourists now pounding down the stairs and away from the treetop walkway.

Alex switched to fireballs, his shoulders sagging under the strain. I knew that with the magnitude of spells he was performing that he had one, maybe two at the most left before he was crawling on the ground—

completely drained.

I bit my lip and glanced over the edge of the handrail at the sixty-foot drop to the ground, complete with plenty of thick tree branches to collide with on the way down. Unfortunately, none of the branches grew close enough to grab onto and climb down. With the barrier on one side of us and the Council goons on the other, we were trapped halfway around the walkway.

And I stood, helpless, only able to watch doom approach in the form of my aunt. The witch mutation did me no good. I might as well be a powerless human.

Alex sent a massive lightning bolt that turned the air around the three goons bright red as the sun, blinding us with the intensity of the energy released, before it dissipated. But still their shield held. He was almost out of power, and dripped with sweat, while Jax and I pressed our backs against the invisible barrier.

Alex gripped the rail to stay upright and swayed.

Jax grabbed my arm. "Do something."

The strain in his voice pierced me like daggers. He didn't deserve this. I just shook my head. "It's no use."

"But you're a witch," he insisted. "Use your powers."

I yanked my arm away unable to meet his eyes. "The only thing my powers are good for is…" My eyes stared through the metal mesh at our feet and rested on the support pillars. "Blowing stuff up."

I pivoted back to look at my aunt, now thirty feet from us.

Blowing stuff up.

I may not be able to attack them directly but I could certainly rock their world. Two sets of support pillars stood in the sections that separated my aunt from us.

My hand gripped Alex's arm. "Alex, get behind me. Now."

His brow wrinkled. "Maddie, you can't use your magic. You might—"

"Shut up. I have a plan," I almost shouted. I'd been made perfectly aware of my limitations my entire life. I didn't need him to remind me.

"Maddie, don't try anything. You'll kill us all." He glanced down at the ground, so far below our feet.

Jax stepped in front of me. "Shut up, Surfer Boy. She's smarter than you think."

I ignored Alex's protest and Jax's support and channeled my energy. I focused on the y-shaped support beams where they met in the middle.

Metal was obviously harder to blow up than fruit, but my channeled energy turned the beam a molten red. For the first time in my life I fully opened the channels in my mind. Raw power disrupted the bonds of the atoms in the beam.

Before my aunt could react, the metal exploded with the force of C-4. The entire structure wobbled. One of my aunt's goons stumbled, then was knocked off balance, and flipped over the waist high rail. He didn't scream as he fell. The thud of meat on dirt announced his demise. Not even a witch could survive a fall like that.

Molten metal and wooden shrapnel shot fifty feet above the walkway. Dark metallic, smoke filled the air, singeing my nostrils. Tourists on the ground screamed and rushed farther away. Wooden boards and metal mesh plummeted to the ground leaving a twenty-foot gap of open air between us and my aunt.

My aunt glanced back at where her companion had been. For a moment she stood, assessing the situation. Then she spun on her heel and walked toward the stairs, the remaining goon close behind. She might have to walk around the entire oval, but she would catch us.

They'd trapped us up here on the walkway, but two could play that game. I focused on the support beam under the section my aunt was approaching. Within seconds a second explosion, this one larger than the last, rocked the treetop walkway between my aunt and the stairs. The section in front of her fell away. She stopped right at the edge.

The aftershock made the entire structure sway like a tree in the wind.

"Maddie, the barrier's gone," Jax called, waving his hand where the solid invisible wall had been.

Spells die with the caster. The fallen man must have set the spell.

A twist of guilt squeezed my gut. I'd killed him. Someone forced to do the Council's bidding who had started out probably a lot like me. I thrust the emotions away. Guilt wouldn't save us.

Black smoke billowed up and temporarily blocked my aunt's view of us.

"Run," I shouted.

The smoke gave us cover. With Jax on one side and me on the other, we half dragged a weakened Alex along the treetop walkway to the stairs. Once on the ground, we caught up with the screaming crowd of coughing tourists and escaped into the melee, careful to step over the board shards and metal that littered the area.

From the dirt path, sixty feet below, I glanced up at

the bottom of the smoldering walkway. One island stood separated from the rest of the oval by two large gaps in the structure. The island swayed, top heavy and supported only by a single set of beams. Two figures leaned over the rail, searching the crowd below.

She wouldn't give up. The realization turned the air in my lungs to cement. I coughed and choked on more than smoke.

Sirens screamed in the distance, help coming to rescue the stranded couple. Despite my desperation to put as much distance between us and my aunt as possible, I had to gawk one more time at the enormous structure I'd taken out with my powers. The corners of my mouth snuck up. Blowing stuff up came in handy sometimes.

****

"Hey, you made the news." Jax held his phone up for me to see.

Word of the terrorist attack on the Royal Botanic Gardens had spread fast. A helicopter view showed the damaged walkway, its two stranded tourists now rescued and safe. Miraculously only one casualty was reported and no other injuries despite the *electrical disturbance*. Authorities were trying to figure out the link between the apparent art theft and the bombing.

I found myself grinning at the news feed. I couldn't beat them with magic, but I outsmarted them. I handed the phone back to Jax and smacked his shoulder instead of hugging him like I wanted to. He'd believed in me on that bridge. "Not bad for a Defect, huh?"

He sneered at the term. "I never thought of you as one."

We stared, silent, for a moment, his copper eyes

179

molten and burning into mine. My breath came faster. My chest seemed to have magnets inside, drawing me toward Jax's arms. I inched closer. Close enough to smell his clean spicy scent.

"Yeah, that was a pretty convincing fight you two had as well," Alex mumbled from the couch.

I'd completely forgotten he was in the room. I blinked and stepped away. The insults Jax had thrown at me now refreshed in my mind.

"You should be an actor, Jax," Alex continued, seemingly oblivious to the distress he caused me. "I believed every word."

Color poured into Jax's face. His jaw firmed while his hands formed fists.

"Can I get a glass of juice or something?" Alex asked. "All that magic really drained me."

"Yeah, sure," I said, hoping to shut him up before Jax killed him. "How do you feel about joining me on the council's hit list?"

"The company is good," Alex stated with a weak grin. "I hope you know now that you can trust me."

He'd broken the most sacred rule of not exposing witches. There was no going back for him. He was an outlaw, like me. Guilt welled up at the thought that another life had been ruined to protect mine. I swallowed it down and pasted on a smile.

"How did it feel to see your aunt?" Alex asked.

I paused, unable to put the mix of emotions into words.

"She was pretty freaky," Jax spoke up from behind me. "She didn't even care when the other guy fell."

That woman or thing bore no resemblance to my once carefree aunt. I swallowed through a thick throat.

The Council could do that to me, I thought, then pushed it away.

"Yeah, she lives up to the stories for sure," Alex chimed in.

I nodded and handed him a glass of fruit punch to wash down the candy bar I'd given him earlier. His cheeks lacked any color. He'd used up his energy reserves. We'd practically had to drag him into the room from the elevator.

The glass slipped through Alex's hand. He jerked upright and clutched at the glass with both hands. Juice sloshed onto the expensive fabric of the couch. The red of the liquid, bright as blood, stained the cream of the cushion.

I grabbed the glass and righted it before any more damage was done, then set it on the table. "Jax, throw me a towel."

Alex brushed away drops of liquid with furious strokes. "I'm sorry, so stupid." His saucer-eyed gaze zoned in on the stain. "Stupid, stupid, stupid. Such an idiot."

The frantic tone of his voice and gestures gave me pause. I'd never heard him be anything except cool and collected. Maybe he'd drained himself more than I originally thought.

I patted the couch with the towel. "It's fine. One simple spell after you've recovered will fix the problem. No one will ever know."

My voice stopped his hands. He blinked and glanced up.

I only glimpsed the expression on his face for a moment before the familiar, collected, Alex returned, but for that moment he reminded me of a small child. A scared child.

His face relaxed, and he sank into the softness of the couch. "Sorry, I guess I'm really tired."

"No worries," I responded, and walked to the kitchen to give him some space. It was probably nothing, just that he had pushed his limits too much or that he was understandably freaked out about the council wanting him dead now. But something felt off. I filed it away for later consideration.

Jax shot me a raised eyebrow, to which I could only shrug. Uncomfortable silence settled over the room.

"Should we examine the painting?" I asked.

Jax shuffled through the stack and pulled out the one we'd been after. Bella Donna. Deadly Nightshade.

I bit my lip. This was it. The answer, I knew it.

He examined the yellowed paper then handed it over to my shaking hands. The beautiful rendering of the plant included the bell shaped five petaled purple flowers, yellow at their centers, as well as the pointed leaves and the ripe dark berries. The watercolor was signed Annabel Price.

The name sounded vaguely familiar, but the connection refused to surface in my eager brain. I flipped the paper over and examined the recipe inscribed on the back bottom corner in a careful hand.

I scanned the ingredients, barely paying attention to the specifics. "These look easy enough. The only thing I don't think we have yet is the nightshade." I glanced at an unsmiling Jax. "I'm sure every herbalist keeps the world's second deadliest plant on hand. Easy."

His expression still grave, he pointed at the recipe.

"That's too much."

It called for four large leaves of nightshade.

My stomach shriveled into a hard ball. One bite of a leaf would lead to a host of fun side effects including hallucinations, tachycardia, and convulsions. One leaf was enough to kill a healthy adult in a most unpleasant fashion.

I crossed my arms and hugged my ever tightening abdomen. How confident was I in my theory? I'd be betting my life on it.

Alex straightened from his slump on the couch. "What is it?"

Jax kept his gaze fixed on me. "With this much nightshade anyone who drinks the tea is dead."

I stared at the toxic recipe.

"We can't drink it then. I mean it's only a theory. We don't even know if it will work," Alex said.

Jax nodded. "For once I have to say I agree with the Surfer Boy. How do we know this isn't a recipe for a disgruntled wife who wants to kill her husband?"

"Exactly, poisoning was a common way to kill people. We'll have to think of something else," Alex stated.

My hand found my locket and twirled the warm metal between my fingers. In my mind I went over the path we'd followed to get to this point. The nightshade was the only viable answer we'd come up with. There were no other options. Someone had to try it. This was my theory, my idea, my quest. Jax opened his mouth again, but I cut him off.

"No. I'll drink it."

Chapter Fifteen

Jax did his best to convince me not to drink the nightshade tea, while Alex halfheartedly offered to drink it with me. In the end, we decided that Alex should stand by in case things went bad to give me a chance at survival. Witch powers could be useful to say restart the heart and other necessary bodily functions, as well as purifying the blood.

It did make sense. All I could do, if I had to help Alex, would be to put him out of his misery with my messed up magic. Besides, this was my theory. He'd risked enough on my behalf already.

With the nightshade procured from a local specialty shop, we returned to the hotel room. I had no excuse to put off proving or disproving my theory.

"Besides," Alex agreed, "I'm too drained from the lightning and fire on the bridge, and we don't have time to wait for me to recover."

I nodded to preserve his male ego. "Just be ready in case anything goes wrong."

Jax, of course, rolled his eyes so hard he likely saw gray matter.

"Let's do this then."

Jax glared until Alex cleared the kitchen, unwilling to let him even touch a single ingredient to prepare the tea. The incident on the walkway hadn't changed Jax's suspicion. Instead, Alex's doubt in my abilities had added yet another brick to the wall of hate between them.

Taking a seat at the breakfast bar, I gripped my hands together to stop them shaking. Jax set the water on the stove to heat and pulled out the nightshade. My foot tapped a rapid rhythm against the chair rail.

With each ingredient that fell into the mug from Jax's careful hand, my heartbeat quickened. By the time the water boiled my heart practically matched the thousand beats per minute of a hummingbird. At this rate it would give out before the nightshade could do any damage.

Once he set the steaming mug in front of me, I licked my lips and took a deep breath. He put his hand over mine. "You don't have to do this."

I gripped the mug. "Yes, I do."

Alex watched from where he perched on the arm of the couch. Without another moment of hesitation, I lifted the mug and gulped the contents. The heat seared my throat. I swallowed the last of the bitter liquid and wiped my mouth on a napkin. "Kind of tastes like drinking wet hay—with a kick."

The boys stared at me like I might grow horns or a tail. Who knew, maybe I would.

I swallowed again. My stomach churned and strained against the flood of fluid I'd just sent down. I focused on my breathing for several minutes until the nausea passed.

Alex walked over and sat on the barstool next to me while Jax paced the room. He leaned in. His gaze stayed on my face. "Do you feel anything? Do you see anything?"

Jax spun and threw his hands out. "Dude, it's been

like two minutes. The chemicals haven't even had time to enter her bloodstream. Back off."

Alex didn't seem to like it, but he gave me space. "I'm just concerned."

Over my shoulder Jax snorted. "More like hoping she'd find the secret for you."

I squinted and blinked several times, the bright light coming in the window almost more annoying than the boys bickering. "Jax, he's on our side. Could you stop clacking like a couple of old hens and close the shades?"

Jax paused in his pacing. "The light is bothering you?"

"No." I glared at him, which hurt. "I just want to make it more romantic so you two can kiss and make up."

Ignoring my sarcasm, he went to the windows and drew the shades. The room dimmed to a comfortable level for my eyes. Sensitivity to light was one of the effects of nightshade. It was beginning.

"Maybe it would be better for you to lie on the couch," Alex suggested.

I nodded and climbed off the chair. The floor lurched beneath my feet. I grabbed for the breakfast bar and held on tight through the continued rocking. A strong hand gripped my elbow. I looked up into the copper of Jax's eyes and traded my grip on the cool granite countertop for his warm hand.

He wrapped his other arm around my waist. "It's hit your inner ear. Hang on to me."

I walked with him to the couch, where I collapsed. My heart tapped a quick beat in my chest. My tongue stuck to the roof of my desert-like mouth. "Can I have a drink?"

Alex appeared out of nowhere with a glass and bent over me. "Do you see or feel anything?"

I tried to shake my head but felt as if it had been filled with lead. I gasped air, my lungs unable to keep up. "I–I can't breathe." Alex pushed the glass into my hand, and I took a small sip. Not sure if I would end up choking or not.

Jax shook his head, which appeared to leave tracks of rainbows through the air in my drug-altered vision. "That's enough. It's not working. We have to get her to a hospital."

"No," Alex and I said in unison. Although my voice was more of a raspy whisper. But the water had helped a bit.

I took another sip, and then sucked in a lungful of air. "Give me some more time."

Jax ground his teeth together but didn't protest any further.

My grip tightened on the couch cushion as I tried to stay calm, but panic washed over me like a cold shower. Light, bright light, stung my eyes. I threw my hand over my now closed lids. It failed to block the painful glare. "Who opened the blinds?"

"The blinds are still closed, Maddie," Jax said. "Tell me what you need."

Light, brighter than the sun, seared through my corneas, glaring from every surface in the room. No matter how I tried to cover my face the light burned through. "It's burning my eyes."

Jax's voice seemed farther away. "She's hallucinating."

I felt his fingertips on my wrist.

"Her heart rate is over two hundred. Her body can't sustain that for more than a couple of minutes."

The excruciating pain tormenting my eyes could no longer distract me from the crushing suffocation in my chest. My body needed oxygen.

Cool fingers grabbed my hand. Alex spoke, "Maddie, try to find the power. Do you hear me? You have to find the power."

I turned my closed eyes toward Alex. The pain faded a bit, the neurons too overloaded to fire anymore. My brain shut down slowly. Through my eyelids I could see Alex clearly, only he was made up completely of iridescent light. His strong and classically handsome features blazed as if a torch lit his entire body from beneath the surface of his skin. "You're made of light."

"What do you mean?" he pressed. "What kind of light?"

Jax's face hovered inches from my own. His gentle fingers lifted the lids of my eyes. "Oh man, her pupils are huge. This isn't good."

Jax shown with light as well, only his had more of a blue hue to it.

"Beautiful," I gasped. My hand reached out to touch the brilliant sight and rested on his cheek. Heat, much more than body heat transferred to my skin where we touched. I gasped. "The power…"

Alex shoved Jax aside. "Where? Can you access it? Try Maddie."

My torso rolled forward, my muscles no longer able to support it, and hung over the edge of the couch. The floor of the hotel room no longer existed. I could see straight through to the earth. Dots of living things, bright with light, white like Alex or more often blue like Jax dotted the air, seemingly hovering on nothingness.

Below us, underneath the shield of dirt and rock, deep inside the earth a liquefied pool of light swirled. Branches ran off it much like rivers off a lake and broke into smaller streams, then brooks, to every living creature on earth, plants, and animals. The power of the earth.

The heat warmed my now chilled body. I reached out—I could almost touch it. "I can feel it." My words came out in a ragged gasp.

Jax held my wrist again. "She's up to two fifty. We have to do something."

My heart gave up its breakneck pace and began to quiver inside my chest. Blood came to a halt in my veins. I knew I was dying.

Jax called my name, frantically, and then I heard him screaming at Alex to do something. I tried to answer, to tell him not to worry, but nothing happened. I floated into darkness, my eyes still locked on the marvelous pool of light. I found it. I'd found the power of the earth.

****

Some people tell stories about dying and near death experiences. Going into the light, Heaven, seeing dead relatives. I would have loved to see my grandmother again, to tell her I'd done something right before I died, but I didn't experience any of that.

I remembered the darkness closing in. Then there was nothing. All of a sudden Jax was yelling at me. Darkness then yelling. That was it. That was my near death experience, not nearly as cool as the movies made it seem.

"Maddie," Jax yelled again. He sat on the coffee table, leaning over me on the couch. "Come on, babe. Fight for me."

I cracked an eye, a monumental task. "Babe?" I croaked. "Since when do you call me babe?"

Jax sucked in a huge breath and wiped his hands over his face before grasping my limp hand. "I thought you were gone."

Alex pressed forward into my still limited range of vision. "Could you touch it? You said you saw the power."

Jax bolted upright and grabbed Alex's arm. He yanked him away from me. "If you don't give her some space—" he shouted with his finger in Alex's face— "I'm going to throw you off that balcony and see if witches can fly."

Alex pushed back and yanked his arm from Jax's grasp. "You think you're in charge of her? I didn't see you cleaning the poison out of her blood then restarting her heart over and over again."

Jax ground his teeth together, and his hands clenched into fists.

The pounding in my skull got worse with every word they screamed. I struggled to a sitting position. Pain shot through every nerve in my body. "God, what did you guys do? Beat me up?"

Jax rushed to help me. "Don't push it. You need to rest."

I pressed my fingers to my exploding temples. "I'll be fine once you two stop bickering like old women."

His face reddened. "You'll be fine? Your heart stopped six times. You were dead, Maddie, for nearly ten minutes. You were dead."

I waved off his concern. "Well, I'm back now so cancel the funeral."

He got to his feet, hands again fisted and white knuckled. "I told you not to try this. You nearly died and where did it get you? Nowhere. It was a reckless move," he yelled.

"Why don't *you* give her some space?" Alex stepped in.

Jax spun. "Why? So she can go and try to kill herself again on some idiotic idea?" He held out his palms. "Maddie, please, stop this. I can't watch you die again."

"I have to find the answer. It's the only thing that matters."

He stopped short. "It's the only thing that matters?"

The hurt in his expression stopped my initial response. "I mean, if I don't find it I'm dead anyway."

"There has to be another way. We can find another way."

I shook my head. "Without the power to fix me I'll always be a, a Defect," I whispered the last word. "I have to find a way."

"You have never been a Defect." He crouched beside the couch and took my hand. "You're amazing. They call you a Defect just because you don't do magic like the rest of them, but I don't buy it." His grip tightened. "The power isn't the only thing that matters. You matter to me, we matter."

I tried to hold his copper gaze but couldn't. "You matter to me, too, but I can't stop. I have to keep trying."

He stood and stepped away from me. "Right. Well,

I can't watch you die."

"Jax, wait. That's not what I meant." I tried to rise from the couch, but my legs wouldn't support me.

"I'm done. I won't stand around and watch you kill yourself. Good luck with finding the power and everything. I'm out of here."

Before I could manage a word, he grabbed his jacket and stormed from the room, slamming the door in his wake.

I stared at the closed door for several seconds while my most-likely damaged brain struggled to catch up. He'd left me.

Alex sat next to me on the couch and patted my knee. "I'm so sorry Maddie. He is a complete jerk."

I stared at his hand, still on my knee. "I'm sure he'll be back after he cools off."

Alex squeezed my leg gently. "We don't need him. I mean, he isn't a witch. He shouldn't be a part of the search anyway."

I tensed my muscles to rise and pushed Alex's hand away. I needed to go after him, to bring him back. Without Jax this entire search seemed futile. I got half way to my feet before my legs gave out. I gripped the armrest and refused to give up, forcing myself upright. My legs shook like a newborn foal's.

"What are you doing?" Alex gasped and rushed to my side.

"I have to catch him," I said between gritted teeth and took two stumbling steps toward the door. "Help me."

"Absolutely not. You literally just had six heart attacks. You cannot be chasing after some fool." Alex's firm grip guided me back to the couch.

"No. I have to stop him. I have to tell him how much he matters." Tears filled my eyes as a different kind of pain filled my chest. My heart sputtered like an engine running out of fuel and blackness spread over the edges of my vision. I sagged in Alex's grasp.

"You need to rest," he said, and settled me on the cushion.

I nodded—no energy left to argue.

After a few minutes my heartbeat slowed into a normal rhythm, and I could at least hold my head up.

"Are you ready to talk about what you saw?"

I settled back into the softness of the couch and pulled a throw pillow into my lap. "I guess so."

Alex listened, completely still, while I described the light pooled beneath our feet. When I finished he sat for a moment, silent, then spoke. "Do you think it was a hallucination?"

I took a deep breath and sighed, which sent knives stabbing into my ribs. "No. I don't think it was a hallucination. I could feel it. I could almost touch the power." My hand lifted into the air then dropped to my side. "But it doesn't really matter. We obviously missed something. I could feel it but couldn't touch it. Plus, they couldn't drink that stuff every time they wanted to access the power."

He nodded and stared at the wall. "I don't understand what we did wrong."

I shrugged, my eyelids heavy.

Alex reached over and took my hand in his. "We'll figure it out. Together. And then we'll have the secret. You and me."

I pulled my hand away but couldn't answer. My body gave up the fight for consciousness, and I slipped into sleep with one thought on my mind. Jax had left me.

****

The constant pounding in my head, along with the smell of coffee brewing, dragged me from the bliss of sleep. Someone moving around in the kitchen brought me fully awake. Warm fuzzies tickled my stomach. Jax.

I sat up on the couch, and the blanket fell away. I peered over the edge of the cushion, and saw Alex putting food and a mug of coffee on a tray. The warm fuzzies in my stomach grew horns and spikes then burrowed into my flesh. Jax hadn't come back.

When I grabbed my phone, there were no texts. No calls. He'd really left for good.

Alex brought over coffee, toast, and eggs. He smiled when he saw me. "You're awake."

I attempted a smile. "Just barely."

"How about some breakfast?"

The act of sitting up sent my muscles into screaming spasms. I bit back a gasp. I guess dying really takes a toll. Alex seemed to be waiting for me to eat the breakfast.

With the exhaustion from the nightshade at a more bearable level, the reality that I had actually died hit me. It hadn't been a nightmare or a hallucination. I died, multiple times. Tremors rippled through my body uncontrollably. I couldn't die without telling Jax how I felt, and I needed to tell Emma I liked her damn clothes, and there were my parents, my brother. I never said goodbye.

"You okay?"

"Probably just low blood sugar." I waved away his concern, and made myself pick up the toast, nibbling the corner. "Thank you. Not just for breakfast, I mean, but for saving my life and stuff."

He waved away my thanks. "I wouldn't let anything happen to you. Besides, I restart people's hearts all the time."

I laughed then regretted it as spasms tightened my ribcage.

Alex picked up a piece of toast and chewed a bite. "I've been thinking about what you saw and the clues. I don't think it was a hallucination. Maybe Jax messed up the tea recipe."

"Jax wouldn't do that." I forced the toast down my dry throat.

"Are you sure? How well do you really know this guy?"

I opened my mouth but then paused. I knew his copper eyes and tousled hair by heart, but how well did I know him? Being a great kisser didn't make him trustworthy.

Jax believed in me, or did he believe in the money he'd make off my discovery? Doubt tickled my stomach with a feathered touch. At first, he'd said he was only in it for the money. They say your first instincts are the most accurate. I thought he was a complete jerk that first day in the lab.

"He wouldn't sabotage the test, whatever his motivation was for being here. He wanted it to work just as badly as we did."

Alex pressed his lips together. "Maybe, but then why hasn't he come back?"

The neural pathways in my brain sat empty, no answer, except that he didn't care about me at all.

"All I'm saying," Alex continued. "Is that we

should consider trying the tea again."

I stared at him, my body shaking with the effort of sitting up. "Right, great idea, kill me again. By *we*, I assume you mean me."

He stood and crossed his arms. "You know I would try it if you could bring me back."

"There's no point to trying it again. Jax wanted to pay for his grad school. He didn't sabotage the test," I argued.

His back stiffened. "It could have been an honest mistake." He walked to the kitchen and muttered under his breath. "He's not perfect."

Far from it, I thought, but if anything he's smart. He wouldn't make a mistake like that.

I bit my tongue. Alex was the only ally I had left.

"I have something I want to ask you," Alex said, returning to the couch.

"Okay."

"Is there someone else helping you? Someone from the council?" he asked.

I pulled a square pillow into my lap and hugged it to my chest. "No, no one from the council is helping me."

"How did you avoid them at the airport then?" he pressed. "I'm only asking because if we have any more allies I need to know about them. I'm in this with you."

"If I had a council member in my back pocket I wouldn't have failed my final in the first place." I dodged the question while my brain raced. He'd used his powers in front of ungifted people. I knew he had to be on my side. But the Monks wouldn't be any help figuring out the secret and the fewer people who knew about them the better. In case we were caught and tortured by the council the less Alex knew about the Monks and how they'd helped me would make it healthier for us all.

"I was hoping you had someone else that can help us is all," he said.

"Sorry to disappoint you. It's just you and me," I answered.

****

It took a full day for me to even feel half-way human, and to fully accept Jax was never coming back. He could be stateside by now. Anger replaced my initial hurt. Anger was good. Anger brought power.

I insisted that we needed to change hiding places, but Alex seemed more worried about me regaining my strength than my aunt finding us. Finally, I packed my stuff, and unable to carry the bags, dragged them to the living room and dropped them on the floor with a bang.

Alex's gaze bounced between the bags and me. "I guess we're moving?"

"My aunt's not stupid. She's going to find us eventually. They know you're with me, so they might check places you've stayed in the past."

He took a seat on the stool. "It might actually be smarter to lay low and stay put."

I leaned against the bar counter, my energy reserves used up by the packing.

His phone buzzed. He read the screen and typed a quick reply. "But, if it would help you feel safer then it would be worth it."

I blinked. My brow pulled together. "What's wrong?"

"Nothing at all. Just a text from my dad." He got to his feet and turned away from me. "Listen, I want you to be able to relax and get stronger. I'll go pack."

He strode from the room, and I tried to decide what had happened. I poured a cup of coffee and blew on the steaming mug, then settled on a barstool to let my muddled thoughts clear. Before the coffee had cooled enough to drink he returned with his bag.

"I travel light," he explained.

A pounding at the door stopped my response. Alex stepped between me and the door. So chivalrous. I wanted to puke. He still thought I needed protecting because I was a girl.

Adrenaline strengthened my shaking legs. Scenarios ran through my mind like jackrabbits on speed. The question being, how to escape this room with my aunt pounding on the only exit? The pounding continued.

"Maddie," Jax's voice called though the door.

I pushed around Alex and threw open the bolt with shaking hands. Jax sagged against the door frame. His left arm hung limply from his shoulder.

I sucked in a breath. "Jax."

One eye squinted down at me, bruised and blackened, while the other was swollen shut. Dried blood crusted his mouth where his bottom lip was split. But the worst of it all, the part that turned my stomach, were the veins under his skin, visible from the electric shocks someone had coursed through his body. Witch lightning.

I wrapped my arm around him, careful not to touch his left arm, and guided him inside. He limped and leaned heavily on me.

Alex jumped into action and dropped his suitcase to take Jax's other side.

"I don't need your help." Jax wrenched away from Alex's grasp.

"Okay. I just didn't want you to fall." Alex held up his hands.

My legs trembled under Jax's weight. I gritted my teeth and walked him to the couch. He slumped onto the cushion with a groan.

I sat next to him, his hand gripped in mine. "What happened? How did they find you?"

He pointed his bruised chin at Alex. "Why don't you ask Surfer Boy there?"

"Maddie, I swear, I don't know any more than you do," Alex said, his gaze bouncing between me and Jax.

"What about the text you got?"

"What about it?"

"You suddenly wanted to leave."

He pulled his phone out of his pocket and tossed it onto the coffee table. "Look at whatever you want. I have nothing to hide."

I picked up the phone and scrolled through the texts. One text had been received twenty minutes earlier from an unknown number. I opened it. "They are close to finding her family. We have to move them again. You would be wise to do the same."

The air in my lungs turned to sand. My mouth dried up like the Sahara. "Are they okay?"

Alex sat in the chair opposite me. "I didn't want to worry you. We'll keep them safe."

I handed his phone back.

Jax pulled himself up. "He's lying. It has to be him. How did they find us at the Gardens? How did they find me?"

"Alex has had plenty of opportunity to turn us into

the council if he wanted to," I said. "Besides, they'll kill him for exposing us if they catch him."

"It's him, Maddie." Jax closed his eyes.

"Tell me what happened," I urged quietly.

"I left to cool off. I needed to get out of here for a while. Seeing you, like that…" He squeezed my hand. "It was like seeing my mom gone. I had to get out of here, so I decided to take a walk. I'd turned around to come back when your aunt and the thug grabbed me."

I controlled the urge to smack myself in the forehead. It never occurred to me that he'd be upset because of the memories of his mother dying.

"I don't remember anything until I woke up in a room somewhere," he continued. "They hit me a few times and asked me where you were and who was helping us. I wouldn't tell them anything. Then they stopped asking questions."

He stared at the air for a moment before he spoke again. "Your aunt kept electrocuting me with this weird blue lightning. She didn't ask any questions though, just shocked me over and over again."

I shivered. "Witch lightning. They use it to make people talk."

"I didn't say a word," he stated again. "But she never asked anything, she just… kept doing it."

"How did you get away?"

"I made up a goose chase for them about a clue I found in the library in Cambridge, one that I kept from you. They wanted to check it out." His gaze refocused on the blank wall. "They left me locked up. I reached the tools in my pocket and picked the cuffs."

"They left you alone and conscious?" Alex chimed in for the first time. "There is no way a human could escape the Council unless they wanted him to."

Jax glared. "I wasn't conscious when they left. And no they left one of the thugs to guard me, but I got the jump on him and knocked him out."

"It sounds way too easy," Alex said.

Jax's fist clenched. "Let's see you do it. Without your stupid spells. Maybe they underestimated me because I'm just a human."

"Take it easy. We're all trying to figure this out," I said.

Alex leaned in and spoke in my ear. "I should check him to be sure they didn't put a tracker spell on him."

I nodded.

Alex closed his eyes to do a scan.

Jax bolted upright. "What's he doing? Keep your magical shit to yourself."

I pressed a hand to his shoulder.

He screamed in pain.

I yanked my hand away and eased the shirt to the side to expose the mottled purple and black skin around the shoulder joint. They'd dislocated his shoulder. From the yellowing of some of the bruises it looked like they'd popped it in and out several times.

My insides turned to molten rivulets of anger. I wanted to kill my aunt.

Alex grabbed my arm. "They put a tracker on him."

Chapter Sixteen

I jumped to my feet and pulled Jax up by his good arm.

We made it half way to the door before the tingle of magic stopped us in the center of the plush carpet. The slight brush of energy was like a magical calling card, an announcement of what stood on the other side of the door.

A knock sounded, no pounding, just a polite rap on the wood. Alex and I stared at each other. We were trapped. Jax had led them right to our door.

"You go, out the window. Who cares who sees you," I said to Alex. There was no way he could safely fly all three of us, but he could save himself.

His jaw firmed. "No way I'm leaving you to face this alone. I knew the risks when I decided to help."

Jax leaned against the back of the couch, too weak to stand anymore.

"We don't stand a chance in a battle," I said. "But I might be able to at least take out my aunt before I go down."

Alex took my shoulder in one hand and gave me a shake. "Maddie, if we fight we all die, even Jax. You're still weak. What chance do we really have?"

My eyes rested on Jax's bruised, broken form. He didn't deserve any more pain. "They'll never let him go."

"I can hear you, you know," Jax said.

Alex let his hand fall from my arm. "We do have something to bargain with. Maybe we can work something out."

Half my mind wanted to blast everything I had at that door, and hope I killed at least one of them, while the other half wanted to get Jax out of here safe. "So we bluff and act like we know the secret?"

He grimaced. "They'll know because we would use it to fight them if we did. But we have part of the answer."

I closed my eyes, then opened them, and walked to the door. If there was a chance, however slight, I had to take it.

"Maddie, don't," Jax called, his voice weak. "Blow them to hell."

My fingers wrapped around the cool metal of the knob and twisted.

The door swung open to reveal my aunt, no expression on her face. At her side stood two thugs, one a replacement for the casualty on the bridge. The wide carpeted hallway sat otherwise empty.

"I'm glad you have seen that it is futile to fight," she said.

The same voice from my childhood memories, but now devoid of emotion, crept over my skin like spiders. Images of her standing over Jax, hurting him, flashed through my mind. Magical energy welled up inside me, ready to blow both of us to pieces.

Her expression remained the same, almost bored. "You would only succeed in killing yourself."

I pressed the energy back into my tissues. Damn council defenses. My revenge would have to wait.

I stepped to the side. They filed into the room, all polite and stuff.

After I closed the door, I moved slightly in front of Jax. "So now what?"

My aunt scanned the room, then her eyes rested on me. "Now, you give us everything you have found. Then we kill you."

I laughed, the sound echoed off the walls. "Just like that, huh?" The smile slid from my face. "I don't think so. You want to know what I know? Then I have a few demands of my own."

"You are not in a position to bargain here, Maddison," she retorted.

My name coming off her emotionless tongue tightened my stomach. I tried for my best defiant expression. "I guess we'll see about that. Good luck figuring out the answer. You guys don't strike me as the most talented outside the box thinkers."

She didn't say anything. Instead, she turned and fired blue lightning directly at Jax's chest.

His body tightened like a guitar string. A strangled scream escaped from his throat.

I didn't think. I stepped into the path and blocked his body with my own. Pure acid raced through my nerves, burning everything in their path. My brain sputtered, misfiring with the overload of input. Muscles tightened to the point of snapping. Teeth ground together. Heart struggled to function.

The lightning stopped. I collapsed to the floor, my vision blackened except for a pinpoint in front of me. My leg muscles twitched with residual electricity.

I felt her crouch over me. "That was not a smart move. You show your weakness for this human."

I gasped in air. "Let him go. And I'll tell you everything I know."

"No," she said and straightened. "Tell me everything you know or I'll kill him as painfully as possible."

Alex leaned into my limited range of vision. "Are you all right?"

"Peachy. Do me a favor and kill her."

One corner of his lips turned up. "I would if I could."

He pulled me to a sitting position. I leaned against the back of the couch next to a semi-conscious Jax. "Maddie," Jax mumbled. "Don't tell them."

Aunt Clara stood in front of the three of us. "Tell me now or the next shock may kill him."

I stared at the face of my once beloved aunt. I remembered her pushing me on the swing higher and higher while I shrieked with joy until Mom scolded her. Aunt Clara had always made me happy. Until they changed her.

Was this how I would end up? A shell of myself with nothing left inside. I'd rather be dead.

I glared up at her. "You'll have to kill us all."

Her face didn't change, not a single bit. "Very well."

She shifted her attention to Jax again.

I gripped his hand and hoped the end would come quick.

"Stop," Alex jumped up. "I'll tell you everything."

My aunt froze, her eyes on Alex.

"Alex don't. They'll kill us anyway." I struggled to get up but failed.

"I will tell you what we know then you leave us

alone," Alex said, more of a demand than a question.

I couldn't stop him. He spilled our discoveries quicker than a tabloid reporter.

My aunt listened.

At least I didn't have to deal with a smug expression on her face.

After Alex finished cataloging our findings thus far, she stepped away and made a phone call. I couldn't make out the muffled exchange.

She turned back around and pointed to Jax. "Take him."

"What?" I forced myself up to a standing position.

The goons grabbed Jax and half dragged his weak body across the room.

"No," I screamed, and lunged toward him. My gaze met his and held. "Jax, I don't care about the secret. You matter, you're the only thing that matters to me."

He disappeared through the doorway, and I fell to my hands and knees.

Alex gripped my arm to support me. I yanked away from him.

"You have earned a chance to save your human." My aunt stood in front of the doorway. "You have two days to find the answer or else he dies. If you succeed he will go free, minus his memory of course, and you will simply be stripped of your witch abilities as you were supposed to be. As for you." She pointed at Alex. "The council will decide if you are allowed to keep your magic after the exposure at the Gardens. If you fail, he dies, and so do both of you." She turned to leave but tossed a phone on the counter. "I will contact you with this. Two days."

She closed the door behind her, leaving us in a

dead silence.

"Why didn't they kill us? They would have enough to continue the search themselves." I said finally, still staring at the closed door.

"I'm a convincing negotiator I guess."

"Why did you tell them anything?" I demanded.

Alex slumped on a barstool. "I was trying to buy us some time, and it worked."

I spun and glared at him. "We'll never figure out the mystery in time. You just prolonged his misery."

"Is that all you care about? Jax? Don't you see that there is more at stake than your love life?"

"I know very well what's at stake, thank you. If you'll remember the best I can hope for is to be stripped and maybe keep my mind whole."

"I risked my life to help you." He straightened up and crossed his arms.

I pointed a finger in his face. "You risked your life to find the secret for your own purposes. Don't try to act like you did anything for me."

"Maybe you need a moment to cool down." He stared back at me. His face a mask of cool stone.

I rolled my eyes, slowly. "I'll need way more than a moment. You don't seem to understand that without Jax, I can't save Jax."

He frowned, his brows pulled together. "What makes him so special?"

I collapsed on the couch, my eyes focused on the pink stain from Alex's juice. My voice came out almost a whisper. "Without him I'll never be able to figure out the mystery."

The cushions shifted under Alex's weight. "Maddie, you're about the smartest person I know.

You'll figure this out. We have to stick together. I know I don't know much about science, but I'm here to help."

My anger faded when I looked up at his face, so sincere, almost childlike in his hope. "I'm sorry. I know you're trying to help. It's just that I thought I had the answer, but I was wrong. I don't have any idea where to go from here."

"We can figure this out. We have to figure this out."

****

Three hours later, I pounded my face against the table a couple times. None of the other paintings were helpful. I'd gone over them all again in hopes we'd missed something.

A steaming mug of coffee appeared in front of me. The tempting aroma gave me the strength to coax my head from the table. "Thanks."

Alex set his own mug on the wood and sat in the chair next to me. "You seemed like you could use it. I also ordered your favorite, a cheeseburger and fries."

My stomach cramped at the thought of food, empty for too long, but all my brain could do was wonder if they were hurting Jax, torturing him. I forced the thought away and nodded. "That sounds good. Now I just need to figure out what we're missing."

"Nothing promising in your stack of paintings?"

"No. I don't think we missed anything there. Hand me the letters again. They had the clue about the beautiful women. Maybe now that we know that, something else will stick out."

He passed the stack of yellowed parchment over, and I began reading the first letter for what seemed like the hundredth time. I'd gotten to the third letter when the food arrived.

I forced myself to take a bite of the burger. It tasted like sandpaper on my dry tongue. How could I eat while they did God-knows-what to Jax? Choking the bite down, I chugged half the soda to keep from gagging. I stuffed a couple of French fries in my mouth and chewed methodically.

By the fifth letter, I'd noticed a definite pattern but had no idea what it could mean. "The friend always visits in the spring, always in May. Could that mean anything?"

Alex shrugged. "I have no idea. Maybe that's just because travel is easier after the snow stops."

I nodded and sank into my chair. "You're probably right."

In the next letter, the duke detailed his wife's delicate health for the third time. It seemed that she was getting progressively worse. I pointed the passage out to Alex. "I wonder why they didn't fix whatever was wrong with her."

"What do you mean?"

Laying the letter aside, I picked up the next. "If they could access the power of the earth, then you would think they could have fixed whatever disease she suffered from. I mean, if they could fix a Defect, any human ailment should have been easy."

His eyebrows raised. "What makes you think they could fix a Defect?"

I kept my gaze on the paper. "There were none when they could access the power. They used to screen all the young kids. Defects didn't show up until after the secret was lost." I finally looked up and met his gaze. "Why do you think my parents became

209

historians? They wanted to find a way to fix me."

"Maybe she had something they couldn't figure out like cancer or something."

I nodded and didn't point out that cancer would have been easier to cure than my problem. But whatever had been wrong with her wouldn't save Jax, so I moved on to the next letter.

The rest of the duke's letters contained no answers. He thought his wife was a *special one*, but I had no idea what he meant by that. Everything I found pointed to the nightshade. The references to beautiful women, the discussion of plant growth cycles and blooming, all indicated that the answer had to do with the plant. Even the duke's oddball reference to cattle and rabbits fit because they could eat nightshade with no harmful effects. Nothing pointed me in a different direction.

Twelve hours since they took Jax. Thirty-six hours left until they killed him.

"I hate to say it Maddie, but I think we have to try the tea again."

I allowed my eyes to remain closed. Jax's bruised face danced behind my lids. I finally opened my eyes and forced myself up. "I know. I'll get it ready."

Preparing the recipe, I checked and triple checked every measurement. Every step in the tea preparation. The herby aroma flooded my mouth with saltwater. I'd put my heart through quite a bit over the last couple days. There was no way to know if it could handle another assault. Alex and his magic could only do so much.

I placed the tea on the table and pushed aside the Bella Donna painting.

"I wish I could do this instead of you," Alex said

from behind me.

"Trust me, you don't want to experience this."

He gripped the back of the chair. "I mean I wish you didn't have to go through it again."

I wrapped my hand around the warm cup of death. I couldn't decide if I wanted this to work or not. If it did, then I would have to trade the secret for Jax or let him die. Then the council would be unstoppable and who knows what they planned to do with unlimited power. If it didn't work, I was likely dead. Great options.

Tremors erupted in the hand holding the mug and sent miniature tsunamis over the surface of the tea. The tremors progressed into a full on earthquake. The cup slipped from my grasp.

Alex made a grab for the mug. "Careful."

Instead of steadying the mug he knocked into it and sent a tea tidal wave over the smooth table surface toward the painting. I dove across the table in an effort to save the Bella Donna.

The tea got there first.

Chapter Seventeen

The liquid washed over the fragile paper. I grabbed the painting and pulled it out of the tea. My heart lodged so far up my throat it felt as if it were stuck in my nasal cavities.

Alex ripped the painting from my hands. "Now look what you've done."

I stared between him and the dripping paper, my tongue quicker than my brain. "Okay, Mom."

His brows pulled together. He glared at me with slits for eyes. "What did you say?"

I opened my mouth to repeat myself when my gaze fell on the back of the painting. Faint script appeared in the formerly blank center of the page. I grabbed the paper out of Alex's grasp.

He tried to grab it back. "What's the matter with you?"

I smacked his hand away. "Shut up and look at this."

He blinked, his hand extended, then refocused on the now visible writing on the back of the painting. The careful calligraphy was etched in blue ink. My mind raced through possible chemical reactions between the tea and the ink that would make the writing invisible until they came in contact.

Parts of the writing were too faint to read. I dipped the paper back into the pool of tea then laid it flat on the breakfast bar.

The writing darkened to a legible paragraph. I leaned over the paper. "What idiots! It wasn't supposed to be a drink at all. No wonder it almost killed me."

Alex remained a few feet away, his arms crossed. "How were we supposed to know?"

"Are you seriously still upset about the mom comment?" I tore my gaze away from the paper.

His jaw muscle bulged, but he stepped closer to lean over my shoulder. "Let's just say that my mother wouldn't have approved of such carelessness. Trust me, you don't want to be on her bad side." He motioned to the paper.

"*Use with caution. The fires burn too hot for most.*"

"It sounds like a warning." I bit the inside of my lip.

"Well, for anyone but a witch the fire would be too hot. It would kill them."

"That's only one interpretation," I said. "We need to be careful."

He kept his focus on the writing. "It sounds logical to me, but of course we'll be careful."

"Soak three chimera blooms for five minutes for quick results. In an emergency they can also be eaten, but the results will be delayed."

"What is a chimera?" Alex pointed to the first sentence.

"A genetic mutation causing a different color flower on two different branches of the same plant," I quoted the botanical garden exhibit we'd seen with the roses.

He grabbed his phone and searched nightshade flower colors. "They only come in purple. You must be wrong."

I blew out a breath, and very maturely if you ask me, resisted the urge to hit him. We didn't have time for this. Jax didn't have time for this. "Look it up if you don't think I'm right."

He searched while he spoke, his voice smug. "I know you're usually a know-it-all with science, but you have had a lot going on. Plus, who knows how all these herbs and toxins are effecting your brain."

I considered shoving the phone down his condescending throat but instead examined every inch of the back of the painting.

"It says a chimera is a genetic mutation that changes the color on a specific branch of a plant due to a random genetic mutation, common in roses."

"Shocking," I said, keeping my eyes on the wet paper.

"Or it's a fire-breathing female monster with a lion's head, a goat's body, and a serpent's tail," he continued.

I'd show him a fire-breathing female monster all right. "I'm going to go with the first definition unless you think we need to start searching for mythical creatures."

He rolled his eyes. "Let's not be a poor sport. There was no hurt in double checking."

I swallowed my reply. Jax didn't have time for my irritation. My hands trembled as raw fear swamped my mental barriers and overwhelmed me. Short choppy breaths were all I could manage for several seconds, and I gripped the table to stay upright. If I lost him—I forced deeper breaths. The painting came back into focus on the table beneath me. Jax needed me at my best. One breath, then two, now think.

Satisfied the back of the painting held no further clues, I flipped the paper over. The difference popped out immediately. On one side of the painting, seemingly sticking out from the back of the plant, one of the branches now bore a red flower. A chimera.

The red five-petaled, star-shaped flower sparked recognition in my brain. I pulled the locket chain from under my shirt and unhooked the clasp. The faded red flower engraved on the front bore a striking resemblance to the painting. I held the locket next to the watercolor.

Alex leaned over my shoulder. "Where did you get that?"

"My grandmother gave it to me." My voice came out choked by my thickening throat.

"Does it say anything inside?"

I didn't need to open it. I knew the inscription by heart. "'For my wonderful wife. Those who are special pay the highest price.'"

His brow wrinkled. "What is that supposed to mean?"

I tucked the locket back in its rightful place over my heart. "I've never been able to figure it out."

"Not much help then," he said, and blew out a breath.

I'd always known the necklace was a family heirloom, but it must have come from farther back then we'd known, as far back as the letters from the Duke at least. Whoever the owner had been, they had to have known the secret.

Alex returned his attention to the painting. "So now we need to find a red nightshade flower. It was smart, really, to hide the clue this way. If anyone ever got close and figured out the answer had to do with Deadly Nightshade they would probably kill themselves with the tea before they figured out not to drink the stuff."

"It worked on us, almost," I said and swallowed bile at the thought of how close I'd come to drinking the lethal tea again.

Alex put his hand on my shoulder and squeezed. "I wouldn't have let you die. I'd have brought you back again."

I sucked in a shaky breath and nodded.

"The question is where do we find the nightshade with the red flowers?" Alex asked.

I pointed to Annabel's signature again and the newly visible line under it *France 1784*.

"France is thousands of square miles of ground to cover. How are we supposed to find red nightshade without more to go on than that?" Alex asked.

I bit my lip and checked my watch. Thirty-two hours and twelve minutes until they killed Jax. "I haven't figured that part out yet."

****

Time was running out for Jax. I glanced at my watch for the tenth time in as many minutes. Hours of searching and we were still no nearer to finding a red nightshade flower.

Alex looked up from his computer screen. "I don't think dwelling on our time constraint is helping."

"You don't think I know that?" I snapped.

"I'm only trying to help you."

I closed my eyes and ran my hands through my knotted mass of hair.

He got up and stood in front of me, his hands on

216

my forearms. "What he needs is for us to focus and figure this out so you can get him back."

"You're right. My freaking out isn't doing him any good."

Alex released my arms and sat back in front of the computer. "So, I can't get satellite images close enough to see individual flowers, much less have the time to search the countryside inch by inch. And there is absolutely no reference to red nightshade flowers in any scientific journal, research paper, or gardening blog."

I paced back and forth from the kitchen to the couch, going over all the information we'd gathered. What was special about France? I stopped midstride. "What about Paris?"

"What about it?"

"The revolution in Paris. That's where they killed the previous council. They used the political unrest to cover the coup. But the council was in Paris."

"So we focus our search on the area around Paris," he said, and tapped on the keyboard. "That narrows it down, but it's still a lot of area to cover."

I resumed my pacing. This time from the couch to the bedroom door. I thought better on the move. My packed bags, forgotten on the floor after Jax and my aunt showed up, blocked my path. I kicked the backpack stuffed with clothes out of the way. It rolled behind the couch, and I paced in the now cleared path.

"I'm searching gardens in the Paris area for hits on red flowers or chimeras. It will take me awhile."

The phone ringing stopped my response. I stared at the cell phone that my aunt had left while my heart tapped out a River-Dance-like pace inside my chest. I forced air into my lungs and reached for the phone.

217

Alex stared, his hands frozen over the keyboard.

I hit the green button. "Yeah."

"Your boyfriend is hoping you've made progress."

My aunt's voice churned acid in my stomach. "We are closer than we were."

"Tell me what you found."

My jaw firmed. "You think I'm an idiot? I'll tell you what you need to know when we make the exchange."

"I'm beginning to wonder if you've hit a dead end. That would be bad for Jax, extremely bad. Remember, you only have twenty-four hours left."

"What? No, we have twenty-eight hours left," I yelled into the phone.

"Consider it motivation. Twenty-four hours."

The line went dead. I gripped the phone until my knuckles went white. The acid in my stomach ate through the lining and into my abdomen.

"What did she say?"

"They moved up the deadline."

I slammed the phone onto the table and flexed my hands to relieve the tension. The frustrated anger boiling over in my chest had no outlet. I needed to hit something—repeatedly. Someone would be better. I continued pacing.

I rounded the couch and booted my backpack across the room. It smashed into the wall and knocked a frame off its hook. The picture shattered on the floor with a satisfying crash.

Alex glanced between me and the mess of scattered clothes and glass. "Feel better?"

I nodded and went to take a step. Pain shot up my foot from my bleeding toe. I grabbed the back of the couch and examined my foot.

"Are you okay?"

I ripped off the broken toenail. Blood oozed from the torn skin. "I'm fine."

Tissues sat on the table next to the couch. I hobbled over and wrapped several around my toe.

Alex brought over a Band-Aid from the bathroom and dropped my father's journal on the table. "You must have caught your toe on this when you kicked it."

I stared at the worn leather, my overtaxed neurons struggling to make a connection from the depths of my memory. I was forgetting something. The connection snapped together. I jumped from the couch. "The journal."

Alex furrowed his brow and gave me a look like he would give an idiot. "Yeah, I just brought it to you."

"No. The journal from Cambridge. We left it in the library when you clobbered Talbot. It was written by Annabel, I'm almost sure the last name was Price, like on the painting. It has to be the same one that painted the picture."

"Annabel was a pretty common name. Without being sure of the last name, there's no way to know if it is the same person," Alex said. "I flipped through the journal when we found it. It has entries about plants and some poems, but I didn't see anything too interesting."

"That's what they thought about the references to botany in the letters," I answered. My jaw firmed. "We have to get the journal. It could be the clue we need to find the chimera."

He held up his hands. "I'm not making much progress anyway so it's worth a try."

I grabbed the phone and dialed my aunt.

She picked up after one ring. "Maddison. I see my incentive worked."

"I need to get back into the library at Cambridge."

Chapter Eighteen

Talbot, sporting a nasty bruise that went all the way down the back of his neck, led us to the elevator. He hadn't said a word since our arrival in front of the library. He swiped his card, and the door opened. We filed in, and he hit the emergency button.

I studied his profile, jaw clenched, nostrils flared.

The doors slid open, and I followed Talbot down the hallway. After the rush from the hotel and the racecar driving up here his pace could have matched a sloth.

"Just unlock the door. I'll take it from there," I said.

His two by four of a spine got even stiffer, if that was possible. He took his time extracting the key-ring from his pocket and examining each key before selecting the correct one.

My teeth ground together while my hands closed into fists.

"Can't believe I have to let a filthy Defect into my store rooms," Talbot said, disgust dripping from his tone. He made no move to unlock the door.

The slur hit me in the gut, just like it always did. The twisting ache spread to my chest. But, to my surprise, it stopped there and faded. The paralyzing shame that usually followed didn't come. I took a deep breath.

"Maddie, let it go," Alex said under his breath.

I shook my head. "Not this time."

Alex tried to grab my arm, but he didn't have a chance. Before Talbot could react, I shoved him to the side and held up my hand, palm out, adjacent to the metal security door.

Pure raw energy exploded from my palm. It was getting easier each time, now that I wasn't holding back. The entire wall detonated, blasting the door and the frame into the storage room, and leaving a smoldering hole in its place. Smoke and dust choked the air. I strode past a drop-mouthed Talbot and stepped over the rubble. Red lights now flashed, my magic setting off the security alarm.

"You–you are going to pay for that," Talbot stammered in a high shriek and raced to punch in a code on his phone to disable the alarm.

"Add it to my tab," I smirked.

Alex followed me inside and grabbed my arm. "That wasn't smart."

I rolled my eyes for his benefit. "I'm already going to be stripped of my witch abilities. Might as well blow shit up while I can. Plus, he started it when he used that word."

The red lights switched off, and the regular white ones turned on. Talbot, clutching his chest like he was having an attack, stomped into the room. "Whatever deal you made won't matter. The council will never let you live. You're all going to die."

I nodded and forced the fear into the pit of my stomach. He might be right but I wasn't dead yet.

The extensive room was once more in OCD order, not a speck of dust, besides what I'd just made.

"You can leave now," I spoke to Talbot. "Unless you want another display of my Defect abilities."

His face went from pale to boiling red in a matter of seconds. His jaw tightened again until the muscles bulged from his cheeks. White knuckled he turned and climbed back over the rubble pile.

I pounded the search into the computer and tapped my fingers while it thought. Alex tried to put a hand on my shoulder, again, but I shrugged it off.

After I scribbled down the reference area and wiped the search, we sprinted down the rows of shelves. The journal was right back where it belonged. I grabbed it off the shelf. Talbot's snail-pace had wasted half an hour. A little less than twenty hours were left.

I sat right there on the floor and ripped open the journal. Annabel Price was written on the first page in the same handwriting as the signature on the painting. I pointed the signature out to Alex. "It's the same person."

The yellowed pages felt slightly rough against my skin. I turned the page and was pulled into the elegant script. The warehouse and my surroundings fell away, and I was enveloped by the literary voice of Annabel. Her sweet and unassuming nature was evident in her words. She wrote about her husband and children, and the joy she took in her family was obvious. She talked about working in the garden with her children.

I turned the page and focused on a pencil sketch. A mother sat on the grass with her young daughter and a baby, surrounded by bountiful plants and vegetation. A self-portrait. Annabel gazed adoringly at her children while they played by her side. The detail caught in the simple sketch held my attention. Her soft features, the laughter on the baby's face, her daughter's joy in holding up the flower for her mother's approval. A pointed, five-petal flower.

I sucked in a breath. I couldn't be sure with no color but I'd swear that flower was a nightshade.

"Look here," Alex pointed out, breaking into my trance.

I followed his finger. On the next page, Annabel wrote about a trip to France. I devoured the words, searching for any clue as to where they'd gone. The trip lasted several weeks since they'd left England at the end of March to spend most of the month of April in France. But she never said where.

I bit my lip. It had to be somewhere in the journal. Jax was running out of time.

I moved on to the next entry, a poem:

~*~

I was formed deep within the earth,
And fire flows in my veins,
The heat burns, the fire churns,
My gift has become my bane.

~*~

My brow scrunched. I skimmed the next four stanzas: ocean, air, the earth, and last one about her spirit. Poetry was never my strong suit. I was much more a write-down-the-facts, scientific kind of girl.

Several more entries talked about trips to France, all in April. It seemed to be an annual event. Halfway through the journal Annabel began talking about her health problems. Nothing specific, just mention of bad days when she needed to rest and increasing weakness. The reference brought the duke's wife, my distant ancestor, back to mind.

Twenty minutes later I bolted up. Alex, who'd given up reading over my shoulder, set his tablet down.

"Listen to this. 'It will be our last trip to France as a family. I fear my health won't allow travel much longer. I will miss the island but will carry the memories we created there with me. I hope the children remember the Isle de Batz long after I am gone.'"

Alex was already typing on his tablet. I stood behind him so I could see the search on the screen. "The island is a fifteen minute ferry ride from the city of Roscoff."

The word Jardin caught my eye, bringing back memories of freshman French class. I pointed. "Click on that, Jardin Exotique Georges Delaselle."

The description of the once private garden, now tourist attraction, came up and Alex whistled.

I shifted from foot to foot and fought the urge to rip the tablet from his hand. "That's it. It has to be."

He scrolled down and read the description aloud. "Founded by a Parisian insurer in the early 1700s the garden is home to over two-thousand rare and exotic plants. After his sudden death, the garden passed through several owners and finally was abandoned in 1959. The Conservation Society purchased the garden and began restoration in 1991."

A chill ran along my spine, and I fisted my hands. "A Parisian business man, he must have been on the Council. After the Council was killed, no one knew the garden was important and it was abandoned. This could be why they still planned to meet in France even with the uprising. They needed to get more of the nightshade."

"Especially if it only grows on that island," he

agreed.

I glanced at my watch. "We need to get out of England."

****

I called my aunt from the car. She answered on the first ring.

"You need to bring Jax to France," I said, instead of a greeting.

"Making demands now, are we?" she answered in her monotone.

"Quit the games and do what I say if you want the secret."

"And where in France are we going?"

Alex sped around a car on the freeway. I grabbed the dash with my free hand to steady myself. "I'll tell you that when we get there. For now get to France."

She stayed quiet a moment before speaking again. "I'm not sure he's up to traveling. Perhaps he'd be more comfortable if I left him here."

My insides turned to liquid that sloshed around with Alex's every swerve. "What have you done to him?"

"Not much. We've just been enjoying each other's company."

Her calmness made me want to scream. "If you've hurt him…"

"You'll what? Blow me up? You might have gotten lucky on that bridge but don't count on it happening again."

"I didn't get lucky. I used my brain."

"Your brain won't do your boyfriend much good, Maddison."

"I'll say this one more time. Go to France. Call me

when you get there, and I'll tell you where to go. You want the answer, you do what I say and bring Jax with you." I hung up the phone before she could respond.

Alex raised his eyebrows but kept his focus on the cars whizzing by on either side.

"I'll check flights to France."

I scrolled down the screen, my stomach lurching every time the car swerved.

"Don't bother with the airport. The Channel Tunnel will be faster unless there is a problem with it."

I paused and stared at him for a moment. "You're telling me there is a tunnel going under the English Channel?"

"Yeah, it's been around for like twenty some years."

"Under the ocean?"

"Look it up. And make sure there aren't any delays," Alex said with his gaze still firmly on the road.

I typed in the search and sure enough there was a tunnel going under the English Channel. Guess I needed to get out more. "It says there are no delays."

"Good, it only takes about forty-five minutes to cross and no hassle of flight check-ins and such." Alex pressed on the gas.

I sat back in the seat and tried not to think about the millions of gallons of water that would be pressing down on us in that tunnel. More like billions of gallons. The pressure would be astronomical. Rough calculations zipped through my brain. I swallowed. If it saved time for Jax, I could deal with a little claustrophobia. I had to.

We ditched the rental car at the station. Despite the no delay claim we had to wait to board the train. My attempt to keep my newly-discovered claustrophobic nerves on the down-low failed miserably. I was calmer when faced with witches.

The wait and the ride took over an hour and a half. But at least the train didn't break down in the middle. Alex shared that horrific story while we waited to board, then tried to hold my sweaty hand. Gross.

We emerged in France in the early morning and rushed from one station to the next train station only to find that we had two hours until the first train to Roscoff left. Time wasted. Time that Jax didn't have.

Fourteen hours and two minutes until he died.

Chapter Nineteen

I alternated between pacing and sipping coffee for what felt like years but actually ended up being only an hour. Finally, Alex grabbed my hand and dragged me to a bench.

"Sit down. I'm going to go get you something to eat."

I leaned against the wooden bench, glancing at my watch every second or two. Thoughts circled my head like hamsters on a wheel. Every once in a while one hamster-thought would go too fast, and the other would spin around the wheel like an amusement park ride. I took the journal out of my backpack and picked up where I left off. I'd been so excited about the name of the island that I hadn't read any further in the entries.

After what she called a *successful last trip* to France, the family returned to England, and she spent several months in her greenhouse with no success. The historians ignored any reference to her experiments with plants, but the hamsters froze on their wheel the moment I read the word Chimera.

~*~

I'd hoped to grow the blooms here in England from transplanted plants and cuttings, but any attempt only results in purple flowers. It must be the specific conditions on the island that allow for the color change to happen in April.

~*~

My breath froze solid in my chest at the last phrase, *color change to happen in April*. The ice crystals cut through my alveoli and entered my blood to spread icy-sharp chills over my body. It was the end of March. April wouldn't be here for five days. Over four days too late for Jax.

Alex returned and found me sitting like a statue on the bench, the journal still gripped in my hand, my unseeing eyes staring down the train tracks.

"What's the matter? What happened?"

I stared straight ahead. It didn't matter that I'd found the clues, found the answer that eluded my kind for over two hundred years. I'd done my best but it wasn't enough to save Jax.

When I didn't answer Alex pulled the journal from my hand and read the page. His eyes widened. "They only grow in April?"

I blinked and dragged myself back inch by inch from the edge. We were too close. In my mind I could hear Jax telling me to snap out of it in that annoyingly hot voice. Right now, Jax was still alive and fighting to stay that way. I wouldn't stop fighting while he had a chance.

"Give me the phone."

I didn't wait for my aunt to respond but spoke the moment she answered the phone. "We have a problem."

"No Maddison, you and your boyfriend have a problem."

"No," I snapped, pushing my fear down deep into my stomach to let my anger take over. "You want the secret, then my problems are your problems."

Silence met my tirade. My stomach folded in on

itself painfully. I might have just signed Jax's death certificate.

"What seems to be the issue?"

I let out the stale breath trapped in my lungs. "I found out there is a time constraint to the secret. I won't be able to access it for another five days."

"Tell me the details and I can pass your request along to my superiors."

"Nice try. All you need to know is that if you kill Jax you'll never find the answer. So give me the five days."

"I'll contact you shortly with their answer."

I hung up. My bravado leaked out of me like air from a balloon. I deflated against the bench and focused on not passing out.

Alex pressed a warm drink into my hand. "Here, take a sip of this. You did great."

"We'll see when they call back. I may have killed him." I sipped what turned out to be cocoa.

"I think you sounded strong. They don't have much choice. We have the clues. It would take them years to figure out what we know." He held out a fresh croissant. "I got you something to eat."

The smell of the flaky pastry turned my stomach in on itself once again. I took a bite of the warm roll and chewed mechanically.

A beep sent the croissant flying. I swallowed my bite. It crawled down my throat like a slug. I fumbled with the phone and hit the green button.

My aunt's voice greeted my ears.

"You have your five days."

My teeth sliced into my lip in an attempt to hold back a sob of relief.

"Don't try anything like this again. This is your last reprieve—and his."

The line went dead. The phone stayed by my ear, my shaking hand unable to move.

Alex put a hand on my shoulder. "Is he…"

"He's okay. They gave us the time."

****

Alex and I took the train to Roscoff and holed up in a vintage but ritzy hotel. The luxury was completely wasted on me in my guilt-ridden state. Any comfort or pleasure brought on tormented thoughts of Jax and his current conditions.

The first day I reread every word of Annabel's journal. She proved to be a beautiful poet, if a bit flowery for my taste. I tried for a day to analyze the poetry for clues but failed to learn anything except that she loved her family and thought about death more than was probably healthy. I couldn't find any more clues hidden in the other journal entries but felt a connection to the long-dead witch.

Before I could drive myself too crazy on the second morning, a soft knock at the door broke me from my thoughts. I opened it and faced the now-familiar face of my monk friend.

He bowed slightly.

"What's happened? Is it Jax?"

Worry creased his brow. "Your friend is alive. I'm sorry we were unable to intervene when they took him."

I shook my head and blinked back the moisture in my eyes. "It's not your fault. You're…" I'd almost said monks but stopped myself. "I'm not even sure what you are."

"We are guardians. 'Ungifted,' as you call it. Our

numbers have not recovered from our last battle with the council. They nearly destroyed us. Our only advantage now is they assume they won," he explained. "We cannot risk all, but your safety is our concern as well."

I had no idea how a group of ungifted would battle the council, no matter how badass and Zen they were. I nodded. I didn't want anyone else dying on my account.

"I have come to offer what help I can. You are alone?"

His question sounded more like a statement. I nodded and opened the door wider. Alex was out scouting and picking up breakfast. "He won't be back for about half an hour."

The monk entered, motioned me to the kitchen, and then he turned the ancient hand cranks to open up the two windows. "We will do this quickly, then. We cannot be sure of his alliances."

My brow pulled together, but any protest stopped at my lips.

My visitor motioned to the sink and set a metal spoon inside, then covered it with a pan lid from the cupboard. "Focus on the spoon. Try to use your energy to destroy it."

"You want me to blow it up?"

He nodded.

"That may not be such a good plan." The smoking metal from Kew Gardens came to mind.

The monk put a light hand on mine. "I am familiar with your talent. You must trust me."

"My talent? Don't you mean my cosmic joke, my deficiency?"

"I say only what I mean."

I stared into the depth of his brown eyes, about level with my own. No worry, no fear, only assurance shown back. "Okay. You asked for it."

I imagined the metal spoon beneath the lid and allowed a small amount of energy through. Within seconds the lid erupted from the sink with the force of the blow and landed with a clatter on the tile floor. Smoking spoon shards lay in the sink.

The monk placed another spoon in the sink and covered it. "Now, instead of trying to destroy it. Release the energy from the spoon."

I waved residual smoke away from my nose, most of it blowing out the windows, a metallic taste on my tongue. "I'm not sure what you mean. Release the energy?"

"Yes, instead of destroying the matter, use the natural energies inside and shift them. Create." He took a step away from the sink.

I crinkled my brow but kept my snarky comment to myself. Okay, create. I focused again on the spoon in the sink and poured energy into the metal. This time trying to imagine releasing the energy from the chemical bonds.

The lid from the pan exploded from the sink once more and crashed into the vaulted ceiling, a good twelve feet above, while fire spewed from the sink in a four-foot column. The monk sprang forward to slap on the water. Steam billowed while I stared with my mouth dropped open. I'd barely used any energy.

He fanned the smoke and steam out the windows while I snapped my mouth shut.

"You are an adept student," he praised with a smile.

I blinked and swallowed the lump in my throat. No one had ever said that to me about my magic.

All that remained of the second spoon was a shimmering powder in the bottom of the sink. I'd reduced it to the elemental metal.

After he washed the evidence of our experiment down the drain, he turned to me. "One other bit of help I can offer. Those with your talent tend to work better with particular elements: some copper, some oxygen, aluminum, and nitrogen. You need to find what resonates with your energy."

I nodded and followed him to the door where I could finally get a word out. "Thank you. For all your help."

"If you are to succeed, you must not underestimate the value of your ability," he responded, and, with another bow, disappeared down the hallway. I closed the door and leaned against it, hope filling my chest for the first time since they took Jax.

****

The smell of fresh baked goods and coffee announced Alex's return. He set the pastries on the table, his brow pulled together.

"Is something burning? It almost smells metallic." He looked around.

I rooted in the pastry bag, suddenly starving, and didn't look up. "Yeah, I was going to make some tea, but I forgot about the kettle and all the water boiled off. I guess I'm a little out if it right now."

"Oh, well, I'm glad you were actually trying to drink something." He watched me take a huge bite of a Danish. "It's good to see you getting your appetite back. You haven't really eaten in days."

"Got to keep my strength up," I mouthed around another bite.

He sat with me at the table and sipped his coffee, a smile on his face. "This is good. It's the first step."

I frowned, not sure what steps he was talking about but too busy stuffing my face to ask.

Over the next day, I took every opportunity I was alone to test out my *ability* on different elements. Hopefully, if the monk was right and I did have an element I could work best with, it wouldn't be some extremely rare one that was impossible to find. First, I tested the metals, precious and common, hopefully no one would be taking a close look at the wiring in the electronics and plumbing pipes. And for some unknown reason, Alex's tablet had stopped working. I lessened my guilt by reasoning that I'd only used a small dot of gold and surely it would be an easy fix. Besides, no way was I using my grandmother's necklace.

Each time, if I focused on the particular element I was isolating, my energy would seek those atoms out, like heat-seeking missiles, only slower and not in a straight line, so maybe like heat-seeking snakes? I'd never tried sending my energy out with such a specific target. The results were shocking. I could feel the element, the frequency it resonated at.

On March thirty-first Alex went out to get some dinner. I sent him across town to pick up Indian to give myself some time.

The plant leaf in front of me curled up in a smoking black ball. I blew out a breath. I'd tested fifteen elements with no luck. At this rate it could take a week to find the right one and tomorrow was April first. I had about sixteen hours before the meet to figure this out.

I pulled up the periodic table on my phone again. After the metals, I decided to start from the beginning and go with hydrogen, then helium and so on. The carbon in the plant leaf was my latest failure.

Up next was nitrogen, the most common element in the earth's atmosphere, but also an essential component of all living things. I rubbed my eyes and contemplated the new plant. The leaves frothed out over the pot like a muffin-top. A little more pruning wouldn't hurt.

I selected a leaf and set it in the sink. I'd wised up after so many practices and turned the ceiling fan on to get the burned smell out the windows. It worked, mostly. I also ferreted out a fire extinguisher. It went next to the back wall of the kitchen, just in case.

The amount of nitrogen in the leaf would be relatively small but should be enough for my purposes. I pictured the atom in my head, named it, and sent out tendrils of energy. Releasing the energy, as the monk had taught me, took way less of my own energy than trying to simply destroy something. The tendrils snaked around the leaf, then inside, to the very molecules that made up the structure.

The moment they latched on to the nitrogen, my muscles stiffened. My eyes flew wide open.

It was as if my energy vibrated at the exact same frequency, in harmony with the nitrogen atoms. For a split second, peace washed over me, like I was listening to the most beautiful voices singing in unison. But only for a split second.

The entire sink erupted in billowing flames. The force of the blast threw me backward. I sprawled against the stone tile of the kitchen floor, arms raised to cover my face from the heat.

Forget turning on the water. The smoke detector blared in high ear-shredding bleeps. I watched the paint on the ceiling bubble and begin to peel off, while acid bubbled up in my stomach. I scrambled for the fire extinguisher before I burned the entire room down.

Just as my hand closed over the nozzle, the flames in the sink sputtered, and, like a candle without oxygen, blinked out. My shaking hands held the extinguisher aimed at the once white, now charred, sink. I stared and waited, smoke swirling around me.

Finally, I approached the sink—extinguisher still at the ready. The once gracefully curved metal faucet hung down into the sink like a drooping flower, melted. A chunk of ceiling dropped to the floor with a thud.

"Maddie? Oh, my God, what happened?"

The extinguisher dropped from my hands with a metallic clatter, and I spun on my heel.

Alex stood, take-out bags in hand, and stared at the smoke-filled kitchen, the smoke detector still blaring. He glanced up and, with a flick of his wrist silenced the alarm.

"I was trying to practice," I blurted out the first thing that came to mind.

"Practice for what? You already took the test." He set the bags on the table and stepped closer to inspect the damage.

The monk's words bounced around my brain. I couldn't be sure of his alliances either, even after the magic on the walkway. "I hoped I could transport Jax out of the garden tomorrow, or something."

He pointed at the remains of the faucet. "Not unless you want him ending up like that."

"I know. Bad idea."

"You need to leave the magic to me." He put an arm around my shoulder to press my torso against his. "I know it has to be hard, but you have to accept you're a, um, that you have weaknesses."

I stood, muscles tensed, he'd almost said it. I pulled away from his grip, my arms crossed over my chest. I'd heard that condescending tone from other witches my whole life, even if they were kind enough not to call me a Defect. I stared out the window, glaring at the world to avoid glaring at Alex.

"I'll do everything I can. But you have to promise me, no more trying your magic." He faced the mess. "I'll fix this if you get dinner out of the bags."

Biting my lip to keep my anger inside, I took paper containers out of the bag and watched Alex rebuild the kitchen. The ceiling put itself back together, like a movie in rewind, while the faucet straightened and resumed its original luster. The sink took on its white sheen while residual smoke blew out the open window. Two minutes later and not the slightest sign of my explosion remained.

My eyes moved over the room. He made it look so easy, so simple, almost as easy as it was for me to destroy it. No, I reminded myself, I'd been creating, like the monk said. I remembered the food in my hands and set it on the table.

A knock at the door caused us both to turn. Alex held up a hand and opened the door to face the concerned expression of the concierge.

"Is everything all right, sir? We had a smoke detector go off and several guests call downstairs to report a fire."

"Our alarm did go off, but the only smoke was coming in through the window," Alex said as the shorter man tried to peer around him into the room. "Feel free to take a look yourself."

He nodded and stepped inside to the now immaculate-suite. "I must apologize for the inconvenience of the alarm. I will check outside for any sign of smoke."

Alex smiled and closed the door behind the concierge.

We ate in silence. Any attempt by Alex to start a conversation I shot down with one word answers.

I finished my Tikka Masala and dumped the container. "I'm going to bed."

"Okay," Alex responded and rose, taking a step closer to me. "Are you all right?"

"Yeah, just need some rest before the big day." I stepped away.

I closed the door to my room before he could say anything else. If I was going to get Jax out of this mess with his brain intact, I had some serious planning to do. Now that I knew what element I worked best with and the effects, I needed to use that to my advantage. Good thing I knew just where to find plenty of nitrogen in a garden.

****

The morning of April first, my sleepless eyes opened at the first hint of dawn. I reaffirmed my decision not to tell Alex anything about my plans. He'd spilled everything to my aunt way too easily. The less variables, the more likely the experiment would succeed.

My plan relied on two things—my aunt and her

goons bringing Jax as promised, and my ability to blow stuff up. Not bad considering my recent experiments.

I walked to the kitchen to pour a mug of coffee. Alex rose from the table, looking rumpled with bags under his eyes.

"Did you sleep?" I joined him at the table.

"Not really. I was up most of the night thinking."

"Okay, anything you want to share?"

He ran a hand through his usually styled hair which now stuck straight up like grass growing off his head. "Well, first we should talk about the plan and who helped you."

I furrowed my brow and did my best to look innocent. "What plan? We get the secret to the greatest power source known to witches, give it to the evil goons, save our families, and get Jax back. End of story. And I already told you no one has helped me except you."

"I know there's something you're not telling me." He rolled his bloodshot eyes. "And I think there's more to the situation than that."

"Right, I get turned into a mindless drone. If I'm lucky. Sorry, forgot that part." I stared at my nearly empty coffee mug.

"Maddie." He reached out a hand to touch my arm. "Don't say that."

I got up from the table and walked to the sink then stood with my back to Alex. "You're absolutely right. I'll be lucky if I end up dead. Who wants to live like that? No free will, no say in your own life." My aunt's blank face flashed in my mind. I dumped the rest of the coffee in the sink, suddenly unable to stomach anything. "I'd rather be dead."

He stepped behind me.

Warm strong arms wrapped around my shoulders. My muscles stiffened. He'd been getting progressively touchier since Jax was taken. I put up with the hand holding and side hugs to not hurt his feelings but this was too much.

The muscles of his chest pressed into my back, and his hands rubbed over the skin of my arms. I tensed and cringed away, but his grip tightened, holding me firmly in place.

"No, please. I don't think I'll have the nerve to say this if you turn around," he spoke into my hair, with his warm breath on my neck.

Claustrophobia and a little fear washed over me. My hands tightened into fists, but I held still.

"Maddie, run away with me. I know you have feelings for Jax, but in time those would fade. We could be together, get married like we were supposed to. We have the answer, we would be the most powerful witches in the world." The words tumbled from his mouth like a flood-gate releasing. I'd never heard this pleading tone from him.

The fear turned to disgust. I tensed and pushed myself out of his arms. He stepped forward and cornered me against the counter, gripping my upper arms.

He frantically searched my face. "Please. Maddie think about it. I would protect you. I wouldn't let anyone hurt you, ever. We could be happy together. I know we could. If you just give me a chance."

"Alex. What are you talking about? I could never leave my family, leave Jax to be killed by the council while we, what run away into the sunset?" I twisted in his grip, the stone of the counter digging into my back. "How are we supposed to hide? They would find us."

"No. Not if I have the power. I can protect you. They wouldn't dare try to hurt us, or I'd take them all out." He tightened his grip on my arms to the point of pain.

His eyes looked crazed, desperate. My heart twisted painfully and jack-hammered. I was trapped, yet, anger poured over me instead of fear.

"What about your family? You can't leave them at the mercy of the council." I tried to reason with him.

"They wouldn't miss me. Trust me. But we could love each other. Just give it a chance."

"No. Alex, stop," I demanded, fury strengthening my voice, and yanked one arm from his grip. "I'm not going anywhere."

He blinked and the desperation left his face, as if a mask had dropped over his features. The typically cool, collected Alex had returned. He glanced at his fingers, still on one arm and dropped them away, turning and walking to the living room.

I stared at his tense back. His hands trembled at his sides.

"I'm sorry. I didn't mean to frighten you," he apologized and only then turned to face me, a smile pasted on his face. "Now that we've cleared all that up, are you going to get ready to go?"

I nodded, shock stealing my voice, and skirted around him to my room. I locked the door and sat on the bed staring at it until my legs stopped shaking—a good five minutes later. I rubbed my bruised arms and tried to make my brain work.

A knock sounded at my door.

"Yeah?" I called but didn't get up.

"Maddie, can I talk to you for a second?" Alex called from the hallway.

I walked to the door, closed my eyes, and pressed my lips together before I opened it just a crack.

He stood with his hands stuffed in his jeans pockets. "Hey, can we just forget about me making a complete ass of myself?"

I still held the door at a crack.

"I'm so sorry. I was up all night, and I got really freaked out about what might happen to you. I guess I panicked."

I contemplated the composed Alex standing outside the door and wondered for a moment which was the real Alex. Anger still colored my thoughts, but I needed him on my side. I couldn't afford to be at odds with him today. I stuffed the anger that remained away and forced a hint of a smile to my lips. "Hey, don't worry about it. I make an ass of myself all the time."

He chucked and took his hands from his pocket. "You want to know the truth?"

"Of course."

"I couldn't stand the thought of you being hurt like they hurt my brother." He wiped a hand over his face. "I couldn't save him, but I really wanted to save you."

My throat tightened around my words. "Alex, I have to save myself."

"I know." He nodded. "So let's go do this then."

"Right." I closed the door and let out a deep breath. I'd completely forgotten about his brother. Guilt for doubting his loyalty bubbled up in my chest. Losing someone to the council was not anything you got over, my family knew that personally.

Brain functioning once again, I dressed for the day. Warm black leggings in case I had to make a run for it, a stretchy shirt for easy movement, and black boots with an aggressive tread for rough terrain completed my outfit. I pulled my hair into a French braid to keep it out of the way. A quick peek at my reflection in the mirror reminded me of a cat burglar, all in black and ready to kick some ass. After a dab of lip gloss for confidence, I added a splash of color to the ensemble with a thigh-length blue cardigan.

I realized I was not only comfortable in Emma's clothes, I was actually enjoying them. Not that I would ever admit it to her if I ever saw her again.

Alex waited for me in the living room. He got up but kept his distance, which helped my still-tender nerves. He took in my outfit with raised eyebrows, especially the combat boots, but refrained from comment.

I studied his face. Strength and confidence shone in his expression, no more crazy, thank God. "Ready?"

"If you are."

I held up the only copy of the nightshade recipe, torn from the corner of the painting, and held it to the flame of a lighter. The yellowed paper caught immediately and flared up like flash-paper. I let go and watched the ashes float into the sink then washed them down. With the only known copy of the recipe destroyed, Alex and I were the only link to the secret.

Alex nodded and held out his hands, as if they were cupped around a small delicate object. He spoke too softly for me to hear then closed his eyes and opened his hands. A translucent golden bubble floated up from his open palms, growing bigger as it rose, until it enveloped the two of us inside. I stared out at the kitchen, now bathed in golden light. For a moment the light flared, then the bubble disappeared, and my vision returned to normal.

"Did it work?" The cloaking spell was far beyond anything I'd even ever thought of trying. It would allow us to slip unseen past the goons that were likely watching our room. To any normal human we appeared unchanged, but witches couldn't see us at all.

Alex nodded and squinted at the empty air. "It's holding. But they're going to figure it out pretty quick. Once they start looking for us it's useless."

With another deep breath I slipped the cell phone my aunt had given me into my pocket.

"Hopefully it gives us an hour. Let's hope that's enough time for us to find what we need." I finished up with, "Time to save the world."

Chapter Twenty

We slipped past the well-dressed men in the lobby of our hotel easily. The council had sent reinforcements. Their gazes slid over our bubble as if we weren't even there. Once we were safely on the ferry heading out across the narrow channel, Alex dropped the cloak with a wave of his hand.

The *Ile de Batz* lay before us, a mere dot in the sea. My map showed a two-and-a-half-mile long by one-and-a-half-mile wide island only a few miles off the coast of France. I spent the fifteen-minute ferry ride glued to the rail. This was it. It all came down to today. We'd find out if I really did discover the answer that generations of witches failed to find. We'd find out if I, a worthless Defect, could save Jax and my family.

We neared the island. My heartrate increased until I had to force air into my quivering chest. Focusing on my breathing brought my heart rate down from a hummingbird pace.

Alex gave me a wide berth, no more taking my hand or putting his arm around me. He seemed to have settled back into the guy who had originally shown up at my hotel door. Not conflicted or confused, just focused.

Despite my wanting to scout out the place ahead of time we'd decided against it because my aunt and her goons had eyes on us. I'd been forced to settle for studying maps of the garden on the Internet. Unfortunately, there was no area marked *secret location of Chimera Nightshade to access power of the earth.*

So I had to make educated guestimates based on the preferences of nightshade plants. Moist soil, indirect sunlight, limestone rich soils, only narrowed it down to about three quarters of the gardens. The good news was that my plan would work near any flower bed, so anywhere inside the garden.

The main village surrounded an active fishing harbor. A ferry attendant was kind enough to give us a map of the island and point out the garden on the eastern side. It was just a quick walk along the footpath that circled the edge of the island.

"Be sure to see the *Trou de Serpent*, where *Saint Pol-de-Leon* cast the dragon into the sea. And the ancient chapel and lighthouse," the attendant urged.

I waved and answered under my breath. "We'll put that on the list. Right after kill evil witches."

The wind off the ocean whipped my hair, pulling tendrils out of my braid. My gaze devoured every corner of the island. When the ferry docked, Alex and I were the first to step off.

The tiny village sported cobblestone streets that at this time of year predictably held little traffic. With no cars allowed on the island, we rushed to the footpath that led to the garden. It took only minutes to clear the fishing village. The path opened up onto brown windblown grassland, and spectacular views of the ocean from the cliffs and beaches. New green shoots pushed up past last year's growth from the awakening plants.

I focused on not tripping over the uneven ground

and ran over my plan repeatedly in my mind. I had to save Jax and my family.

"That's it," Alex said, and pointed to a sign ahead.

Palm trees poked up from behind a high stone wall, and a rock-lined raised bed held a mass of succulents and surprisingly tropical-looking plants. The sign on the gate read *Fermee*.

Alex stopped in front of the locked gate. "Let me guess, that means closed."

I scanned the fence for any alternative way in and checked my watch. Eight forty-five. If we were lucky the council hadn't found us yet. If we weren't lucky, they could be on the next ferry. "Can we climb the fence?"

"Hang on." Alex waved to a uniformed man walking by inside the garden. "Excuse me."

The man grinned and pointed to the sign. He spoke in a French accent. "Sorry, we are closed."

Alex nodded and held out several hundred dollar bills. "We were hoping for a private tour."

The man blinked a few times then he smiled and reached out to take the money. "Sorry to keep you waiting."

He unlocked the gate and waved us inside.

"Why waste my energy if good old-fashioned bribery works?" Alex whispered.

I glanced at the empty path behind us, then at the open expanse of the channel, and the lone ferry boat chugging its way across, nearly back to the mainland. I swung the garden gate closed. Step one in my plan, find the nightshade.

Our guide, Philippe, led the way through the garden, pointing out various plants for us. The meandering dirt paths roamed over too much area for a quick search. The trails split and rejoined with seemingly no order or reason. This was a lot different than looking at an overhead picture of the paths.

My guts twisted and churned tighter with each corner we rounded. All the plants seemed to be sub-tropical in nature, tons of succulents and a wide range of palms. Many came from far off places like Asia or Africa and were dormant in the cold weather. Not a likely place to find a deadly nightshade bush.

Philippe droned on as we wandered down the paths about the types and varieties of the plants as we passed, giving us our money's worth. This was way too slow.

I caught Alex's frown and nodded my agreement. I stopped Philippe mid-sentence. Rude but… no time for manners when you have an upcoming appointment with death. "Do you have a collection of dangerous plants or anything?"

Philippe's brow crinkled. "Dangerous plants? There was a collection like this when the garden was purchased but we removed. No, we do not keep anything like that now. We keep only the most exotic and wonderful plants."

The edges of my vision went dark, closing in until only a pinpoint remained. Blood roared through my ears. I grabbed a rocky retaining wall to steady myself. "What if they took out all the nightshade?"

"It will be okay. We may be able to find another place it grew."

"Not before they kill him," I whispered, and closed my eyes.

"Nightshade?" Philippe asked, his brow furrowed at my obvious distress. "You speak of Belladonna?"

I refocused on the gardener. Barely able to form the words. "Do you have any?"

Philippe threw his hands out. "Everywhere." He shook his head, his face scrunched up. "It is the weed. We cannot get rid of it, whatever we try."

I pressed my hand to my chest to keep my heart from leaping out. My grip tightened on the rocks. I held on to avoid dropping to my knees.

Alex motioned to the footpath. "Show us."

Philippe walked up a path, waving his hands in the air. "I pull one, two come back. I pull all here." He motioned under a tree. "It come back over there. Horrible, horrible plant."

I sucked in a breath, and then almost choked on my words. "What color are the flowers?"

Our guide paused in front of a large, raised bed inhabited by what had to be the most enormous aloe plant on earth. "Flowers? Ah, they are purple, blue."

I stopped walking, frozen with one foot in the air.

"But some red," Philippe continued.

I set my foot down. Alex's wide eyes met my own.

Philippe motioned to the Aloe plant with a wide grin. "This is Louise the fourteenth."

I blinked.

"He hate the belladonna. But they love him," Philippe said then climbed into the bed and lifted one of the enormous aloe leaves. "They like the shade."

Under the leaf were the same woody branches I'd seen in the pictures on the Internet. Leaves graced the branches and what appeared to be little flower buds. But no flowers.

Philippe grabbed the plant around the base and yanked.

"No," I gasped.

The nightshade tore from the earth, dirt clinging to its exposed roots. Philippe glanced up, his brow wrinkled at my exclamation, and held the plant out toward me.

I waved to the plant. "We need it alive."

He frowned at the broken vegetation in his hand then shrugged. "We have many more."

Alex stepped close and took the remains of the plant from Philippe. He held up the broken weed and squinted. "How are we going to tell if it's purple or red?"

I sucked my lower lip in and chewed. "Can we try to rip open the buds? It's going to be hard to tell. If they aren't developed enough the flowers won't have any color yet."

We didn't have time for this. That ferry boat would have docked and been loaded again by now. Alex's spell only gave us a head start. They could be on the ferry, heading to the island right now, and we were no closer to the red nightshade than we were twenty minutes ago.

With another glance over my shoulder to check for my aunt and her thugs, I climbed up the rocks and crouched next to the aloe on steroids. Under another enormous leaf I found five more nightshades, just awakening to spring. All the plants bore leaves and buds, but none had broken open into bloom yet. I selected the largest of the buds and climbed down to the path.

Philippe watched with raised eyebrows. He was probably wondering if a few hundred bucks was worth chaperoning a couple of insane Americans around the gardens.

Alex and I carefully pried open the delicate buds with our fingernails. The largest we were able to open without much damage to reveal nearly translucent petals that were just starting to show pigment deposits of purple in the tips.

With a frustrated growl, I dropped the fifth shoot on the ground and moved on to the smaller buds. These were even harder to open. I finally cut through the base of the blossom with my fingernail and unrolled the petals to reveal no pigment whatsoever.

Plant juices smeared my fingers and my fingernails had an interesting green version of a French manicure. I threw the final bud to the ground and put my hands on my hips to pace. We needed more time for the blooms to develop.

I spoke under my breath. "Alex, the plant-aging spell from the final. We need the blooming stage."

He closed his fist around a stem with small buds on it. "Block his view."

I stood in front of Philippe and gestured to an adjacent bed of plants. "What are these? I've never seen anything like them."

That was all the encouragement he needed. The gardener turned to the bed and started off on a long and extremely energetic explanation of the rare plants. I made appropriately encouraging responses, but my eyes were on Alex's glowing hand. When he opened his fingers, the stem bore two perfect flowers. Purple flowers.

"We don't have a lot of time," I spoke under my breath so as not to disturb Philippe's soliloquy, handing Alex another branch and keeping one for myself. Hey, I had a fairly good track record with this spell. I closed my fist around the buds and focused my energy, doing my absolute best to keep the flow to a trickle.

Alex opened his hand and showed me two more purple flowers. I opened my hand and exposed three purple flowers. Not more than a second after I opened my fingers, the plant exploded. Bits of purple and green splattered Alex's white shirt in an interesting tie-dye effect.

"Sorry," I said and tried to brush the bits from his shirt.

"Please leave the spells to me." He waved off my efforts and tried another plant. Five attempts later, he dropped the last into the pile at our feet.

"You need more plants?" Philippe asked from over my shoulder. I flinched, not realizing that the gardener's attention had returned to us.

Alex held up a hand to silence him. "Give us a minute, please."

I sent Philippe a small smile to soften the bite in Alex's tone. The gardener nodded but cocked his head to one side, watching us.

"Could you try calling your aunt?" Alex asked and ran his hand through his hair.

I threw my hand out to the sides. "Now that we've been here, they probably already know about the garden. They might figure that they don't need us anymore and get rid of him."

"There are a lot of plants here. You could explain that we need the flowers, and they won't be ready for a couple days."

I put both hands on my forehead. "She won't care. We have to figure it out ourselves, and fast."

"You are looking for the blooms? We have the flowers in the greenhouse," Philippe offered.

My fingers paused in their assent through my wind-blown hair. Guess we should have listened to him and saved ourselves fifteen minutes of performing bud autopsies with our fingernails. "Can you take us there?"

A broad smile spread across his face. "*Mais bien sur.*"

We followed him through the maze of paths until a greenhouse the size of the high school gymnasium came into view.

I remembered the green rectangle on the map and wanted to smack my own head. I should have thought of the greenhouse. Jax would have remembered if he had been here. My stomach pinched at the thought of him.

A woman in uniform pushed a wheel barrel toward us on the path. She frowned at our group and asked Philippe a question in French. He waved and answered.

The woman nodded and continued on with a polite smile. I whispered to Alex, "He told her we're students from a university."

We walked through the open door to the greenhouse. The humid warmth enveloped me like a summer breeze that smelled of dirt and green growing things. We followed Philippe along an aisle of wooden potting benches filled with pots and flats of seedlings at various stages of development.

The sun shone through the tinted glass to give the place an even greener glow. Philippe motioned to the plants we passed, naming the variations.

We rounded a corner in the back of the building. I froze unable to do anything but stare.

In front of us lay an entire pile of nightshade plants—in full bloom. The heap of ripped up plants topped a trash pile, the flowers and leaves already hung limply from the branches.

With a squeak, I tore through the pile and found what we'd been searching for. I cupped the bloom in my hand. Half dead. Red. Nightshade.

"You see?" Philippe said from behind me. "They like the shade, so love the greenhouse. We pull out all the time. Usually purple flowers, but in the spring, some red. These I saw this morning. The first red blooms of the year."

My hand quaked, several pathetic petals floated to the ground. I grabbed the one intact bloom in my hand and shot Alex a please-stop-me-from-strangling-him look.

"We can use the flowers," Alex said and stepped closer to examine the single bloom. "Annabel's recipe called for three dried flowers."

Alex sifted through the pile, and he pulled another uprooted red belladonna from the trash. The plant bore one branch with two red flowers. We had one dose. "They would also have been dried for transporting them to England."

Behind us Philippe made a growling sound. We turned to see him bent over under a baby palm ranting under his breath. "Everywhere, pull one, two come back."

As the leaves of the palm shifted I caught a glimpse of the five tipped flowers of a red nightshade. My hand flew up and reached toward the plant in a futile attempt to save it.

Alex reacted even faster. I felt the zing of energy

that he shot Philippe's way.

"Stop," he demanded.

Philippe froze, literally, with his hand around the base of the plant.

I glanced around to be sure no one could see Alex's display of magic. Lucky for us, the other gardeners were working in the front of the greenhouse, far out of sight. I didn't care about council rules, but we didn't need freaked out gardeners to deal with too.

Alex chuckled, enjoying his handiwork. The poor gardener held his position like a plastic action figure then tipped to the side. I rushed to break his fall before he toppled over onto the concrete. My arms caught his stiff body and eased him to the ground, still in the same position.

My voice held no conviction. "That wasn't nice."

"But it was funny," he chuckled. "And I stopped him from pulling the nightshade. Didn't I?"

I sucked in a breath and blew it out while I fought to keep the corners of my mouth from turning up. A familiar feeling crept over me, envy. He made it seem so easy.

"Let me give his memory a little help before I let him go."

"Be careful," I cautioned and held my breath while he adjusted Philippe's memory. It was a risky process but hopefully such a recent memory would be right on the surface and easy to extract and replace without harming any thought processes.

"That should do it," Alex said and released the frozen spell.

Philippe immediately pushed himself off the floor. "So clumsy, I did not see that rock."

Alex offered a hand and pulled him to his feet. "Could I borrow a shovel and pot?"

"And a plastic bag if you have any?" I added.

Twenty minutes later, we left the greenhouse, a bag filled with every nightshade flower we could find in each of our pockets. We had enough for three doses each. Plus, I'd stuffed one dose in my locket when Alex wasn't looking in case the goons searched us.

Philippe agreed, after refusing Alex's bribe, not to tell about our search for the red belladonna. Alex tried to insist on putting a memory spell on the gardener, but I adamantly refused to let him mess with the man's mind anymore. Besides, I couldn't picture Philippe betraying us after he promised to keep it a secret.

Nine-forty-two. If they weren't here already they had to be closing in. My twitchiness increased exponentially as we made our way through the paths. There were a lot of places to hide in a garden this size, and I did my best to peer around every corner.

"You want to go all secret agent and crawl through the underbrush?"

I glared at Alex and rubbed the back of my neck which felt like tiny spiders were crawling on it. "They're close. I can feel them."

My hand snuck into my pocket to touch the bag of flowers.

"What are you doing?" Alex reached for my hand. "You can't take it now. It's way too dangerous."

I pulled my hand out, with it, a bag of common purple blooms that I'd collected. I held it out for Alex to see. "I wasn't planning to."

"What are you doing with that?"

I looked at him from the corner of my eyes.

"Thought it might be good to have a backup plan."

He stopped and put a hand on my arm. "Don't you think I should know what the backup plan is?"

We stood in front of Louise, the 'roided-out aloe. My muscles tightened of their own accord. My gaze darted from one path to the next.

Aunt Clara stepped from behind the raised bed fifteen feet in front of us, holding Jax by the arm. Bruises marked his face, some fading to yellow, some fresh and an angry red. He gripped one arm under the elbow across his torso to support it. His gaze met mine, one eye nearly swollen shut, both bloodshot.

Chapter Twenty-One

I sucked in a ragged breath and pulled away from Alex's grip. Warm tendrils of relief washed over me. "Jax."

"You were supposed to call, Maddison," my aunt scolded.

"I lost your number. Besides, I knew you were watching. Let him go."

My aunt released Jax with a shove. "You have your boyfriend. Now you give me the secret."

Jax limped down the dirt path toward me. Igor and another council drone stepped from the shadows on either side of us. I rushed to Jax's side and slipped an arm around him to support some of his weight.

"Are you okay?" I asked under my breath, afraid of what the answer would be. I could only hope they hadn't stripped his memories. He might not even know who I was.

"Peachy," he mumbled through gritted teeth.

"They didn't mess with your head?"

"Who are you?"

My insides crushed in on themselves like a black hole. I stared into his bloodshot eyes and sighed when I saw the sarcasm.

"Like I would know if they did," he added.

I resisted the urge to pat him down and check for injury. Instead I settled for putting my cheek on his shoulder and breathing him in. I'd missed him.

We reached Alex and turned to face the three goons. "You weren't supposed to hurt him."

"He was a bit slow at learning the rules," my aunt answered.

"You can shove your rules," Jax called to her, his spine stiff as a two-by-four.

She shook her head slowly.

"Jax." I stepped between him and my aunt.

"Yes, now get to the point," Aunt Clara ordered. "Hand over the secret."

I reached in my pocket and pulled out the bag of purple nightshade flowers. Jax glanced at the bag, then at me, but stayed quiet for once.

Beside me, Alex was not so helpful. "Maddie, I don't think that's a good idea."

I turned and held his gaze hopefully conveying the shut-the-hell-up message. "This was the deal. They let Jax go, we give them the answer."

He pursed his lips but nodded.

"Here." I threw the bag at my aunt's feet. "This is what you've been after for the last two hundred years. Four of these blooms and you have access to the power of the earth." One bloom would have been enough, but I had to be sure.

My aunt reached down and grabbed the bag, her face still a mask of indifference. She examined the flowers in the bag then returned her eyes to me. "Prove it. You take them first."

I laughed. "You want to give me access to the power? Great. You'll be the first one I kill."

She stared, assessing me, then held out the bag to Igor. "Eat four of them."

It might have been my imagination, but I could have sworn he glared at me for a split second.

Igor took the bag from her hand and downed four blooms without question, without even a grimace at the bitter taste.

"Are you sure you want him having the access to the power and not you?" I taunted. "Maybe you should take it too."

Her calculating stare shut me up.

She watched the test goon for a minute, and when nothing seemed to happen returned her stare to me. "If you've lied to us you will all die right here."

Jax crushed me to his chest, a wall of bruised, limping, strength.

My aunt raised her eyebrows at his chivalry.

He spoke softly, "She was always going kill us no matter what."

I nodded and glanced at Igor. He didn't look so hot. It was kicking in—step two of my plan.

I glanced at the gardens on my left and right, hoping they were freshly fertilized.

Igor stepped to the side and gripped the low barrier adjacent to a raised garden bed. His breathing quickened, he clutched his chest, sweat pouring from his face. All those muscles didn't do much good against the nightshade.

My stomach knotted, tight as a noose, at the memory of the effects of the plant.

My aunt noticed her companion's distress. "Tell me what you see."

"It's everywhere. So beautiful," Igor held out a beefy hand to touch nothing but air.

She stepped closer, her attention completely on

him. "Can you access it? Can you use it?"

He nodded. "I think so, I can feel it. It's amazing."

With that he fell face first into the dirt, not even holding up his hands to break his fall. My aunt felt his neck for a pulse and then turned to us.

Jax stepped closer to me. "Should we run?"

"Not yet," I whispered.

"He's dead," my aunt announced.

"Don't look at me," I shot back. "He even said he could feel the power. Maybe the guy had a heart condition."

Her eyes bore into me, unblinking.

We'd found the nightshade, then taken out one of the goons with the decoy flowers. Time for part three of my plan. Blow stuff up.

"Get ready," I whispered to Jax.

Without even trying to control my power or hold anything back, I focused on releasing the energy from the very fertilized, nitrogen rich soil in Louise's garden. It just so happened to be nearest my aunt and the remaining goon.

Sorry Louise. I thought at the aloe plant.

A fireball the size of a bus erupted. Flames and black smoke billowed up from the massive crater in the ground. Plant parts and dirt hurtled through the air along with the limp forms of my aunt and the remaining goon. The shock wave knocked Jax, Alex, and myself off our feet and onto the dirt path. I stared up from the ground and marveled at the explosion's magnitude.

We didn't stick around long enough to see the extent of the damage. We ran.

"We should split up," Alex warned.

"Meet us at the chapel ruins," I agreed, and pulled

Jax down a twisted path that, if all the hours of studying the map of this place paid off, should lead to a side gate.

Alex nodded and bolted down the opposite path.

Behind us shouts bounced back and forth. I silently swore. I'd been hoping to put an end to this right then and there. The damn council protections saved them. I ran as fast as my shaky body could manage. Jax limped beside me. Panting and about ready to toss my cookies, we reached the gate. The door stood open. Had Alex beaten us?

Hills of dead grass spread before us. My legs trembled, and my muscles searched for any scrap of energy my magic had overlooked. It was like running a marathon, then doing a triathlon, then being chased by a pack of rabid wolves. With a deep breath I ran up the first hill about as fast as a five-year-old. Actually, most five-year-olds would probably have smoked me, then stood at the top taunting me while I stumbled up.

I gripped Jax's arm and stopped to catch my breath.

He steadied us, his hands tight on my sides. "Are you okay?"

"Fine," I panted. "Any sign of Alex?"

He held me longer than necessary then stepped away. "No. But he may be taking a longer way around. Let's get to the church."

The toppled stone walls of a church came into view. No sign of Alex. I chewed on my lower lip and focused on making it the last hundred feet to the ruins.

As we approached, I read the warning sign posted in several languages outside the ancient church. "Unstable structure. Keep out."

I picked my way through the rocks that had once formed the chapel walls and sank down on a boulder, every muscle trembling. I rested against what remained of the back wall of the building. Cigarette butts strewn around the rocks attested to the fact that we weren't the first to disregard the notice.

The sun shone down through where the roof should have been. Jax wove around large pieces of fallen walls.

"Why don't you sit down? You've been through enough. I'm sure you're exhausted." My eyes roamed over the multitude of injuries I could see, and my imagination filled in many that I couldn't, by the way Jax moved.

He shrugged and stayed by the window. "It looks worse than it is."

Jax was here, alive. I'd forced myself to believe they would make good on their promise, but part of me had known they would kill him. The urge to touch him, feel him close, overwhelmed me. My skin tingled at the thought of him being so near. I forced my legs to bear my weight and walked to his side.

He jerked at the pressure of my hand on his arm then turned to face me. I ran my fingertips slowly over his cheek. Those copper eyes, what I could see through the swelling, met mine, and I thought I saw a tear before he blinked it away.

"I was sure I'd lost you. I'm so sorry I got you into this," I whispered.

One corner of his mouth pulled up. "Got me into it? You couldn't have kept me away."

"Jax. You're all that matters."

He pulled me into him. My arms wrapped around

him, and it felt as if the piece of me that had been missing snapped into place.

I broke off the kiss and hugged him tightly, my face in the crook of his neck.

"You're all that matters to me too," he whispered into my hair.

I had Jax back, now I needed to keep him alive. Time to move on with my plan. "Do you see Alex?"

He rolled his eyes but peered over the half wall. "I don't see him."

The anxiety bubbling in my stomach heated to a full blown boil. Alex was the only one of the three of us that wasn't exhausted or injured. "It shouldn't take him this long."

"I hate to say it but, we may have to leave without him," he said in a tone that said the exact opposite.

"How can you still not trust him?" I'd had my doubts in the beginning, doubts in the middle, and I guess I didn't share my plan with him, so doubts in the end. But still, he'd exposed himself to the council to help us. "We'll give him another minute."

"Don't count me out yet." Alex rounded a corner of the rubble wall. "I got a little held up."

Aunt Clara followed, a gun in her hand with the barrel inches from Alex's side. Dirt and plant material covered her torn clothes and exposed skin, but other than a dry cleaning bill she seemed no worse for the wear. "That was a cute trick but all it did was delay the inevitable."

The last of the goons rounded the corner behind them, a large gash on the side of his head seeping blood.

She held up Alex's bag of red nightshade flowers.

"Throw yours over to me."

With a glance at the gun, I pulled the bag from my pocket and tossed them half-way to my aunt.

She ignored the bag lying on the rocks, and instead studied me. "Search her." She waved to her companion.

Rough hands jerked my pockets out and emptied them on the ground. "Nothing."

Her companion returned to her side.

Jax grabbed my hand and pulled me slightly behind him. With a shove from my aunt, Alex stumbled across the ground to our side. He tripped over a protruding rock and landed on one knee next to me. Before he stood I met his eyes. He glanced at his closed fist and opened it just enough to expose three red nightshade flowers.

I shook my head slightly, we had no way of knowing if this was actually the complete secret, and I couldn't save him like he'd done for me if things went south. He held my gaze and threw the flowers in his mouth while my aunt couldn't see.

A couple chews, a gulp, and a grimace later, the experiment began. He rose to his feet and turned.

It would take a little time, hopefully not too much, for the nightshade to take effect. We needed a distraction.

"So. What now? You call the council and take us in?"

My aunt's lips spread in the closest thing I'd seen to a smile. "I already have my orders."

"You don't know the entire answer; the flowers are only the first part. You still need us."

"If there is any information you want to tell us to prove that you are worth something now would be the time." A new voice spoke. From around the corner appeared a woman. Everything about her screamed OCD, from her impeccable suit to her perfectly done hair and makeup. Her blond bob didn't even seem to move in the sea breeze.

Beside me, Alex sucked in a breath and stiffened.

She picked her way around the rubble wearing heels, not nearly the practical shoe I'd chosen, and lifted my bag of blooms from the dirt. Her brow creased as she examined the simple flowers and took up a position next to my aunt. The gun still trained in our direction, we waited and watched the newcomer.

"Mother?"

Chapter Twenty-Two

"What are you doing here?" Alex demanded. "I have everything under control."

I stared at Alex's angry expression. One thing was for sure, he wasn't surprised to see his dear mother here. Upset, but not surprised. His glaring eyes revealed pupils that were too dilated for the sunny day.

Mrs. Warner huffed and shook her head slowly. "I had to come clean up your job. Once again." She turned to my aunt. "Set up a perimeter and make sure we aren't interrupted."

My brow pulled together. His mother was obviously working with the council. Had Alex known?

"I was doing fine on my own," Alex came back in a voice that reminded me of an insolent child. "I just needed a little more time."

She laughed, a harsh sound that left me drenched in dread. "A little more time for what? To play house? Your task was easy, use your appearance and charm to get the girl to trust you, let her lead you to the secret and find out who helped her. You couldn't even do that much."

The blood surrounding my heart turned to sludge, forcing the muscle to pump harder. Jax had been right all along. I turned and faced Alex. "You bastard. You've been working with the council this entire time?"

"I knew he was a fake," Jax snarled from beside me.

Alex took a step away, toward the side of the chapel ruins. His gaze darted back and forth between Mrs. Warner and me, unable to rectify the two of us in the same space. "It wasn't supposed to happen this way."

My mouth dropped. My neurons flooded with anger and violent thoughts—really, really violent thoughts. Like feeding-him-to-a-meat-grinder violent thoughts.

Jax tried to move past me, but I held him back. He might get in one blow but Alex could easily kill him with his powers.

"I knew it was you who called them in at the Gardens," Jax spat. "Did you tell them where to find me too?"

Alex's face twisted when he looked at Jax. "You can thank Maddie for your torture. She kept messing everything up. I had to give her a better incentive. You at least served a purpose there."

I assessed if I had enough power left in me to blow Alex to hell where he belonged. My reserves were still dangerously low. I'd be able to make a puff of smoke if I was lucky, then I'd likely pass out.

"So why wait, you have the answer, why keep hanging around?" I demanded. "Why all that stuff about us running away together?"

He stiffened at the mention of his outburst this morning and glanced sideways at his mother.

"Don't tell me you actually got attached." Mrs. Warner turned her glare on her son. Her mouth puckered in distaste. "To a Defect?"

Alex shook his head. "No, no. I was just trying to make sure she trusted me, to find out who helped them at the airport. I would never, that's revolting."

He shifted his attention back to me, his face a mask. "After the disaster with the tea, I wanted to be sure we had the real answer before I got rid of you."

"So that whole story about your brother was a lie."

"No, that was true." He met my gaze.

His mother spoke from the entrance. "He couldn't control his powers and failed his test. So unfortunately he had to be dealt with like any other Defect."

I stared, unable to comprehend such words coming from a mother. "Your own son?"

"It was unfortunate that he did not survive." She brushed it away like we were talking about a pet goldfish. "But the more important objective is to keep our secret safe from humans. A Defect running around causing problems with their powers draws too much attention from the media to cover up. It can't be risked." She glared at her son. "That stunt at Kew Gardens took all my best men to fix."

"So that is what this is still about? Don't you think unlimited power is going to throw a wrench in your world view?"

She took a few steps into the rubble. "Keeping our secret is all that is important. Reading the history books about witch hunts and trials, burning at the stake, obviously has not conveyed the terror that presided over those days." Her hand waved toward the mainland. "The last council wanted to announce our presence to the world, and some witches did. They wanted to help change the political problems, end wars, disease. They ended up dead, killed by the very people they so wanted

271

to help."

I'd heard this tale many times. It was the first chapter we studied every year of witch elementary school. Eight years of pounding it into young witch skulls that the most important thing was to keep humans from finding out about witches. Talk about brainwashing. "How will having the power of the earth help keep our secret?"

"It will certainly make it easier to keep rebels like you in line," she smirked, and added an evil grin for good measure. "I imagine you'll make a good drone, just like your aunt." She glanced behind her through the door. "Where is your aunt? Setting up a perimeter shouldn't take this long. Ah, good help is so hard to find."

My aunt rounded the corner of the rubble and stood next to Mrs. Warner. "We won't be disturbed."

I thought of the nightshade hidden in my locket but knew taking it now wouldn't save us. Time was running out.

I glared at Alex. His pupils filled his entire iris and sweat covered his skin.

It was beginning.

"Alex, come over here out of the way before you find a way to mess something else up. Honestly, I have to do everything myself. I think I've spent half my life cleaning up after you and your brother," Alex's mother griped, her eyes still on me.

Had she given her son a second glance, she might have noticed the sheer hatred that filled his face. At the mention of his brother he winced, seemingly in real pain from the memory. I took a step back. Not good to be near an unstable mass of explosives that seemed ready to go off. Luckily for us, his attention was directed solely at his mother. I wasn't about to attract his notice.

"I said come here," his mother demanded. "You're worse than your brother sometimes."

Alex's cheeks flushed red, rage rolled off him like fog over hilltops. I pressed Jax against the stone of the wall, as far from Alex as we could get in the confines of the chapel.

"Mother," he growled. His eyes now had no color at all save black, and the enormous pupils combined with his hatred made him look like a demon brought to earth.

His mother stopped and turned her attention to her son. "Don't take that tone with me. I'll have your powers wiped before we leave France."

"No, you won't. You won't ever threaten me again. Or tell me what to do."

Alex's hatred seemed to register with his mom, but not the severity of the situation. She scrunched her brow. "You are going to regret speaking to me that way young man. I'm beginning to think you actually do have feelings for this girl."

He raised his hands, and sparks of energy crackled between his outstretched fingers like lightning. Alex flicked his wrist, and a bolt blasted a rock into pieces.

I craned my neck to see if Jax and I could scramble over the stone wall while they fought for dominance. The stone around us stood at least seven feet tall, no chance of slipping away unnoticed. Once again, I considered downing the nightshade in my locket but knew this would be over before it could possibly take effect. I returned my attention to the scene in front of us to wait for an opportunity to make a run for it.

His mother's eyes went round, but she held her ground. "Alex what have you done? Never mind, we'll clean this up just like we always do. Now try to calm down and see reason."

"I have the secret. I have the power. You are going to do what I say now," he spit out and grinned, his eyes never leaving Mrs. Warner. "No one is ever going to tell me what to do again."

Aunt Clara pointed her gun at Alex and waited for the signal from his mother.

Mrs. Warner put her hands on her hips. I recognized the *mom voice*. Every mom seemed to have one. "Alex, listen to me and calm down. You got want we wanted. Now we're going to work together."

She spared a glance over her shoulder to make eye contact with Aunt Clara and gave her a nearly imperceptible nod. My aunt aimed her gun at Alex's chest and fired.

A scream started in my throat, but before a sound made it past my vocal cords, Alex swept his hand to the side. The bullet curved in the air and struck the wall about a foot from my ankle, taking a large chunk of stone out of the wall.

Mrs. Warner seemed scared for the first time, her mouth hung open, her eyes fixed on her extremely angry son. "Alex…"

"You were going to kill me?" he shouted. "Kill me? Like you killed Jason? I don't think so, Mother." He spat the last word and clapped his hands together.

His mother turned to run, but she didn't stand a chance. The bolt of lightning hit her before she could take a single step. For a split second, a shimmering dome appeared over her before the council's defenses crumpled under the power of the earth. Her body erupted in smoke and flame then exploded with the force of C-4 explosives. The shock wave from the blast sent Aunt Clara flying into a pile of rock, knocking her unconscious.

The other goon didn't fare so well. Closer to Mrs. Warner, his body took more force from the blow. His head hit the wall with a crack, and he landed with his neck at an awkward, unnatural, angle. His eyes were open and staring but no longer seeing.

Jax and I crashed into the stone wall with enough force to crack bones. Jax's arms squeezed me, his hands over my head to protect me from the blast. Rough rocks scraped my skin and rocky shrapnel pummeled every exposed surface like tiny razors.

Aftershocks rattled the ground beneath our feet. Alex's hatred for his mother had been well-founded and ran deep.

I opened my eyes, expecting to see gruesome remains but saw only charred earth where Mrs. Warner had died. The raw power instantaneously turned her body to ash. The heat of the blast Alex produced also melted the smaller rocks into molten puddles.

"You always said I couldn't do anything right, Mother. Well, now I did, and you can't hurt me anymore." Alex stood, his arms still raised, staring at the blackened earth. "I did it. I killed her."

He held up his hands and watched the lightning bolts jumping from finger to finger then looked back at the burned spot where his mother died. "Why couldn't you just love me?"

He turned his crazy, manic eyes to Jax and me,

frozen against the stone wall. "Step away from him Maddie. I don't want to hurt you."

I inched closer to Jax. "Forget it. I'm not letting you kill him."

"Maddie, listen to him." Jax tried to step away from me.

"No." I grabbed his arm and pulled him back.

Alex's face twisted with betrayal. "You would die for him? An ungifted? Then, I have to kill you too. You know too much." He raised his arms but paused. "If you had come with me this morning. But no, you love him." Alex jerked his chin at Jax. His eyes narrowed. "We could have been happy. But you ruined it. She would have loved me. You stole her from me."

I stood in front of Jax, my arms out to throw up what magical protection I could manage. Not that it would save us.

Alex raised his arms again but winced and stared at his hands. The sparks still jumped from his fingers but this time they were going into his skin instead of out if it. "What's happening?"

The sparks increased. He fell to his knees and grabbed fistfuls of his hair with both hands in obvious pain. Screaming. "It's burning. Make it stop."

Tiny arcs of electricity jumped over his skin leaving smoking patches of flesh wherever they touched. Alex continued to scream, tormented by pain in his head and body. "The power, it's burning me, no, no, no."

Jax and I stared for a moment at his writhing figure. I wanted to be happy that karma caught up with the person who betrayed us. But I couldn't. The warning from the painting ran through my head. *The fires burn too hot for most.*

"I'm glad you didn't take that stuff. One spell isn't worth the risk. We need to get out of here before your aunt wakes up," Jax yelled over Alex's screams. "We can find someone who works in the gardens to get him help, if they haven't called the police already."

I forced my eyes away and took a tentative step toward the doorway.

A loud crack sounded from the wall behind us where the bullet had impacted the stone, followed by the grating of rock on rock. Jax's hand shoved my back and sent me flying through space. Time slowed to a crawl. My body twisted, and I was suspended in midair.

A six-foot square of stone wall fell. I watched, unable to stop the two-ton chunk of death careening through the air. I didn't need physics to see that the arc ended directly on that dark head that I loved so much. Jax tried to leap out of the way but only made it a few inches before the stone crushed him to the ground like a paper doll.

I slammed into the rocky ground, my hand outstretched toward where Jax had stood.

"No," I cried and scrambled forward. Adrenaline spurting into my blood by the gallon gave my muscles extra strength to send me hurtling over the rocks in my path. The logical side of my mind knew that no bones could survive an impact of that magnitude. Every bone would be crushed to slivers, the organs and tissues... jelly.

I refused to accept that verdict and pushed the nightmarish image from my mind. A lifeless hand extended from beneath the gray tomb. Swallowing the bile that clawed its way up my throat, I lifted the familiar fingers into my own and took in every detail with my adrenaline sharpened senses.

"You can't die. You can't. Not now. We got away, we won." A whisper of sound from beneath the stone stopped my protest. The lifeless fingers in my hand twitched. Then wrapped around my trembling and still tingling hand.

The barest hint of a whisper reached me. "Maddie."

I jerked and tightened my grip. "Jax? Jax hang on."

I shifted gears from grieving to rescue-mode and assessed the situation. A smaller rock propped the massive stone off the ground to form a right triangle with the slab forming the hypotenuse, or longest side. Six inches of air separated the tons of stone from the dirt. Six inches.

"There's no way I can lift it," I whispered to myself.

Behind me, Alex had ceased his screaming, thank God, and was rocking and whimpering—still in a fetal position.

"I don't think I have the energy to transport him. And I've never done anything alive," I said out loud.

I traced my finger along the hills and valleys of Jax's battered knuckles. Ideas raced through my mind. Not enough energy. Too risky. Not enough time.

I considered using magic to lift the slab off of him. Discussions of complications with pressure injuries came to mind. Perversely, the slab was likely keeping him alive while it slowly killed him. Besides, I doubted I had enough energy to lift a pebble, much less a two-ton slab.

I needed more power. My eyes moved over my

aunt's unconscious body and fell on Alex's now still form. His breath came in short gasps, and smoke wafted up from his ear canals.

Jax's voice rang in my mind. *One spell isn't worth it.*

One spell.

Chapter Twenty-Three

I ripped the locket from under my shirt and opened the clasp. Three blood-red blooms rested in the interior where I'd hidden them for an emergency. This definitely counted as one. I'd have unlimited power. But only one chance to use it and then I'd end up like Alex. I dumped the contents into my hand.

I forced the pokey, half-masticated, plant down my throat. I would definitely need vinaigrette next time. Once again, I gripped Jax's hand and waited. No superhuman strength. No rush of power.

I put my cheek close to the ground so that I could see the top of Jax's skull, pressed between the stone and the ground. "Jax, I'm going to get you out. Jax can you hear me?"

No answer, no movement. I scrambled to find a pulse in his wrist. Faint and thready, but the pulse under my shaking fingers assured me that he was unconscious but still alive.

"It's okay, I'm going to get you out," I repeated even though I knew he couldn't hear me.

I tried to estimate how long it had taken Alex to gain access to the power, maybe five minutes. With my fingers glued to the pulse in Jax's wrist, I planned how to save him. One spell, I'd have one chance to save him. Then I'd be in a useless ball right next to Alex.

I could move the slab, if he wasn't injured too

much. I wouldn't be able to heal him. I needed a one-step fix all spell. The minutes ticked by, Jax's pulse was unstable but continued to beat.

My stomach rolled. I put one hand on my abdomen and groaned. Poisonous plant and stress. Bad combination. My heartbeat picked up, like it had when I drank the nightshade tea. It had begun.

My hand caught my gaze. The skin glowed from within as if pure light had replaced my blood. Warmth flowed through my veins, beginning in my feet and pouring through my mind.

With one last squeeze I released Jax's hand and stood over the slab. I glared at the offending stone while I tried to decide what to do. I blinked, thinking my eyes were playing tricks on me. I could have sworn I could see Jax's body under the stone. Several blinks and an eye rub later I still saw his broken body.

Energy radiated from Jax's living form from under the rock, much like an x-ray, only way better. I tried to keep my mind analytical, clear of emotion, and with my new x-ray vision worked my way up his body, completely crushed feet, tibia and fibula of each leg broken in at least five places, compound fracture of the femur, hips crushed. With each injury my stomach twisted in on itself.

While painful, the breaks weren't what bent my hope to the point of snapping. It was the gelatinous mass of organs in his abdomen. His liver, kidneys, and intestines, were totally unidentifiable. His chest cavity held a set of mangled but working lungs, and a barely beating heart that struggled to pump blood.

As I suspected, the pressure from the slab was the only reason his blood still flowed through his damaged veins instead of staining the dirt.

The second I moved the slab, he'd bleed out. Not even the power of the earth could bring back the dead. At least not any spell I knew about. Besides, I wasn't really the return-from-the-dead-zombie-boyfriend type. That left no alternative but to find another way to save him, because losing Jax was not an option.

I closed my eyes against the image of his broken body. A spark flared in my brain, a stroke of inspiration.

****

Talk about making complicated things even more complicated or impossible. The plethora of inside out fruit carcasses in my basement provided plenty of evidence as to the dangers of transporting. And I'd decided to add another twist to the spell.

Once I transported Jax from under the slab the pressure keeping him alive would be gone, and he'd bleed out instantaneously. There would be no time for me to go through and heal the injuries, even if I could and wasn't writhing on the ground next to Alex. Jax would be dead within a few seconds.

I needed to transport and heal simultaneously. His cells and damaged tissue would retain some memory of their position before the injuries. All I needed to do was rearrange them to their former positions during transport. Easy peasy. Hey, I did transport a grape. Which, after I was done with it only tasted slightly like an orange.

No time to freak out. Before I could psyche myself out too much, I sent out blazing tendrils of energy. They wrapped around Jax's broken form like rabid vines of ivy and roots began to grow into his tissues.

With my eyes closed, I hesitated for a split second, doubt crowding in. I firmed my jaw and dispersed the molecules of his body. He existed only in the energy attached to the atoms.

With the unlimited energy at my disposal, I struggled to hold back the enormous flow that wanted to rush into my spell. I was kind of like building a damn for the Mississippi river out of tinker-toys. Too much energy would blow the spell, and Jax, sky high. I knew from experience.

I clamped down my control and restricted the energy flow to a trickle. Sweat poured down my face, my entire body vibrated with the effort of controlling the energy for even a few seconds.

The molecules followed the leash my spell formed to the clear patch of dirt a few feet from the slab. I collected the stragglers, my hand shaking. If I lost focus for even a millisecond, let a fraction of the energy go awry, I'd lose him.

Power flooded my brain, putting pressure on the channels in my frontal lobe that made me a witch. The pressure built to a painful level, pipes near bursting, but I held on. My spell directed the energy to rebuild the molecules, but not damaged as they had been, whole as they should be. The memory was in them, only fainter than the broken body.

My memory supplied an image. Jax the way he should be, whole and healthy. The first molecules joined together, then more.

I held on to the completed parts as I forced more to join. The molecules fought to escape like small children amped on sugar, longing to run free. I corralled the mutiny and, with a tiny blast of energy, held them tight while coaxing the order I needed. My muscles trembled. My head throbbed, ready to explode.

A *pop* sounded. Jax lay on his side in the dirt, his organs on the inside and not a scratch on the outside. Even the bruises and cuts from the beatings he'd suffered were gone. He looked like the Jax I'd met a few weeks ago in the lab.

I sank to my knees beside him and gasped for breath, my entire body shaking and my brain full of energy to near bursting. The light radiating from his body confirmed correct positioning of internal organs. I soaked in every detail of his peaceful face while I waited for the pain to start like it had in Alex.

Then I realized Jax wasn't breathing.

I waited. Waited for Jax to take a breath. Waited for his heart to start beating. His body remained lifeless. My heart crept up to my throat and kept right on going until it took up residence in my nasal cavity.

His heart wasn't beating. I shook his shoulder. "Jax. Don't give up on me."

I grabbed his torso in both hands and pounded his shoulders into the dirt, about to lose my mind. "I can't lose you. I won't lose you." My voice cracked, "You have to fight."

I sucked in a breath. He needed a jump start.

It only took one mental image of me blowing his heart to bits to make me reconsider using the power. Better go with the old-fashioned way. I fisted my hands over his sternum and pressed down. Over and over again, I pumped Jax's chest, stopping every twenty-five counts to breathe air into his lungs.

After fifty, I paused and pressed my fingers into the artery on his neck. Nothing.

"Come on," I screamed.

I resumed my thrusts, more forceful this time, until my hand on his chest registered movement. A thump. Then another. I leaned over his face. "Jax. Jax wake up."

His eyes flew open. He sucked in a gulp of air and focused on me. "I guess I'll keep you around." He sounded breathless but strong.

My shoulders slumped. A chuckle rocked my torso. "Glad to know I'm good for something."

Jax pushed himself onto his elbows.

"Wait. You should take it easy," I urged, my arms shaking, my head spinning.

He smirked and hopped to his feet. "Are you kidding? I feel great." He glanced down at me. "You don't look so good." His smile dissolved from his lips. "Maddie, what did you do? How did you get me out of there?"

I rolled onto my side and pressed my hands to my temples, a futile attempt to stop the pressure of energy that demanded to get out. "I had to save you."

He looked from me to Alex, both of us curled up on the ground, grabbed me by the shoulders and shouted, "You took the nightshade? It could kill you."

"A simple *thank you* would be fine." I squinted my eyes against the pressure.

His frantic gaze searched my face. "What should I do? Tell me what to do."

"I have to let it out," I gasped. "My head is going to explode."

"Let it out then. Blow something up if you have to."

A few feet away on the ground, Alex stirred and

285

whimpered.

Gripping Jax's hand, I released the clamps I'd put on the channels in my brain. Raw power rushed through me like water through a burst damn. I aimed the power up, away from me and Jax and any other living creature. Rain. I thought to give the raw power direction. Make it rain.

"What's going on here?" my aunt demanded from behind Jax, the gun still in her hand.

Surprised jolted through my body at the sound of her voice. My muscles seized. My thoughts hung suspended in their neurological path. My attention shifted away from my spell for a split second. That was all it needed to morph. Instead of rain, the energy dispersed and flew into the air in a bright explosion. Just like Fourth of July fireworks. The morning sky lit up in a blinding display of color. No fireworks display in history could match the brilliant colors of the power of the earth blazing through the sky. Not what I had in mind but…nice.

"Pretty," Alex cooed in a childlike voice.

"Stop that," demanded my aunt. "You'll draw attention to us."

"Too late," I responded, then realized that with the power out of my body the agony had left as well. While Alex still rocked and moaned on the ground in obvious pain, I felt completely fine. I held a hand out to Jax. "Help me up."

He steadied me, and I rose to my feet. Jax's brows drew together. "Are you okay?"

"I feel fine," I said, a bit distracted. I watched the iridescent colors fade from my vision, and the world returned to normal. The effects of the nightshade were wearing off.

In the distance we heard voices, my fireworks had attracted attention from the locals. We turned to my aunt. I wished that I hadn't used up the power for a bunch of fireworks, and I could at least give her a descent blast so we could get out of here. With what power I had left, I couldn't hope to break through her defenses.

"What are you planning to do with us now?"

"That's for the council to decide."

****

I watched the island disappear with my hands wrapped around the chilly metal of the ferry's rail. The power of the earth left my cells rejuvenated, filled to bursting with power. I contemplated jumping in the white caps and swimming to America.

Alex had to be carried off the island and was still in considerable pain. He continued to complain of burning in his brain and body. He was on a stretcher, doped up on pain meds. The paramedics that my aunt called to help him were under the impression that he had suffered some kind of stroke from the apparent neurological damage. I wasn't about to correct their assumption. Telling them he had fried his brain with the power of the earth would likely earn me a drug test and a trip to the neighborhood nut house. Besides, pain meds were probably the best thing for him at the moment.

I reached out to grasp Jax's hand. He not only suffered no ill effects from his time as a pancake, he had more energy, and claimed he felt smarter, as if his brain had more neural connections. Maybe someone should smash me over the head and put my gray matter back together.

"What do you think they plan on doing with us?"

I shrugged. "One thing is for sure, we're valuable or we would already be dead."

"We're going to figure a way out of this." Jax squeezed my hand.

"I know." I looked at his now unblemished face. Those copper eyes melted the last of the rock of doubt I'd carried around with me all my life. It dripped away along with the fear it had brought.

The council couldn't figure out the secret for hundreds of years, we did that. I did that. I could sure figure a way out of this as well.

Chapter Twenty-Four

"Maddie, where are you going at five in the morning?" Mom asked from the stairs.

I sighed, so much for my quiet exit. My life had done a one-eighty since we left that little island off the coast of France. "Sorry, I tried not to wake you. The council called. I have to meet them at six to pull power. Then I have class and I'm meeting Jax so I won't be home till late."

Her brow pulled together. "That is the fifth time this week that they've called you. Can't they at least let you sleep?"

Actually, it was the eighth time I'd been called in to pull power this week, but I wasn't about to tell my mom that. "You know, fate of the world stuff. Can't wait for normal business hours."

Turns out I was a channel that the power of the earth could travel through without burning my witch powers to a cinder, like Alex had experienced first hand. From what little I'd been told, Alex's powers were pretty much useless after the power of the earth burned and scarred his channels. Even the smallest spell caused extreme pain and usually failed.

The monks, or Guardians, as I called them now, had been right. I did have an ability after all.

The council tested the power on several other *volunteers* before they realized that the only person who could handle it was a Defect like me. My wider channels were made to draw the enormous energy and funnel it into several other witches so they could manipulate the power and perform spells.

Problem was I was the only live Defect around since they'd killed or stripped so many like me of their powers for the last couple hundred years. That suddenly gave me almost celebrity status in the witch world.

"I'm worried about you." Mom moved down the stairs and wrapped her arms around me.

I forced more energy than I had into my voice. "No worries, who needs sleep when they have the power of the earth?"

It was true that the power left my cells brimming with energy, ready to run a marathon, swim the English Channel, or solve the mysteries of the universe. But then eight hours later came the crash, and I had to pay the price for that false high. My body wanted to sleep for days, or if I was lucky, a couple hours until the council called and I had to pull power again, and the cycle started all over.

"It can't be healthy," she admonished. "You need to set some boundaries."

"I'll be sure to bring that up." I kissed her on the cheek before I spun and bolted out the door to avoid any further concern.

Sparky's yap followed me the entire walk down the driveway. When I reached the side walk the yap alarm suddenly stopped. A smirk spread over my face. Parker would never learn. Hopefully, he'd sent the dog someplace warm this time.

My new car, provided by the council so I wouldn't be late because of my old hunk-of-junk, purred at the curb. The October mornings brought a definite chill to the air, and I enjoyed the remote start on this fancy vehicle. For some reason, my body couldn't tolerate the cold anymore.

I settled in the heated leather seat and breathed. The light inside the window turned off, and I watched the house, imagining my family warm and safe in their beds. Being the only Defect left gave me some bargaining power. They got my help whenever they needed to, and basically I was on call twenty-four-seven, but my family was protected and safe. My parents even got their choice of research topics, and finally, the respect they deserved. Plus, they wouldn't have to worry about money. Ever.

I didn't even mind the term Defect anymore.

As long as I was useful to the council everything was fine. But I wasn't dumb enough to think that things couldn't change pretty fast. I put the car in gear and pulled away from the curb. Better go be useful.

****

Jax bent over a microscope, his attention absorbed by the tiny object on the slide. I paused and leaned against the doorway to enjoy the view his fitted shirt and jeans offered. Yep, yummy.

One of the other things I'd been able to bargain for—Jax. His mind would stay intact. I refused to budge on that point, plus he got an unexpected scholarship for a free ride all the way through his graduate degree. We called it payment for his services in uncovering the secret. And I was no longer betrothed. I could date and marry whoever I chose. Even an ungifted. For now.

They needed more Defects, it was a gene passed

down to children. I was a scientist. I could see where this was going.

For the time being, we both attended Northwestern, me a freshman and Jax a junior. MIT offered me a spot, but I wouldn't consider leaving. Besides, we had it pretty good here as the only two undergrads on campus who had their own lab to work in, thanks to the council perks. We devoted our time outside class to genetics research, both the witch kind and the disease-causing kind. Jax was finally able to make some progress on finding a cure for Tay-Sachs, the disease that took his mom. Turns out magic and science work really well together.

"Are you going to stand there and stare at my ass or are you coming in to help me?" Jax asked, never lifting his gaze from the scope.

I shook my head. The whole near-death experience had some benefits for Jax. Not only did he seem to gain some IQ points, basically his entire body worked better, especially his senses, which were more acute. Like superhuman acute.

"What was it this time?" I walked across the room.

He straightened and smirked. "I smelled your espresso."

"I'm not the only person in the world who drinks espresso you know."

"Yeah, but who else is going to stand there and check me out?"

I raised my eyebrows. "Any girl with a pulse."

His gaze took in my V-neck sweater and boots, before he smirked. "Emma again?"

I rolled my eyes. "She loves taking me shopping to spend my *inheritance*." I cocked out one hip and struck a pose. "What do you think?"

"You look awesome. But I'll take you in your jeans and T-shirts any day." He pulled me into his arms and buried his face in my neck. "You smell good too."

I enjoyed the solid, defined muscle, under my hands. He raised his head and cupped the back of my neck to pull me in for a not-so-G-rated kiss.

After a minute Jax pulled away. "Your dad's waiting outside the door for us to quit making out. I hear him pacing."

I sighed. "Can't you turn your superpowers off for a few minutes?" I stepped out of Jax's embrace. "It's safe to come in, Dad."

He poked his head around the corner then stepped in carrying a stack of books. Dad had two research projects going, one the council knew about and one they didn't. The secret one involved the family histories of Defects. We knew of several that had been killed in the latest generation, and because we'd determined that the trait was genetic, we were tracing it back to try to determine other possible Defects the council had missed.

Ironic that before the coup and the new council taking over, the ruling families of witches had been the ones with the Defect gene. For the last two hundred years, they'd fallen into disgrace and shame because no one understood their ability.

Whoever controlled the Defects controlled the power. We needed to find others before the council did.

"I found a new possible line, now that I know what I'm searching for it's a lot easier. This family seems to have a lot of descendants that never developed their powers," he explained, and opened the family tree he'd been working on.

The other manifestation of the Defect gene was for the person's abilities to never open so they appeared to be an average human and would never even know they were born into a family of witches. We weren't sure, however, if they could pass on their abilities to their children.

I nodded and leaned over the tree. "Do you think there may be one that the council missed?"

He nodded. "It's possible. This particular family line nearly died out, but it looks like there may be one descendent left. A girl who, from the looks of it, never developed her powers. But I'm not sure, yet."

A tremor began in my hand and spread up my arm. I made a fist and pulled my hand off the table. A deep breath did nothing to stop the shaking. I walked a few feet away and pretended to look inside my backpack for something. With my back to Jax and my dad, I held out my hand. It shuddered violently and tiny red sparks jumped from finger to finger.

I'd noticed the tremor a couple weeks ago. Now, every time I pulled power it seemed to get worse. The sparks were a new development. I sucked in a deep breath and grabbed my notebook from the backpack.

When the sparks stopped, I turned to my dad, still bent over the family tree with Jax. "Dad, do you have time to research something else for me?"

He looked up. "Of course, what do you need?"

"Could you find out about the disease that killed the duke's wife?" I asked, doing my best to sound nonchalant.

His brows pulled together. "I can see what I can find out. Why?"

After finding out that the Defect gene was a sex-linked trait and most defects were women, we theorized that in the married couples that were council members, the wife would be the one to pull power. That meant the duke's wife would likely have been a Defect. I shrugged. "It has been bothering me why, with the power of the earth, they couldn't fix her. Just curious really. No big deal if you're busy."

"I have time. And I agree, it would be good to know if there is a limit to what the power can do. I'll get started this afternoon and let you know what I find."

He gathered up his papers and left with a wave.

I'd tried reaching out to the Guardians to see if they had any idea what was happening to me, but being surrounded by the council constantly made any contact impossible.

I started toward the bench to set up a scope, but Jax caught my hand.

"What's going on?" he asked, his face serious.

His over protectiveness both endeared and drove me batty. I understood he was afraid of losing another person he loved, but, well, it could be a bit stifling.

"Nothing. I couldn't stop wondering what happened to her," I lied.

He held my gaze for a moment, copper eyes daring me to show that I was being untruthful. I didn't even blink.

Jax nodded. "As long as you're okay, that's all I care about."

I kissed his lips. "I'm fine." And I was for now.

I turned to the bench and pulled out my scope, my hand still shaking. One thing was certain, I needed to find another Defect. Fast.

A word about the author...

Emily grew up loving to read and escape into stories. She began writing her own at the age of twelve. In college she focused on science and graduated with a degree in Environmental Biology. After college she began writing again but quickly realized she had failed to take a single writing or grammar class. Luckily, she's a quick learner.

Emily now lives in Colorado with her wonderful husband, three amazing children, and way too many animals. She still enjoys making up stories and can't seem to leave out the paranormal elements because they are just too much fun.

http://emilybybeebooks.com